THE THIRD JUNGLE BOOK

THE THIRD JUNGLE BOOK

by *Pamela Jekel*
illustrated by Nancy Malick

ROBERTS RINEHART PUBLISHERS
ODYSSEY BOOKS

Copyright © 1992 by Dr. P.L. Jekel
Illustrations copyright © 1992 by Nancy Malick
Published by Roberts Rinehart Publishers
Post Office Box 666, Niwot, Colorado 80544
and Barbara J. Ciletti
2219 Judson St.
Longmont, CO 80501

Published in the United Kingdom, Ireland, and Europe by
Roberts Rinehart Publishers, 3 Bayview Terrace, Schull,
West Cork, Republic of Ireland

Published in Canada by Key Porter Books,
70 The Esplanade, Toronto, Ontario
Canada M5E 1R2

Printed and bound in Hong Kong

Library of Congress Cataloging-in-Publication Data

Jekel, Pamela Lee
    The third jungle book / by Pamela Jekel : illustrated by
Nancy Malick.
        p. cm.
    Summary: Presents new adventures of Mowgli as he
grows into manhood among the animals of the Indian jungle
and seeks knowledge of the Law of the Jungle.
    ISBN 1-879373-22-X : $19.95
    [1. Jungles—Fiction. 2. Animals—Fiction. 3. India—
    Fiction.] I. Malick, Nancy, ill. II. Title.
    PZ7.L51435th   1990
[Fic]—dc20   90-36410
                                        CIP
                                        AC

Contents

Preface

On a recent trip to London, I happened to blind-bid an estate lot of antiques, primarily mid-Victorian, for a client of mine who is renovating his townhouse in San Francisco. I was frankly disappointed in the pieces, for most of them were the small, ungainly sort of overly ornate monstrosities one so often finds from that era. Not to my taste, but I knew he would like them.

However, one piece aroused my curiosity. It was an old overland trunk, of the kind which one imagines has seen countless miles on the Orient Express or the old Cunard Lines, and it was solidly, substantially, locked. I removed it from the inventory list (subtracting the cost from his bill, of course) and carted it home.

I set it in the middle of the living room and stared at it, warming a glass of brandy in my palms. There might be nothing at all inside, I told myself, nothing of value. Perhaps just a lot of mouldy old letters or dusty, rotting velvet capes. But the lock was unique—a twisted brass affair with an ornate, rather oriental carving of a banyan tree—and there was something about the trunk itself which drew me. It had been undisturbed, an uncompromised mystery, a Pandora's Box of virgin secrets, for over a hundred years. After tantalizing myself with possibilities, I downed the brandy and cut off the lock.

Actually, I must confess to another disappointment. I was hoping for a long-forgotten deed to some prime Hampton acreage or perhaps some negotiable bonds. Instead, I found a packet of brittle sketches, done in pen-and-ink, I guess, of some ruins; a walking stick, cracked along the head; a pile of old, useless rupee notes; a faded photograph of some woman, with the name "Carrie" scrawled across it—and a parcel of yellowed papers tied with a leather strap, probably not even as old as I'd thought.

I read them, of course, but I couldn't make much of the story. Some sort of child's nursery tale, I suppose, that the original owner saved out of sentiment, with no real beginning and no ending, either. Hardly likely to be a commercial success. However, an editor friend of mine offered me a grand for the sketches, the photo, and the papers—and since that paid for the trunk five times over, I was quick to oblige him. His only stipulation was that I write this letter, telling how I came by them.

There is still some doubt, I gather, as to the validity of the papers, themselves. I want to make it perfectly clear that I take no responsibility for any claims whatsoever concerning them. But if anyone's interested, the trunk is for sale to the highest bidder.

signed,
P.J.

FIRE IN
THE JUNGLE

If with the Herds, you'd learn to go,
Then sniff the air and stamp the earth,
And watch for brush which hides the foe,
For you must run, e'en at your birth.
Run, for there's nothing fleeter,
Run, where the grass is sweeter,
Run, each bleating kid must know to
Run!

If with the Herds, you wish to race,
Then do not stop to reason why,
The last hooves up in any chase
Will surely be the first to die.
Run, for there's nothing fleeter,
Run, where the grass is sweeter,
Run, life is swift but death is slow, so
Run!

Song of the Deer

It was the time of the ripe mango in India, when the earth is baked flat and dry by the blazing sun. The cattle in the ploughed fields stumbled under the yoke, and the herdboys were sand-blinded. The well was dry beneath the village peepul tree.

Yet beyond the parched fields where the shadows grew more dense, the jungle stretched long cool fingers of green, and the dust winds ceased. Here, the creatures followed their own rhythms and obeyed their own laws.

Now, the Law of the Jungle is like the light spring rain, seeping into every nook and lair, leaving no Jungle People untouched, as old as the water itself. If you have read the first book about Mowgli, the Jungle Boy, then you will remember that he had to spend the first part of his life learning the Law from Baloo, the old Brown Bear.

Once long ago, a woodcutter and his wife had been working in the jungle, when Shere Khan, the Tiger, surprised them from the brush. They ran away in terror, leaving their small brown baby hidden under the leaves. The child found his way to a wolf's lair and there, unafraid, he crept into the den and pushed aside the mother wolf's cubs for a turn at her warm belly.

Mowgli, the Frog, Mother Wolf had called him, and raised him as her own. Mowgli, the man-cub, the other wolves called him when he was brought to the Pack Council for acceptance into the Seeonee Wolf Pack. Two of the strongest voices in the jungle, Baloo, the old Brown Bear who taught the young wolves the Law, and Bagheera, the Black Panther who turned aside for none, became his friends. And so, Mowgli came to learn the jungle ways.

Now, Mowgli lay stretched out on the lowest branch of a banyan tree, listening while Baloo told him, for what would surely seem the hundredth time if the boy could have counted, the reason he must learn the Master Words.

"Even I cannot remember every tongue in the jungle," Baloo said patiently, "and most never learn to speak any save their own.

But ye art the smallest and softest among us, and so ye must be the wisest, as well. When thou art facing grave danger, as will surely happen, for the jungle is the jungle, thy life may be saved by knowing the Master Words of each tribe. Now, speak them for me again."

"It is too hot for my head to carry so much this day," Mowgli said drowsily. "My tongue feels as thick as this branch."

"None too thick enough," Bagheera purred gently from a higher limb. "Ye still have not learned to choose the sound over the rotten. Move a little higher and stop kicking, Little Brother."

Mowgli sat up and stretched lazily, sliding down the tree to the ground. "Let us move the lesson to the bathing-place, and I will tell ye both every Word in the jungle."

"Which thou dost not know even yet," the Bear grumbled. "But lead on, wolfling, and perhaps thy head will work better when wet."

The three slipped through the jungle silently. Bagheera moved swiftly in the underbrush, scarcely twitching aside the leaves; Baloo rolled his great bulk with surprising ease, and Mowgli padded between them, laughing and catching at branches and flowers.

They reached the bathing-place, a deep, shadowed pool ringed by sunned rocks, favoured by the Hunting People on long, hot jungle afternoons. The Snake People had their own lagoon, as did the Hoofed People, and few used that of the other, save at times of drought.

Mowgli dove into the black waters jungle-fashion, sliding in chest deep without a splash. Baloo submerged himself so that only his eyes and nose peeped out, and Bagheera glided through the water to come up drenched and gleaming on a flat rock in the sun.

Mowgli swam to Baloo, curled his arms and legs around the great brown neck, and lolled contentedly in the cool water.

"Now, the Master Words," Baloo said firmly.

"We be of one blood, ye and I," Mowgli answered, with the snap of a wolf's jaws at the end of the eerie barking call.

"Good," Baloo said. "That will do for the Hunting People. And for the Birds?"

Mowgli warbled a cry that sounded like the alarm of a peacock stranded in a neem tree, ending in a most raucous screech.

Baloo cuffed him gently, ducking him under water.

"Ow! Fat old bear!" Mowgli splashed away in a huff.

"That call will bring Tabaqui, the Jackal, to see what new meal is afoot, but no other help that I can tell, Little Brother," Bagheera said, stretching his long talons out to inspect them.

"He knows it," Baloo grunted. "He enjoys trying my patience."

"_What_ patience, O bad Baloo?" Mowgli sulked, climbing back onto his shoulders. And he gave a clean, perfect call of a hunting hawk, and then drummed on the bear's neck with his fists.

"So, for the Birds," Baloo said with a quiet smile of pride.

"There is no Word I do not know, eh, Bagheera?" Mowgli crowed.

"To say is one thing, to know is another. And there is one yet, I have not heard from thy mouth," the Black Panther said silkily. "Hast thou not taught him the Word of the Hooved People?"

"I cannot pronounce it well," Baloo said sheepishly. "I had thought to take him to Kakar, the Barking Deer, to hear it meet and proper."

"What need I with the Word from the Hooved People?" Mowgli asked fretfully. "They cannot hurt me or help me, I think. I need only learn the call to herd them to my brothers, that I might share in the kill. The herds are made of silly fools who only stamp and bleat and run to and fro."

"Thy manners, manling," Baloo said gently. "Tolerance is a rare flower that withers too easily. And often, the smallest blossoms, when clustered together, have the strongest scent."

"The cub speaks some truth, even if with an unlovely tongue," Bagheera said. "The herds are like other tribes I have known who prefer to follow that which disturbs them least. This is common to many nations, ay, even in the jungle." Bagheera had been born among men, as you may remember, and so he knew of what he spoke. "Still, there is much he can learn there, if he will."

But then a jungle mynah flapped down and bent his head to the pool. All the Hunting People listen when Patwari, the Mynah, speaks, though he does so incessantly, for he rides the herds to eat the insects off their hides, warning of intruders. He knows the movements of all the beasts of the plains, and one set of hooves is the same as another to him, so long as they kick up the dust and the bugs.

The mynah cocked a yellow eye at Bagheera's sleek flanks and wide jaws. "Good hunting all," he whistled wryly.

"Good hunting," Baloo answered courteously.

"Indeed, it would be," Bagheera purred, "were the day not so long and the shadows so scant. What moves?"

"The grass is dry by the river, Your Honour," Patwari recited quickly, "and the herds move closer to the trees." He ducked his head in the pool, throwing water on his wings, ruffling and sneezing in a frenzy of pleasure. "The blackbuck say the Rains come soon, but the chital say they will never come again."

"So they always say," Bagheera said. "And the bud-horns?"

"Fat and running well, Protector of the Poor. Their dams must search far for fodder, though, and the dust tightens every gorge."

"Except thine own."

The mynah gave a brazen croak. "Except mine own. Shall I tell my Lord you will favour us this night?" Patwari's current lord was the gaur, the horned buffalo, and well Patwari knew that not even Bagheera would try his ripping talons on such a thick-necked prey.

"Tell him what thou wilt," Bagheera yawned, deliberately showing both gleaming, white canines, a red curled tongue, and half-way down his hot gullet.

The sight of the huge teeth made the mynah start and pull his head into his feathers nervously. "Good luck go with you, Your Honour," he stuttered, and flew quickly away.

Mowgli laughed delightedly. "By the time the shadows disappear, all the plains will know Bagheera has teeth longer than Patwari's tailfeathers."

"This, they know already," Bagheera said. "But it is good to remind them, Little Brother."

As is the way of the Hunting People, the friends slept the rest of the sun away. Then, when the sough of the wind changed, Bagheera lifted his head and stretched out his claws, shuddering with readiness. Mowgli woke to the whisper of the dry grass and the palm fronds, the hoot of a roused owl, the hurried scuttle of some night creature foraging in the bamboo, the chirr of a cricket, the flutter of a bat's wing, and far away, the lullaby of all India—the howl of the jackal pack. Night had come to the jungle.

"Tonight, I hunt with thee?" he asked Bagheera quietly, hoping it was so.

Mowgli was still too young to know much of death. The times when he would kill his first buck, destroy the Red Dog, and even slay Shere Khan, the hated Tiger, were still far before him and are told in another place. This night, the taste of blood was still fresh and new to his lips, for Baloo had showed him that honey and nuts and fruits could be fine to eat, and he had only just learned to drive game into his brothers' jaws, that he might share the meat they took down.

"Woof!" Baloo said drowsily. "This is not my path, Little Dreamer. I leave thee to thy game," and the old bear padded off to find a tree full of sleeping bees.

Mowgli jumped up, instantly awake as young boys are, and eager. "It will be *most* good hunting together!" he said, wriggling with pure joy.

"Not quite together, Little Brother," the Black Panther said dryly. "But, ay, tonight we go among the Hooved Ones. See ye stay behind my flanks, and rub some of that marsh on thy jowls, else the moon will betray us. And tell me again, thou wilt kill all save what hooved beast?"

Mowgli said quickly, "I may kill all I can catch save the cattle. For by the sake of the Bull that brought me into the Pack—the Bull thou hast paid for me and so for thine honour as well, O Bagheera"—and here, the great cat purred gently—"I must never kill any cattle old or young. That is the Law."

"Well spoken. And now, we shall see what runs hot-foot in the grasses."

The moon was fat and high when Mowgli and Bagheera finally reached the edge of the jungle, and dark clouds bunched and crowded across the night sky. The two hunters crouched in the tall grasses and gazed out over the flat plains. Before them, a wide *dhun* or veld stretched as far as they could see, dotted with vast herds, darker moving shadows on the lighter ground. Bagheera's eyes glowed with a green fire, and he kneaded the ground rhythmically, a deep hum coming from somewhere inside him.

Mowgli opened his eyes as wide as he could, straining to see the herds in the distance. "Would that I had thine eyes," he muttered to Bagheera.

The big cat chuckled low in his throat. "There speaks a man-cub. Now, hssst! Watch their ears, Little Brother, and keep downwind."

A large herd of chital deer browsed nearby, their eyes a cluster of blue stars in the waving grass. Further off, Mowgli could hear the muffled bellow of the nilghai, the tall blue cows of the plains, and the snort of the gaur, the great black bull with the curved horns, keen nose, and poor eyes. He knew that the red dots in the blackness were the eyes of the sambhur, higher from the ground than he was tall, the huge deer with the maned neck.

Bagheera was creeping closer to the spotted chital, his head barely parting the grass. The does, fawns, and yearlings grouped in the centre of the herd; some lay in the brush. The sentries browsed at the edges, their antlers clicking together as their heads dipped and rose, their eyes always moving, their ears twisting towards the shadows.

Mowgli slid behind Bagheera, careful to keep well back of his switching tail. The hot wind began to gust, the grasses rustled and the herd shifted nervously. Still the Black Panther crept closer.

Mowgli tasted the wind for smells and signs and could find only the dust and the grasses in his nose. The chital before them browsed again, and Bagheera bunched his haunches under him to spring, his ears back and flattened to his head.

A distant sambhur gave a sudden alarm call, a "po-onk, po-onk, po-onk!" and each chital leaped to its feet. Bagheera froze, and Mowgli dropped to his belly, hiding his face from the deer. When he peered through the grasses again, all the herd looked towards them, trying to see the danger through the thick brush.

And then Bagheera did a curious thing. While Mowgli watched in amazement, the big cat rose slowly and sauntered from the grasses out onto the open plain, in full view of the herd. They started; a fawn bleated in terror, and for an instant, it seemed they

would bolt. But Bagheera never looked once in their direction. The Black Panther ambled to a spot of ground, snuffed it carefully, and lay down on his back. He began to purr, a crooning hum in his throat that sounded like the sweetest, most private lullaby.

The chital sentries stamped and snorted; the herd clustered close together, and no head turned away from the cat.

Slowly, with no sudden movement, Bagheera began to twist and turn in the moonlight, switching his long tail back and forth in the grass, and batting his paws at some unseen butterfly in the air. His green eyes were half-closed in pleasure; he curled his huge body up and swatted at his own tail, and his purr grew louder still.

A nervous murmur ran through the herd, and those yearlings sheltered inside the circle of deer craned their necks to get a better view. One young buck snorted loudly, rushed to the edge of the sentries, and stamped both hooves as though in challenge.

But Bagheera never turned his head. Now, he was chasing his tail round and round, giving excited mewing, growling sounds, for all the world like a giant, half-mad kitten.

The herd stood silent now, in wonder, and a few yearlings ventured out towards the cat, their nostrils reaching for the half-familiar, well-feared scent, their ears twitching towards these teasing sounds. A sentry bleated a warning, but the hum of Bagheera's purr all but blotted it out. Still, the wind rose, and Mowgli raised up on one elbow to see more clearly.

A cloud moved across the moon, and in that swift black moment, Bagheera leaped, hurling himself at the closest yearling. The chital gave a startled bleat and bolted. The herd sprang as one deer away from the snarling panther, and there was only the thunder of hooves, the dust, and racing shadows. Mowgli jumped to his feet and shouted in the confusion.

When he reached Bagheera's side, the cat was methodically cleaning his great talons of chital hide. He panted, and Mowgli could see his heartbeat shake him back and forth.

"Ye have missed!" Mowgli said in wonder.

"It happens," the Black Panther said. "Even to Bagheera."

Mowgli hunkered down beside him and examined the clumps of hide and hair on the ground. "That is one yearling who will not soon forget. Almost, did they come close enough."

"Almost. But they were skittish this night. We do not hunt alone."

In the distance, Mowgli heard the giggling, whooping, screaming from the shadows that said a hyena pack also prowled the plains.

A sudden crack of thunder rumbled across the sky. Mowgli put his nose in the air. "I taste a storm," he said.

"The Rains will soon be on us," Bagheera sighed.

"It is in my stomach that something comes on the wind."

"Thy stomach is young, and thou hast not seen many Rains," Bagheera said quietly, licking one huge forepaw. "The herds are large, and ye have not been this close, I think. Dost thou still think the Hooved Folk of little matter?"

Mowgli frowned thoughtfully. "They are eaters of grass, and as such, fodder for such as we, the Hunters, is it not so? No little matter, but neither are they Masters of the Jungle."

"Uum," Bagheera purred under his whiskers and said no more for a long moment. Finally, he stretched and looked over the plain, taking his bearings once more. "Well, one of us at least is empty, and Master or no, an empty stomach makes a careless eye." His tail switched once, twice, and then stiffened. "So, to the foolish, foolish deer."

In a while, the two were once more hidden in the brush, watching another herd. This time, Bagheera had chosen a small group of blackbuck. Ordinarily, Mowgli knew, the large deer with the high spiraled horns would be the last choice, but the chital were now huddled in a nervous group in the middle of the plains with no near cover, and the hyenas were worrying the nilghai.

For a herd with many young, the blackbuck were uncommonly scattered, and only one old vigilant *harni,* or doe, stood guard. Again, Bagheera crouched low in the grass, his eyes watching each head, his ears pricked forward for the stamp of a hoof.

"Stalk behind them, Little Brother," he whispered, "whilst I move closer. But beware their horns. I have seen older cubs than thee gored and trampled, too eager to be first at the kill. Give tongue when thou art ready."

Mowgli slid backwards through the brush, holding the grasses still with his hands until he passed through them, willing his breath to be silent, his feet to be sure. When he reached full cover, he rose and moved swiftly behind the herd, staying downwind, watching the guard doe always for the sudden lifting of the head, the snort of fear, which would say he had been discovered.

Another crack of thunder rolled through the night, and Mowgli used the cover of the noise to creep so close to the herd that he could smell the warm hides of the does, could hear the mumble of the yearlings in the short grass.

"Ai!" a fawn bleated sleepily, "this grass hurts my mouth, it is so stiff."

A yearling muttered, "Then do not tear it up, if ye cannot use it, sprigling."

Mowgli could understand part of this, of course, for the talk of the young, even of different creatures, is more the same than different.

"Will we run again tomorrow?" another fawn asked wearily, stretching his bony legs out and shaking each one.

"Uhnn-uhnn-uhnn," his dam murmured. "When tomorrow comes, we run for tomorrow."

"Would I were born a bullock," the fawn whimpered. "They lie in the cool mud all day and eat what is at hand."

The doe shoved the fawn with her haunches in reproof. "And they are one blood with the pig. We are the Deer."

Mowgli shifted up on one elbow and tried to peer through the herd to the grass beyond. He knew Bagheera lay hidden somewhere in the brush, waiting for him to drive the quarry into his jaws.

There was a sudden flash of light, a sharp brraack! of jagged heat-lightning from somewhere close behind him, and Mowgli ducked, blinded by the flare. His eyes were closed, and he could see, outlined against the white sky, the frozen shapes of the deer inside his eyelids. He sat up and rubbed his eyes.

For a long moment, all was silent—and then another rumble, louder than the thunder, came swiftly towards him, the pounding of a thousand hooves, and he suddenly smelled smoke on the wind. He looked up and saw a line of fire moving fast across the plains, eating up the brush, moving towards the river, and he leaped through the milling animals, trying to reach Bagheera. But he stumbled against a running blackbuck, its eyes rolled back white in terror, and he fell to his knees. As though by a silent signal, the hooves wheeled as one away from the fire.

Instantly, the herds were upon him, and he was smothered in their hot, swaying, pounding bodies as, flanks pressed together, bleating frantically, they rushed over the plain, and he was pushed along, almost trampled, thrust forward with their mass. He clutched frantically to the maned hide of a sambhur, somehow separated from its herd and taller than the blackbuck around it, and lifted his feet off the ground, trying to raise his head above its shoulders. Mowgli knew if he fell again, he would be food for the kites by dawn.

He gave the call of the Master Words again and again, cursing himself for not learning the words of the herds before he went among them.

"We be of one blood, ye and I!" he shouted in every jungle tongue he could remember, but in the chaos of noise and panic, he could scarcely keep his breath, much less be heard above the din. He pulled himself up with all his strength, the last of it, he dimly realized, and threw one leg over the galloping sambhur's back. He hoisted himself up, clutched the plunging animal's neck, and raced across the plains before the fire.

"Wahooa! O Bagheera! Ahai! Bagheera!" Mowgli cried when he could, and he caught himself just in time as a huge gaur crashed into the sambhur's side and almost knocked him down beneath the pounding hooves. Through the dust and the smoke, Mowgli could see nothing but moving shoulders and haunches; he could hear only bleats and snorts and bellows of fear and rage—and where was Bagheera?

Then, above the din, he heard the single scream of the Black Panther, roaring in a terrible anger, a hideous shriek that meant a great killing was at hand. Bagheera's call seemed to shiver through the moving herds, and Mowgli felt the sambhur shift and check its flight. He pulled himself up and looked over the swaying masses and saw Bagheera running towards them. The great cat's coat was bristled all about him, and he looked twice his size, his jaws open and his huge teeth flashing.

The herds were close to the river now; the fire had grown tree-high, and smoke clouds billowed about their heads. Mowgli saw Bagheera's plan at once and twisted the sambhur's mane hard to the side, forcing him to turn, and he felt the mass of the herd swerve away from Bagheera's charge, towards the riverbank. Now, as though they saw their route clearly, they ran blindly for safety, instinctively towards the only thing which might stop the flames and away from their other enemy, the roaring panther.

They reached the bank, plunged over the side, and Mowgli felt the sambhur's legs begin to swim rather than gallop. He let go the mane and fought his way through the struggling creatures, sliding from one back to another, thrashing through the current, and finally dragged himself up on the riverbank.

Bedraggled and exhausted, he sat and watched the fire coming towards the water. All around him, chital deer, sambhur, nilghai, and blackbuck pulled themselves out of the river, shaking and bleating and snorting. A few, belly-up in the current, would never run again.

There was another rumble of thunder, and the rains began, the sudden drenching cloud-burst that signals the coming of the monsoon. The herds turned their heads to the sky and let the water wash over them. A silence came to the riverbank.

The fire was brush-high and moving slower now, with less to eat as it got closer to the river, almost as though it sensed its own death. The white flames were turning orange, the cracklings and snaps were fewer, and finally, as the flames reached the damp grass near the water, they sizzled and spat and stopped altogether, sending up huge billows of white smoke and hissing steam into the downpour.

As the smoke cleared, Mowgli could see that though part of the plain was blackened, much of the vast grasses was still untouched. The rush of the herds and his own peril had seemed all the world to him just moments ago, yet now he could see that it was just a small space in time. The herds began to cross the river again slowly, picking their way across the shallow spots, barely glancing at their dead brethren, back to the veld.

Mowgli heard a cough behind him, and Bagheera climbed out of a tree, gliding from branch to branch and then to the ground.

His eyes were slits against the rain, and his black coat stuck to his flanks.

"Why do they go back?" Mowgli asked, pointing to the herds straggling across the river to the plains. "This will not be the last time they run from the orange death."

"It is all they know."

"Some could live in the jungle."

"What one does, they all do."

"They die from such a thinking," Mowgli said, glancing at the carcasses floating slowly downriver.

Bagheera shrugged gently. "They live by it, as well."

Mowgli thought this over in silence. "There is one other I shall not kill, after this night," he said quietly. "The Bull and now the Sambhur. But for his shoulders, the herds would have had me." He shuddered as he felt once more the fear of the mad rush in his mind. "For silly fools who only run to and fro, they make a mighty thunder." He glanced up to the tree Bagheera had climbed down. Up in the thickest branches, a young chital sprawled, its neck at a twisted angle.

"Thou hast killed? Before or after ye turned the herds to save me?"

Bagheera closed his eyes thoughtfully. "Whilst turning, I think. It does not matter. Thou art safe, Little Frog," said he tenderly. "And a kill is a kill. We hunt by rules. There is order to our world and reasons why we kill. Why kill one and not another? Why follow one set of trails and turn aside from others just as fresh? Why will a wounded cow stand apart from the herd to be seen and not try to run? It is part of the conversation of death, a language you must learn, Little Brother. A choosing by both the hunter and the hunted. Those who are ready to die, give. In this, there is order. In this, there is meat which fills the belly, unlike that given in a pan to a dog or behind bars from the hand of Man."

"You remember Man?"

"Very well. But Man has forgotten what he once knew, that there is more to the hunt than killing. That dying is as sacred as living. And so, there shall be no time you kill that you have not been given permission."

"When I spring upon a young deer from behind and he does not know I am there?"

"He has given you permission by playing a deadly game of carelessness, and he has lost. Another time, you might meet the same deer and catch only the dust from his heels. It is Good Hunting." The Black Panther turned his head and sniffed the air contentedly. "Dawn comes. The year turns, and the Rains are here."

Around them, the forest stirred with a thousand small sounds as the Jungle People ended the long night of hunting. Chil, the Kite, balanced above them, wheeled over the river, choosing his spot to feed on the dead.

Mowgli sighed slowly, suddenly weary to the bone. "Full gorge and a deep sleep, O best of friends," he said to the cat.

"Thou wilt not share the kill?"

Mowgli turned away. "Baloo says the Law comes before all else, even before the stomach. Most particularly when the stomach is as small as mine. I should have listened then. So I will go to ask something of Kakar, the Barking Deer," he added over his shoulder. "Something I should have learned before."

"And the foolish deer?" Bagheera smiled slowly.

"I shall leave it to their masters to call them such." Mowgli grinned sheepishly, ducking his head.

This is the Master Word of the Hooved People, which Mowgli learned from Kakar, the Barking Deer. It is overlong, when compared to the Master Words from other jungle folk—part law, part anthem—but Baloo assured Mowgli that he need learn only the final verse.

Litany of the Herds

Ears that catch the slightest shift of every blade of grass,
Legs that leap and hooves that kick and tails that flash alarm,
Does and kids to centre, all, until the Killers pass,
Always ready, swift as wind, ye never shall know harm.

When the buck-necks swell once more and rut is on the land,
Gather ye together then into each separate troop,
But when the sucklings stumble forth, heed the Herd's command,
None shall cross or come before the safety of the group!

Claws will rip and teeth will tear, but dust shall they become,
Pug-marks to be blotted out by each spring kid's hoof-fall,
All heartbeats join together, to make a single hum:
"The Herd lives on! We be of one blood, Hooved Ones, all!"

WHERE THE ELEPHANTS DANCE

Keep the silence, listen deeply,
Do not speak till thou art sure.
Ears outweigh tongue for a reason—
Let Time be the arbiter.
Trunks up, trunks up!
As it has been, so it shall be.
Thus, the Jungle Lords decree.

Never hurry at thy wooing,
Never hasten at thy meal,
Pleasures rushed leave hollow spaces
Scars which new heats will not heal.
Trunks up, trunks up!
Strength, resolve, and dignity.
So, the Jungle Lords decree.

Keep from those who cause disorder,
Those who lie or gorge or steal,
When thy son has cast his milk-tusks,
Foes will be dust 'neath his heel.
Trunks up, trunks up!
Keep the Law in all degree,
This, the Jungle Lords decree.

Maxims of Hathi, as told to his sons

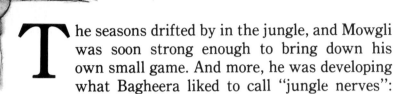

The seasons drifted by in the jungle, and Mowgli was soon strong enough to bring down his own small game. And more, he was developing what Bagheera liked to call "jungle nerves": that unconscious ability to sense danger about and then move to avoid it. When he had grown tall enough to stand well above Baloo's shoulders, the bear took him to see Hathi, the Lord of the Elephants.

"Is Hathi Lord of *all* the jungle?" Mowgli asked as they traipsed through the shadowed thickets to where the elephants roamed.

"Nay, Little Brother," Baloo said, pushing a creeper aside that Mowgli might crawl under it easily. "The jungle has no Lord. But Hathi is one of the oldest and the mightiest of all the forest folk. He remembers when Kaa, the great Rock Python, was smaller round than thy leg. And so, it is seemly that ye meet him and learn from him what ye can."

"What can he teach me that ye cannot?"

"Chiefly, he can teach thee of Man. If he will."

"I have no need to learn of Man, Baloo," Mowgli said quickly. "I am of the Pack. Of the Free People. And those who speak of me and Man in one breath do not see what is. But I would like to see great Hathi, face to face, nonetheless."

"Pick up thy feet, Little Dreamer, else ye stumble on these vines. Face to face with Hathi thou wilt not be unless he kneels. And that, he does not do, I can promise thee."

After two days' travel, the bear and the boy reached the Waingunga River, where Hathi and his tribe spent the hot spring months. They heard the vast troop of elephants well before they reached their grounds, heard the stomping of huge heels in the mud, the splash and spray and squeals of bathing yearlings, the deep gurgling snuffs of browsing old ones, and the occasional creak and crash of a nut-palm when they shoved it to the ground.

Baloo brought Mowgli to the edge of the forest and there, they waited to be recognized before they went forward among the herd.

Twenty or more huge elephants stood on the riverbank, rocking and squirting themselves in the cool water. Smaller, hairy youngsters ran between the massive tree-trunk legs, squealing and throwing mud. In the shade of the nearby palms, the rest of the herd browsed, plucking fruit and leaves from the trees, while sentry parrots screamed and preened among the branches.

Under the spreading canopy of an ancient neem tree, one lone bull elephant stood apart from the rest, flanked by three younger males. He plucked a trunkful of grass, dusted it against his great knees, and put it in his mouth thoughtfully, eyeing the bear and the boy at the edge of the thicket.

"Yonder stands Hathi," Baloo said quietly. "And his three sons by him."

Mowgli glanced questioningly at the bear.

"We must wait," Baloo whispered.

Finally, one of the young males ambled slowly over to where they stood. He cocked an eye at Baloo and then at Mowgli, who stood by the bear's shoulder, his hand twisted in his fur.

"Good hunting, O Son of Hathi," Baloo said courteously.

"Good hunting," the elephant gurgled. "What does the wise teacher of wolves do in this piece of the woods?"

"I bring Mowgli, the man-cub, that he might learn at Lord Hathi's knee. He would know something of Man."

Mowgli knew better than to speak, but he twisted his fingers more tightly in Baloo's neck-hairs.

"Of Man?" the elephant asked, turning a cautious and keen eye on the boy. "Which? There are more colours of Man than there are nuts on that palm. Would he learn of the Wild Men of the woods, the little brown scorpions who hurl arrows and scream from the banks of the Sarda? Or of the Gonds, who creep about, laying traps with piercing sticks? Or of the White-Faces, the worst of all? They are all brothers to the *Bandar-log*, tail-less monkeys, but more dangerous." Hathi's son shook his great head vigourously, his tusks down in contempt. "A long walk to speak of such."

Baloo answered him calmly. "Still, we have come. Wilt thou commend us to thy Lord?"

The elephant shrugged with disdain, a heaving of shoulders and sagging hide, then wheeled slowly and ambled back towards the edge of the thicket, never glancing again at Baloo and Mowgli who followed.

"This sapling has taken leave of his roots," Baloo murmured, half to himself. "Hathi has reared himself a renegade."

"I fear this is a fool's errand—" Mowgli whispered, but Baloo cut him off harshly.

"_Chup_! [Be silent!]" he muttered. "Listen and learn."

The procession finally arrived before Hathi, the Lord of the Elephants. Baloo sat before him, up on his haunches, and Mowgli squatted down in the grass, glancing uneasily at the huge beasts on all sides.

Hathi rocked patiently back and forth, a mountainous gray mass of wrinkled hide with wary white eyes and fanned ears pitched forward, as if to catch the slightest breath from his visitors. His trunk switched gently from side to side.

Mowgli looked up, up, all the way to the top of Hathi's bald and wrinkled head, a massive blot against the sun and sky, but the sun blinded him and his neck cricked, and he had never felt so small in his life.

"Good Hunting, Baloo," Hathi rumbled, a slow, mighty heaving of sound and wind.

"Good Hunting, O Hathi," Baloo said cheerfully. "I bring the man-cub, Mowgli. Thou hast perhaps heard of him? I have undertaken to teach him whatever small wisdom I can, for the sake of the Free People." Baloo nudged the boy gently.

Mowgli stood, unsure what he was to do. The closest part of Hathi to him was the long, snake-like trunk. It looked strong and heavy as a tree at the top, but the bottom seemed delicate and tender, like the smallest fingers on his own hand. Without thinking, he put out his palms towards the questing trunk and said, "Good Hunting go with ye, O Great Hathi Who Blocks Out the Sky, and with thy sons, as well. I, Mowgli, the wolfling, ask leave to walk through thy piece of the world." He stood, his palms outstretched, waiting.

The pink pointed tip of the trunk grazed his palms gently, and Hathi breathed a windy sigh, as he took in the boy's scent. He chuckled then, a blowing out of grass-smell and small thunder.

"A mannered manling," Hathi said, cocking his white eye over

Mowgli's shoulders. "Thou hast given him a gentle tongue, Baloo." He laid the great trunk carefully on the boy's head. "Thou art welcome, Mowgli. Wolfling or manling or both."

Baloo said with pride, "He brings a good head to the teachings. Already, he knows the Master Words. But"—and here, Baloo hesitated—"there are things I may not teach him, O Hathi. Ye know the reasons. And yet, I would he learn them, for his heart's sake." He ducked his head quickly. "There are those in the jungle who love him and would keep him safe. He is but a little frog now, but the time will come . . ."

"Well thought and well spoken, Baloo," Hathi gurgled gently. "It needs no other reason. Is he strong enough for the Trek?"

Mowgli began to grow impatient with being discussed as though he were not there. "I am strong enough, O Hathi, but whither wouldst thou lead?"

Baloo rolled his eyes at this interruption, but Hathi turned to the boy with all courtesy.

"It is the season of the Dance, Little Frog, and then of that which comes after. Few eyes have seen it, other than those of the Tribe. It shall be a long journey, and thou wilt eat much with those big eyes of thine—a man's eyes, to be sure," he said under his trunk to Baloo, "but if thou wilt grow thine ears as large as thine eyes, thou wilt take back fodder for many seasons. And thou shalt know that which even thy teacher dost not know."

Mowgli grinned. The idea delighted him.

Baloo looked away for an instant, as though he had something else he would ask and could not. "It is good," he muttered, "and he shall be well, I am sure—"

One of Hathi's sons, the first elephant who had approached them, interrupted Baloo with a snort, his trunk switching fretfully. "It is a long Trek, and thou art wise to worry for his wellbeing. It is no place for a *man*-child, even one who speaks with a jungle tongue. If he would know the ways of Man, let him learn from his *own* tribe."

Baloo's eyebrows raised at the young elephant's rudeness.

Mowgli stiffened with indignation, but he said calmly, "This is twice, thrice, that ye have called me by such a name as I hate. I had thought that such large ears could surely hear the peepings of this frog well enough. Perhaps I needs must shout." And he stood up and faced the angry elephant. Before Baloo could stop him, he cupped his hands and roared out, "I AM MOWGLI, OF THE WOLVES, O DEAF ONE, AND BROTHER TO NO MAN-PACK! CANST THOU HEAR ME NOW?!"

Elephants, as you know, are extremely sensitive to sounds and find loud noises as disturbing as gunshots in a temple. The brace of elephants visibly rocked back on their heels, and there was a long, breathless moment while they recovered their composure. Mowgli did not flinch, but he felt Baloo beside him, shifting closer in case of danger.

Finally, Hathi chuckled wryly. "Nay, wolfling, there was nothing of Man in that bay." He cast a baleful eye on his son, whose ears still shivered with Mowgli's shout. "This one's eyes are sometimes as weak as his ears, Baloo. I am certain that he did not know thee for the moment. Wilt thou excuse him?"

"It is nothing, O Hathi." Baloo waved aside his apology. "The sun is bright today, and I, myself, near tripped over my own paws for squinting. But if the Trek is overlong—"

Hathi lifted up his trunk in a silent salute. "He shall ride on my own back, Teacher of Wolflings. Do not fear."

Now, Baloo chuckled ruefully. "A broader back, I could not wish for him, O Hathi. I am filled with bat's chatter and little worries which bite like fleas. Mowgli"—and he turned to the boy with great dignity—"remember thy tongue, watch thy hands, and keep thy heels still. And now, if thou wilt come down to the river, I will help make thee ready."

When Baloo had him knee-deep in water and out of earshot, he said, "Thou must keep a watchful eye on that great gray one, Little Brother. He is in musth. Duck under, now."

"What is musth?" Mowgli asked, coming up sputtering.

"Something which befalls many creatures, when they are half-way between a cub and a yearling. This one is perhaps fourteen seasons, I wager, and it is full on him. Thou wert not half-wrong, when thou said he was deaf." Baloo licked the boy's cheeks gently, taking off the last of the dust from their travels. "When the musth is on the bull elephants, a sour wetness comes from openings between their eyes and their ears, and they are near-blinded with ill temper. In their musth season only, they will gore the very sands for offending them and rut on anything which walks. When it passes, they are once again the Lords of the Jungle, and reason rides their backs."

"And what is this Trek which Hathi talks of? Ye wish me to go?"

"I would not have brought thee if I did not. Thou wilt be safe with Hathi, no matter if the whole world is in musth. Raise thine arm, Little Brother, and wash off that mud. Thou hast a chance to see and learn more in a moon than most Jungle Folk will know in a lifetime."

They emerged from the river and rolled together on the grassy bank to dry. "Why will Hathi take *me*, Baloo, and no other? And why canst thou not come along?"

Baloo shook his head firmly. "Ask thy questions of Hathi, if thou wilt, Little Brother. For the next moon, he is thy dam, thy sire, and thy Pack, eh? And I will wait for thee with old honey and new grubs when the night-sky changes once more."

Before Mowgli could speak again, Baloo padded off into the jungle, leaving him among the elephants.

For six days, Mowgli rode through the forest on Hathi's back, rocking back and forth unceasingly with the elephant's rolling gait. The first day, he was eaten up with excitement and curiosity, and Hathi had to tell him, over and over, "Sit thee still, little thumbling, else thou wilt slip and break thy head like a cocoanut."

On both sides, in a vanguard, the sons of Hathi strode along solemnly; behind them, in a long line of swaying gray mountains, the rest of the herd walked head to tail. Mostly silent, the troops of elephants moved through the jungle with surprising ease, startling monkeys and peacocks who warned of their coming. The calves darted between the moving legs, always watched carefully by the vigilant cows; the bulls stayed back, bringing up the rear.

The second day, Mowgli felt he had been beaten with a badger's tail, and the backs of his legs were chafed and raw from Hathi's rough hide. By now, the herd had settled down into the long, rolling gait of the elephant which eats up the miles and flattens mountains. The calves no longer squealed and galloped, but walked along, sedate as their mothers. By the third day, Mowgli

24

felt as though he had never been anywhere but astride great Hathi's back, that he had been born there and would die there, and so he began to open his eyes and see.

On the fourth day, as dawn broke and the troop began to move, Mowgli sat high on Hathi's head and looked about. The sky was yellow with the coming sun, and the fruit bats were flying home to roost, hanging themselves in the shadows of the mango trees, quarreling and flapping as they jostled for sleeping space.

"O Hathi," Mowgli asked, "what is it, to be an elephant?"

Hathi thought for a moment, as always, taking his time. "It is being born feet-first, thumbling, instead of head-first like thy brethren. It is calling no beast *Hare,* Lord, and it is making choices, always remembering that each must make his own choice, even unto death. Thou hast heard it said, 'Each has his own fear'?"

"I have heard it. But what can Hathi's kindred ever fear?"

Hathi swung his great head aside for an instant, checking the source of raucous screams from the plains just beyond the jungle path they followed. A large pack of jackals squabbled over a fallen nilghai; the vultures bobbed and prayed over the carcass, and a hyena shrieked again from the thicket, trying to drive off the mob. Mowgli waited patiently for Hathi's answer.

"Wouldst thou hear a tale?" Hathi gurgled, swinging back into full stride.

Mowgli leaned forward over the great beast's head and patted his brow gently. "I listen, O Hathi."

"Once, there was a jackal who fell into a tub of indigo dye in the village," Hathi said, his huge heels moving rhythmically through the brush. "And so he thought, 'I am now the best of all colours and should be advanced in life.' He called together the rest of his tribe and declared himself King of all the Jackals."

Mowgli chuckled and hunkered down closer to Hathi's head.

"All the jackals called him King as he commanded, and he gathered together a following of tigers and hyenas to keep him company."

"A fine company," Mowgli murmured dryly.

"So the jackal thought. And thus, he banished the rest of his kin as unfit to be in his presence. But the elders of the jackals knew him for what he was and had been. So one night at full moon, they gathered together on the highest hill and began to howl. Of course, the King of the Jackals joined in full throat. And the panther, who is not easily fooled, saw that he was, after all, only a jackal and killed him. Such is the fate of any fool who deserts his own kind and joins his enemies."

Mowgli scowled in puzzlement. Finally, he said, "It is a fine tale, but I cannot see where it leads. We spoke of fear, eh? What fear is there in this?"

Hathi switched his trunk up and snatched at a passing leaf. "The fear of losing oneself, Little Frog. The fear of forgetting who thou art and where thou belongs and by doing so, of losing thy way and thy choice."

"And this is what it is to be an elephant?"

"Even so. Take this leaf," Hathi said, passing it up to Mowgli, "and shade thyself. We come to the open plains."

Hathi wheeled slowly out of the dense jungle and down a hill towards a broad river. He lifted his trunk and trumpeted, and the signal went down the line that they would bed here tonight.

While the elephants rested and browsed and bathed, Mowgli slipped back into the jungle. He gave the Strangers' Hunting Call, which must be repeated until it is answered whenever one of the Jungle People hunts outside his own grounds: "Give me leave to hunt here because I am hungry." From far away in the thicket, he heard the expected response, "Hunt, then, for food, but not for pleasure," and he silently thanked whatever beast had so answered him. Before dusk came, he had killed a small ground squirrel, eaten, and returned to the river to clean himself.

Hathi stood alone, squirting dust all over his huge gray sides, and Mowgli strolled over to him. "How many more suns do we travel, O Hathi?" he asked.

"Two, more or less," the elephant said.

"And what will we see when we get there?"

Hathi's voice turned gruff but his eyes twinkled. "Patience, man-child, patience. Thou must always needs know what will happen next? Wait till the Wheel comes round."

One of Hathi's sons approached them to report. "Two lame and at least half a dozen sore," he said, "but none who cannot travel at sunup."

"And Mayat?" Hathi asked. Mayat was an old grizzled tusker, older even than Hathi, and his eyes were crusted and wrinkled with age. Mowgli wondered that he had made such a trek.

"He says he will outdance thee."

"And he may, he may," Hathi chuckled to his son, shaking all over for the fun of it, as elephants will.

Night came to the river, and the herd began to settle down, the cows calling to their calves to come from the water, the yearlings shoving each other for space among the trees, the old ones snoring before their great heads touched the grass.

Mowgli had learned that many of the elephants needed surprisingly few hours of sleep each night. The calves and old ones drowsed from sundown to sunup. However, most of the grown tuskers lay down for two hours just before the moon was at its highest; then they stood up, switched sides, and lay down again for another two hours as the moon set. The rest of the dark hours, they spent browsing, mumbling to each other, and standing shoulder to shoulder, gazing out over the plains, rocking, rocking, always rocking.

Mowgli found a low-branched sal tree and wove together several vines to make a solid hammock swaying twelve feet above the ground. He climbed in, rested his head on his arms, and watched the moon move across the night sky. Though they had travelled many miles, he had done little walking himself, and so he was weary but restless. He wondered idly what Bagheera hunted tonight and whether Baloo was thinking of him.

Two elephant cows talked softly beneath Mowgli's tree, each unaware that he could hear them above.

"I have never seen so hard a musth before," one she-elephant whispered. "Batha is mad with it and will not be appeased."

Batha was Hathi's son, the young bull who had first approached and then insulted Mowgli on his arrival to the herd. The boy pricked up his ears and listened closely.

"He has worried the back of the lines all day, until even his own brothers must scold him. It is a great shame for Hathi."

"It is a greater shame for Batha," the other cow said wryly.

"And it will not be forgotten, either." She grunted with weariness and shuffled foot to foot.

"And yet—" the younger cow whispered "—and yet, he has some cause, and perhaps it will be forgiven. It is hard to be the youngest son of Hathi, eh? With two older brothers to stand always before him, to know that for always, he has no place of his own, and will never stand where his father stands."

"There are other herds."

"But none so large, so fixed in the eyes of the jungle. And whither he goes, Hathi's name goes before him." She shook her head gently. "I do not envy him his path."

"Nor do I," the older cow said, "but I mean to stay out of it, henceforth. Aa-uugh! My backside is sore with his prodding and my ears ache with his naggings and were I a yearling, his shoulder would feel my tusks."

"And thou wouldst get gored for thy pains. He may be the youngest of all Hathi's sons, but his swords are sickle-sharp and fast as an adder's strike. The Herd will lose a good one when he goes."

"Perhaps he will not."

"Has he any other choice?"

The two elephants browsed slowly away, and Mowgli lay in the darkness thinking over what he had heard. Finally, he slept deeply and dreamed of bathing in the shadowed lagoon, splashing about like an otter with old Baloo.

Mowgli awoke as the moon was setting. His skin felt sticky in the night-heat, and a stiff dryness had settled into the back of his throat. He slid quietly down from his hammock and padded across the bank to the river. All about him, elephants lay in the shadows, their huge bulks sprawled, snorts and gurgles coming from their trunks.

He stepped into the cool water up to his ankles, his knees, and then bent over to drink from his cupped hands. A quick surge of current pushed against his legs, he heard a soft swish, and suddenly a large tail thwacked him across the back of the neck, almost knocking him headlong into the water.

Mowgli staggered, grabbed at something moving swiftly by him, and was face to face with a huge mugger crocodile, its mouth gaping and grinning, its evil red eyes gleaming in the black waters, its leathery body whipping through the shallows like a snake. The mugger slashed across with its tail once more, reaching up to smash the boy into the water over his head, right into its waiting jaws. Mowgli gasped for air, whirled for the bank, and looked up to see Batha, Hathi's son, thundering towards him.

The great bull elephant trumpeted in rage, his ears flapping, and crashed into the water up to his knees. Before the crocodile could turn and flee, Batha snatched him up by the tail, his trunk lifting him high over his head, and smashed him once, twice, down on the riverbank. Then, with a scream of victory and defiance, the elephant whirled the mugger over his head and tossed him high into the branches of the sal trees.

Mowgli gaped in shocked wonder. Now that the mugger was out of the water, silhouetted against the last of the moon, his black, ugly tail did not look so large—now that his jaws were closed. His broken body hung, boneless and slack, pinned between two branches, and a great cloud of bats rose over him, squealing and chattering in protest. Batha stood shivering and muttering loudly on the bank, his tail and trunk switching violently from side to side.

"A *calf* knows better than to wade knee-deep in moonlight, manling! It is lucky for thy young hide that yon mugger was as foolish as thyself with as few seasons on him, else thou wouldst have ridden his belly by dawn!"

Mowgli pushed back the wet hair from his eyes and waited for his voice to recover. Finally he said, "Hathi picks his sentries well, O Batha. My life was forfeit, save for thee."

He looked up and saw many of the elephants standing quietly, watching, aroused by Batha's trumpet of rage and warning. Hathi strolled silently to the front of the herd. He glanced up at the crocodile hanging in the moonlight.

"Well and quickly done, my son. Mowgli, thou art unhurt?"

Mowgli walked silently to the great gray leader and put his hand on his huge trunk. "I am well, O Hathi, and I owe a mighty debt to thy last-born, best of all sentries, who watched over even this wandering calf." He turned to Hathi's son and added quietly, "I am very young and small and have no wisdom, but I shall repay this debt one day, Batha. If ye ever need the help of these"—and he held up his two hands—"ye have but to call."

Batha muttered wryly under his trunk, "And the parrot said to the falling tree, 'Wait, brother, till I fetch a prop.'" He turned with slow dignity and strode silently back to his guard post.

The elephants went back to their sleep, and Hathi said quietly to Mowgli, "Thou hast a good head under that great thatch of hair. But thou must learn to use it."

At dawn, the herd moved once more, and when the sun was high, they reached the foothills and began to climb slowly, moving past deodora cedars and pines. By nightfall, the air was chill, and Mowgli slept nestled between Hathi's massive legs for warmth. The moon rose over the mountain, and a strange secret restlessness rippled through the elephants. Mowgli woke to find them up and rocking all around him, and Hathi lumbered to the centre of the waiting crowd.

"It is time," he said softly, and he put down his trunk, swung Mowgli up to his neck, and almost before the boy had settled his knees, the huge elephant was moving up the mountain.

Mowgli heard a blast of furious trumpeting far away, and he started, wondering what other herds moved this night. Hathi climbed higher and higher, and Mowgli could see the tops of the trees under the moonlight for miles and miles, could hear the forest awake far below him. Around him now, Mowgli could hear stampings and snortings, the sounds of breaking branches, the pulling of heavy shoulders and heels up the hills, the mumble and grunts of the great beasts around and behind him. It seemed to him that the shadows were crowded with bulky shapes, and the hills were alive with elephants.

"Oho!" he said half-aloud, half to himself. "What a to-do is here! Perhaps the dance begins!"

At last, Hathi came to the top of the hill, and he stood at the edge of a vast circle of land, ringed by tall trees. The plateau was flattened, with scarcely a blade of grass. Mowgli rubbed his eyes and stared. The circle was ringed not just by thick trees, but by elephants as well. Fifty, sixty, far too many for him to count, huge elephants stood shoulder to shoulder, tusks facing centre, rocking side to side silently.

Outside the clearing, Mowgli could hear others crashing up the hill, working their way towards the plateau, and finally edging their way into the silent circle. There were huge tuskers with scars riddling their shoulders, their mountainous bulks rippling in the moonlight; there, ranks of young cows stood, with small ears and hairy youngsters peeping out from under their stomachs; there, troops of grizzled old ones leaned on their comrades, their tusks blunted and broken with age—all of them, every elephant in the jungle, it seemed to Mowgli, stood together on the mountaintop.

He crouched low on Hathi's neck and shivered with a fine sense that he was a rank outsider, seeing a thing which only the elephants had seen before.

Hathi took one rolling step into the middle of the circle, clucking and gurgling to himself, and all came to attention. He waggled his ears and tossed his trunk and suddenly trumpeted, a loud scream which Mowgli would never have believed was in him. They all took it up then, trumpeting in the darkness, splitting the silence of the forest with the most piercing bellows and high screeches, rocking more violently to and fro.

Hathi lifted up one forefoot and then the other and stomped one-two, one-two, steadily, a rising thunder of mighty heels. The rest followed him, together now, a rhythmic stamping like a war-drum, pounding, pounding, boom! boom! Even the calves joined the stomp, glancing up curiously, feeling with their tiny trunks up their mothers' sides for reassurance, rocking with the beat of the huge feet.

The booming went on and on, the earth seemed to rock and shiver under it, the shoulders swayed before him, and Mowgli covered his ears with his hands. Never in his life had he witnessed such power, such awesome thunder. He was both hypnotised and frightened by the din, and his heart seemed to beat in time to their heels.

Now, the circle began to move and dissolve, and the elephants stomped while they paced, couples striding together, comrades greeting each other, yearlings stamping forth to show off their new tusks, all the time stomping, stomping, in a steady rhythmic pace, as though they were all of one mind, one pair of heels. A low, rhythmic chant rose from the herd, a song which rolled up through the night, almost coming from the earth itself, a many-versed song which all the elephants seemed to know.

The thundering feet pounded and rolled around him, and Hathi moved from one elephant to another, silently touching trunks. Mowgli felt the brush of huge sides against his legs, saw a hundred white rolling eyes in the shadows, heard the click of tusks as they crossed and bumped and the dry rustle of trunks woven together in passing. Once, a trunk came up and touched him on the knee in soft exploration, and he flattened himself closer on Hathi's back, trying to disappear into the great folds of skin.

After what seemed a full night of noise, the stompings and the chant began to dwindle. Finally, they ceased altogether, and once more, the circle was a silent ring of elephants, rocking shoulder to shoulder. Then, one by one, they filed out, trunk to tail, following a path in the moonlight. Hathi was one of the last to leave the circle, as though he moved almost reluctantly away from the dance. He followed an ancient gray tusker in line, hunching his shoulders over like an old man, deep in thought.

The line of elephants emerged on a high cliff. Mowgli could see a deep crevasse before them, a black fissure in the mountain which seemed to go down forever. A small group of tuskers was dragging fallen trees out of the crack in the earth, small pines and brush which evidently had been laid there as cover. As Hathi moved closer, Mowgli peered through the darkness and gasped.

The crevasse was filled with dead elephants—skeletons of long-gone tuskers, broken skulls and ivory, bits of tail and an occasional brittle hide, all revealed when the brush was pulled away: the elephant burial-ground.

Now the line of elephants dissolved again, as silently, slowly, with great dignity, each trunk touched, up and down the scores and scores of beasts. Gradually, they seemed to separate into herds and then fall back away from the crevasse. Hathi stood to one side, his sons by him, in total silence.

There, in the moonlight, a line of old elephants stood alone, separated from their tribes. Some were almost white with age; others were younger, but their eyes were rheumy and they limped with weariness. Mayat, the oldest tusker of the herd, was with them. They stood shoulder to shoulder, facing the crevasse, switching their tails slowly. Off to one side, the tuskers who had uncovered the brush stood patiently rocking, their trunks down and their ears back.

"O Hathi," Mowgli breathed, unaware that he had spoken aloud, "wilt these feed the earth this night?"

"Softly, Little Brother," Hathi said, the first words he had spoken to Mowgli since the dance began. "They choose to die, in this place, in this way, after the Dance."

"The old ones come all this way just to die?"

"To dance. The dying perhaps comes after. Better this choice, with the herd as ever, their tusks hidden away from those who would defile them, than alone and exposed, their bones left to feed the kites. Now, h'sh. They are old, not deaf."

As though by a silent signal, the elephants turned away, leaving their old comrades to choose their own time. Then Mowgli understood. Some would take to the pit tonight, the minute they were away from their herd; others would live for a day, a week, browsing nearby, waiting for their time to come. And when they had met their fate, then the waiting sentries would cover them safely. And there, the old ones would rest forever, hearing the Dance season after season, sleeping on the bones of their brothers under the top of the mountain.

The herds slipped down the mountain again, going more slowly this time, straggling out in different directions, silently lifting trunks in farewell. Hathi heaved himself down the steep terrain, grunting with effort, and Mowgli knew that this night had cost him.

"How many Dances hast thou danced, O Hathi?" Mowgli asked quietly.

"One for every ring in my tusks," he said, "and more which I do not recall. Each year before the Rains, we come, when the young ones are strong enough to make the Trek, before the old knees get too stiff with the damp aches."

"And no other jungle eyes have seen this?"

"None since I can remember. There is only one place to watch, eh? From on a dancing back. Thou hast been the first. Dost thou understand why thy teacher brought thine eyes to me?"

"That I might see the Dance?"

"That thou might see the Death, Little Brother," Hathi said gently. "That thou might see the Choosing—the choosing of death and the choosing of life, for it is all one. And that is the elephant way."

Mowgli lifted his head and looked around him, sniffing the air, suddenly wearied to the bone. Dawn was coming to the jungle, and the valley below them was smoked and misted with dew. Hathi trod the hill trail slowly, almost as though he were reluctant to leave the mountaintop, straggling behind the rest of the tribe which had spread out to scatter to their separate grounds. Mowgli dozed, his head dropping forward on his chest, his knees rocking with Hathi's even stride. A fleeting dream moved behind his eyes, of elephants dancing in the moonlight, woven together at trunk and tail, and the scream of the peacocks echoed through the night.

The peacocks! Instantly he was awake and alert, for even in his dreams, he knew that peacocks do not scream at night. Ahead in the distance, Mowgli heard another sharp cry, a shout—the sound of *shikari,* hunters! He sat up quickly.

"Wake thee, thumbling," Hathi said calmly. "The end of the Trek is at hand."

"I hear Man!" Mowgli hissed. "What is it?"

"It is the Gleaning," the elephant murmured. "Each season, Man comes to this place. He does not know we dance; he does not know the tusks which he seeks lie in layers on the mountaintop. He only knows that each season, many of our kind gather in this valley, and he has learned that he can take some of us here."

"But why—" Mowgli's voice rose in shock and wonder "—why, if ye know this, do ye not go another way, choose another place to dance, to die? Why do ye not fight?" The boy's fists were clenched in anger and sorrow, and his heels were drumming on the elephant's sides. Hathi had edged himself deeper into the thicket, and he stood in the shadows on the hill, gazing below at the moving herds.

"We fight," he said, "but always, some will be taken. Some

hunters try for the cows, and these we fight. But these *shikari* do not want our cows. They seek the young males with the new ivory, or the old bulls who have gathered few wives. These Men take those with the longest and finest tusks, unscarred and un-blunted by battle."

They watched, hidden in the trees, as the scene turned to confusion and terror below them. A troop of koonkies, trained elephants, ran towards the herds, war-elephants with shouting men on their backs. The hunters were firing muskets and urging their elephants on with sticks, circling the wild herds who milled and screamed in confusion. A group of cows clustered together, their heads in a circle, their calves behind their legs. Snorting and flapping their ears, they challenged the men to charge, but the hunters ignored them. Instead, they turned towards the stampeding bulls, rounding up the young males who ran in all directions, trumpeting and stamping defiance. A few old tuskers were already captured, shouldered into a circle by the working elephants, and quickly roped and pegged at the heels. Some of them plunged and yanked at their tethers, squealing in fear; others stood dumb-ly, shivering with the shock of bondage.

And then, Mowgli saw Batha, Hathi's son, running across the valley, away from the cows, with two trained elephants at his heels. He stopped and whirled on them with a savage challenge, but the great bull trackers surrounded him on both sides, shoul-dering him so that he could not move, while the men on their backs shouted and threw ropes all over his head and neck. When the men and their elephants drew away, Batha was tied and bound, pegged by both back heels to wooden stakes driven fast to the ground.

Mowgli gasped, "We must save him!" for he knew by Hathi's silent trembling that he, too, had seen his son taken.

"Nay," Hathi said quietly. "It is the Gleaning. I have other sons." And indeed, Mowgli could see that most of the herd, includ-ing Hathi's two other sons, had escaped into the jungle. The valley was almost empty now. The hunters began to gather their cap-tives: four males, two of them old bull tuskers, two of them young males with new ivory. Each captive was flanked by koonkie elephants so he could not fight, and though the prisoners trumpeted and stamped, they were finally led away.

Mowgli was silent until they reached the river, thinking over all he had seen. Hathi stopped at the water and waded deeply into the cool depths, lying down on one side. Mowgli sat on his huge flanks, scratching him all over with palm leaves, but he could not drive away what he had witnessed.

Finally, he asked, "What will happen to the captured ones?"

Hathi heaved a huge sigh. "They will be taken to a city of Man. There, they will be rubbed all over with soft hay, given all the sweet grass [sugar cane] they can eat, and picketed with others of our kind who know how to calm them. The hunters' wives will sing to them gentle lullabys at night, and the hunters' children will take them to the river to bathe each day. In time, they will learn to do the bidding of Man, they will carry his kings on their backs, and may even come to love his ways."

Mowgli scowled fiercely. "Speak true talk, O Hathi. Surely they could never forget the jungle."

"Perhaps. Perhaps not. But listen to a true thing, if thou wilt. Nothing stays, nothing passes which does not return. Life is not just," the elephant said, "but it is inevitable, eh? Lower on my stomach, Little Frog."

Mowgli was silent for a long moment, scratching Hathi until he shivered with pleasure in the water. "This, then, is what Baloo would have me see? This is what I was to learn of Man?"

"This is a part," Hathi rumbled. "No one in the jungle knows all there is to know of Man. Even the wisest do not understand his ways. But this, the elephant knows, that Man sometimes catches us best by using our own hearts. And that is all I can teach thee, manling, of thy kind. Nay, do not puff and snort and shake thine ears, thou art *Man,* thumbling, and much as many love thee"—and here, the old elephant gazed at him with a rare tenderness—"their hearts are pegged as surely as Batha's heels. And in this, there is little choice. We may choose to live and die, eh? But we cannot choose to love."

"Why—if I am, indeed, a man-child—why wouldst thou teach me such a thing? Let us get to the yolk of the egg," and Mowgli leaned over the elephant's face and gazed into his eyes. "Why didst thou take me on the Trek, O Hathi? For love of Baloo?"

"Nay. For Baloo's love of thee. Rememberest thou the tale of the jackal I told thee on the trail? Thou thinkest thou art one with the Free People, the wolves. Truly, thou *art* of the Free People, but they do not run on four legs, Little Frog. The freest tribe is Man. And when thou goest from thy people, as the jackal did, thou dost hunt destruction, thine and those who love thee. Better thou shouldst learn the power of thy heart and the love we bear thee, and do as thou wouldst be done by."

"And this was the knowledge which even Baloo, my teacher, does not know? The way love binds?"

Hathi stood suddenly and shook off the mud from his heaving flanks. He rubbed one hind leg against the other in thought and then said, with a deep laugh all the way up his trunk, "Ay. It is an old wisdom, but sometimes even the old heads cannot learn it. Even if Baloo knew the perils of the love he bears thee, he could not loose himself. Hearts are like horses. They come and go against the bit and spur. And now, Little Brother—for I shall call thee this ever after, eh?—the Trek is done. Get thee back to thy jungle and only remember when it is thy turn to hold the rope, that sooner or later, each jackal must one day howl with his own."

Mowgli left the old tusker on the riverbank then and made the long journey back to where Baloo waited. By the time he reached the bear's welcome hug, he had dismissed much of Hathi's words as too heavy for his heart to carry so far. But he never forgot the Dance of the Elephants or the Choosing or the Gleaning. And he never again waded knee-deep in the moonlight without first watching over his shoulder for a swift tail and snapping jaws.

This is the song Mowgli heard the elephants sing at the place of the Dance. He could not remember all the verses, of course, but these few will give you an idea of what he witnessed on that moonlit night.

The Elephants' Dance Song

Forward, backward, left foot high,
Rocking, chanting, all say ay!
Trunks go up and left foot down,
Make the mountains all resound!

Feel the rhythm, right foot raise,
Follow as the circle sways,
We are now on hallowed ground,
Left foot up, and right foot pound!

Trek is hard and way is long,
Yet we come to sing our song,
Each to each and each shall choose,
What to welcome, what refuse.

Round and round the seasons wheel,
Feel the beat of heart and heel!
Life and Death from us shall glean,
Still, the elephants convene!

THE PORCUPINE AND
THE POISON PEOPLE

Ere claws were red and jaws bore teeth,
We slid from out earth's egg.
We kill, for death our jaws ensheath,
We need no useless leg!

Ssst! Uncurl coils and down hoods all!
And strike not at thy kin.
We have Good Hunting when we crawl.
O lidless eyes, sleek of skin.

We, yesss, whom all hearts rightly fear
When the night is full of eyes,
We track and follow with no ear,
Our death-tooth in disguise.

Hissss, now, and whisper all as one,
Our foes must tread with care.
For they know that we turn from none,
Of Poison Folk, beware!

Song of the Poison People

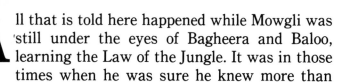

All that is told here happened while Mowgli was still under the eyes of Bagheera and Baloo, learning the Law of the Jungle. It was in those times when he was sure he knew more than five of the Jungle People put together, and all days were alike to him, filled with good things to eat, shadowed places to sleep, and cool deep pools which beckoned when the sun was high.

Because of his adventures in the Cold Lairs with Kaa, which you may perhaps remember, all of the jungle knew him for a growing voice of strength. Indeed, the *Bandar-log*, the monkeys, feared him as they feared the great Rock Python himself, and many feared the knife which he wore always around his neck, even though his hands were still those of a boy.

One day, Mowgli came through the forest on his way to the bathing-place, and he spied Bagheera stretched out on a low limb. The Black Panther often slept away most of the hot hours, saving his speed for the night. Now, he sprawled among the leaves, and his tail hung down, switching gently to and fro as he dreamed.

It was a full moon before the Rains, and Mowgli's flesh felt dry and stretched as Kaa's before he cast his skin. He was restless and ever so slightly irritable, and he spied around for some mischief to do his friend.

A large fat creeper wound down at the base of Bagheera's tree. One end tapered to a narrow tail; the other was flat and large, just like a green tree snake, one of the jungle's most poisonous. Mowgli quietly cut the creeper and wound it round his arm so that it formed curves and coils. He climbed silently up the tree, hiding behind its trunk, until he was on Bagheera's limb, never letting it jiggle with his weight.

Now, there was little that the Black Panther feared in all the jungle. But Mowgli knew, as few others did, that Bagheera had a mighty horror of the Poison People, for he often surprised them in the treetops while hunting the *Bandar-log*, and he knew that a single bite meant swift and painful death.

Mowgli crouched behind the tree trunk, holding his coiled creeper. Bagheera slept on, just a few feet away. Mowgli gave a sudden, perfect *hisssss!* And when Bagheera opened his eyes in startled fright, the boy tossed the green creeper at the panther.

There was an explosion of panic as Bagheera scrambled to get away, and he burst from the tree, grappling for clawholds. His eyes huge as two amber moons, he fell to the ground with a short squall of terror.

Mowgli laughed so hard, he almost fell from the tree himself, hugging the trunk and howling until the tears came to his eyes. Below him, Bagheera coughed dryly, testing each leg gingerly, cleaning ribbons of bark from under each claw.

"Most amusing, Little Brother," Bagheera said when he finally caught his breath.

"O! O! O, Bagheera!" Mowgli panted between laughs, "even the chital have never seen thee move so fast! I am sorry, but I could not help myself—didst thou truly think me an adder? Oho, thine eyes were bigger than Hathi's!" And the boy slapped his thighs and cried with delight.

"Thou hast become quite the tree-frog," Bagheera said, and his voice had a hard rumble that Mowgli had heard rarely. "I scarcely heard thy stalk. Perhaps—" and here, the panther looked up at the boy with his two eyes gleaming like hot rocks in the sun "—perhaps I hunted too hard last night. Truly, thou art no man-cub, but a man."

Mowgli sensed Bagheera's anger now, and he tried to stifle his laughter. But each time he pictured the great cat scuffling from the tree, his tail stiff with fear, he had to cover his grin with his hand. "Not a man," he said cheerfully. "Still thy brother, eh?"

"A man who plays at death," Bagheera purred silkily, as though he had not heard the boy. "Indeed, thou art ripe enough to visit Ikki, I think."

Instantly, Mowgli was diverted and alert, ready for a new adventure. "The porcupine? What is he that I should talk with him?" He began to giggle again. "Baloo calls him 'the Pig with the Irritable Back.'"

Bagheera stretched languorously, keeping one eye on the boy. "Pig he may be, and prickly as well, O Man, but be it so, he is very fond of games. More than any in the jungle, Ikki knows how to laugh, for he fears nothing and no one. And it is in my stomach that thou deservest a game or two after all thy lessons, eh?"

Mowgli said swiftly, "Do not call me Man, Bagheera. Ye know I am not." He narrowed his eyes suspiciously at the panther, who only purred and stretched unconcernedly. "Why have I never heard this of Ikki?"

"Thou wert too small and green for wit. Now, thou art ready." The cat examined his claws carefully. "Unless thou art afraid?"

Mowgli snorted through his nose and swung down from the tree. "There is nothing else to do, and the Rains will never come, and no one in this piece of the jungle knows how to laugh. So to Ikki I shall go, O Bagheera. And whilst I am gone, thou might remember that even great Hathi enjoys a good game now and again."

Bagheera stretched out in a patch of filtered sunlight and closed his eyes. "I shall keep it in mind, O Well of Truth."

And so, Mowgli set out in search of Ikki, the Porcupine. He knew the bristled beast lived out by the rocks, near a thicket of paw-paw trees, and he tramped through the jungle eagerly, hoping to find Ikki well-fed and ready for good play. He fingered his knife as he walked, muttering to himself.

"*Some* folk forget a basic wisdom," he said, gesturing with his finger as he was wont to do. "Dignity is fine and well, and *I* would surely never forget this, but the belly is made for laughter just as it is made for fodder, and the heart needs both."

A peacock screamed over his head, it seemed to him as though in agreement, and he added, "*Some* folk would do well to learn a little lesson, even from a *man*-cub!"

Mowgli found Ikki scratching under a fallen log, grubbing about for new worms and termite larvae.

"*Ohe!* Ikki!" he called loudly, for he knew that porcupines are a trifle deaf, and none among the Jungle Folk wants to surprise one.

The lumbering creature turned slowly to see who called him, his nose wriggling to and fro to catch the boy's scent, his little piggy eyes squinted against the sun. "Who calls? What foolishness of a peacock splits the—oh, it is you, wolfling. This is *my* log, and there is not enough for two." And he huffed around until his back was to the boy, his nose deep in the rotted wood.

Mowgli grinned and asked, "Is this the Ikki I have heard so much of, then? The only other in all the jungle who knows how to laugh? Looks to me like a belly on four legs who never played a game in his life."

Ikki cocked a curious eye at the boy. "Games, is it? You came a far leg for games, grubling." Mowgli noticed that the porcupine did not address him with the same speech of courtesy that the Hunting People shared. Ikki sat on his haunches and looked him up and down. "Why not play your games with old, fat Baloo or that creeping shadow you run with, boy? Bagheera—is that his name? O yes, I think I recall." And the porcupine snorted with delight at his own impudence.

"I see I have come to the right place," Mowgli said, grinning with mischief, "O Mighty Prickly Pig who has the stomach to mock his betters."

Ikki suddenly chattered with rage, stamped his feet, and rushed at the boy, every bristle rattling with threat. Mowgli retreated up a low sal tree as fast as he could scamper and peered down at the porcupine in confusion, his heart pounding.

"Hee, hee, hee!" Ikki squealed, shaking his quills back and forth in merriment. "You can dance like Mao the Peacock when I sing you the right tune, cub!"

Mowgli chuckled wryly and slid down the tree again. "A true master of wit. Thou art mad and many times mad."

"That's more like. I have pricked Hathi himself in his softest places," Ikki said sweetly, "and if you could think me a little *more* mad, I would be more pleased. Now, if it's rambles ye want, ye can follow my tail." He switched his barbs to and fro and waddled off to his favourite paw-paw patch.

Now, Ikki was young for a porcupine, as Mowgli was young for a man. Together, they both shared that same sort of restless, under-the-skin contrariness that comes to most youngsters, while they still are able to take life lightly. And so, Mowgli vowed quietly to himself that he would make Ikki squeal in a different manner before he left his company.

They foraged through the thickets, eating their way placidly from one fruit tree to the next, exchanging banter and insults and generally trying to impress one another with their impudence. Mowgli pointed out that Ikki was pigeon-toed and walked like a fattened goose. Ikki allowed that this was so, but he'd rather walk like a goose than go all naked into the world like a grub, as Mowgli did.

Mowgli happened on a patch of mangoes, one of Ikki's favourite foods. Now, Ikki had few favourites, for he was one of the jungle's most finicky eaters. And so, the boy saw a way to prick the porcupine. He plucked an unripe mango from the tree and hid it in his palm. Then, he began to pick and eat the ripest mangoes, making a great slurping noise with their juice.

"What's that you have found there?" Ikki cried, running over to see. "Mangoes! Move over, cub, and let me show you the proper way to choose the ripest!" He sniffed and slavered and chewed his way through a few quickly, his eyes closed in ecstasy.

Mowgli knew that Ikki's eyesight was dim, and that he depended more on his nose to "see" the readiness of the fruit than on any other sense. And now, with his nose and whiskers all covered with ripe mango, he was virtually blind.

Mowgli pulled out the green mango and pretended to take a huge bite from it. "*Ohē,* Goose-gait, this is the best of them all! Never have I had such a honeyed fruit!" And he made as though to devour the whole mango. But Ikki pushed his nose greedily into Mowgli's palm.

"Let me have a taste, cub," he said frantically, "and I'll leave all these little yellow ones for you." The porcupine took a large bite of the green mango and chewed it eagerly. Then, with a sudden snort and a cough, he spat and hacked and wheezed the bitter fruit out of his mouth, stamping and back-rolling his tongue, whipping his head from side to side in disgust.

"Au-aughrr! Phew! Blatttch! Man-cub, your tongue is as witless as the rest of your mouth!"

Mowgli shouted with laughter, rolling on the ground and holding his sides, pointing at the grimacing porcupine with glee. "Ha! The game was well played, Piggy One. Admit it! Admit it!"

Ikki waddled quickly to a nearby stream and thrust his whole muzzle underwater to try to rid himself of the acridness of the unripe mango, one of the most bitter tastes in the jungle. Finally, he slumped to the bank with a huge sigh, taking a few mouthfuls of green grass for comfort.

"I'll admit you're a quick study," the porcupine said reluctantly. "Shall we call a truce?" And he looked up at Mowgli with a trusting gaze.

"I suppose, if truce we must," Mowgli said, hunkering down beside him. "But I had hardly begun."

"That's what I feared, grubling. Truce it is, then."

The two comrades rambled through the forest, seeking a place to bed through the hot hours. Ikki, like the Hunting People, preferred to do most of his feeding during the night, though he would never pass up the opportunity for a full stomach when it presented itself.

They came to a spreading peepul tree which was curiously empty of the *Bandar-log*. The monkey tribes often chose this tree as their favourite, for the sap of the peepul is so sweet and sticky that young monkeys chew on its twigs as children of the villages chew on sugar cane. Fortunately, its branches are broad and well-leaved, making it a good choice for a napping place.

Mowgli swung himself into the branches to rest, calling down below to Ikki. "Good sleep, O Prickles. We hunt again at sundown. Wilt thou rest beneath me?" And he peered down to mark the porcupine's position.

"I'll be right here," Ikki called up cheerfully. "Close your eyes and dream."

Mowgli crept under cover of the broad peepul leaves and quietly went to work. He quickly wove together a few of the creepers and leaves to make a basket. He cut a gash in the bark of the tree and tied the basket underneath to catch the dripping sap. Then, pleased with his cleverness, he leaned back to doze away the afternoon.

Meanwhile, the porcupine was beneath him, investigating an anthill under the peepul. Ants, too, are drawn to its sticky sap, and these were mounded in large colonies, irritable as all working ants are. While Mowgli slept above him, Ikki dug a deep trench around the base of the tree and the ant mounds, careful not to disturb the foraging insects. He lined the trench with leaves, that it might hold. Then, glancing up to be sure Mowgli had not spied him, he circled the tree, laying down a ring of scent in the lined trench, voiding it from the glands he carried under the base of his bristled tail—a scent which all insects recognise as danger and will turn from, if they can.

Hours had passed, and the upper limbs of the peepul were quiet as Mowgli dozed on. Ikki chortled with delight and began to root vigourously at the ant mounds, busily driving the insects out of their burrows. They surged up angrily, saw their arch-foe before them, and made as though to flee. But they were confused by his scent which surrounded them, and many hurried up the tree trunk to escape.

Mowgli awoke to find his legs swarming with angry ants. Thinking him a monkey, another enemy, they bit his feet and fingers as he tried frantically to brush them away. He heard Ikki laughing below as he swatted desperately and jumped to a higher branch.

"Give them the Master Word, O Wise One!" Ikki giggled. And he waddled further out away from the base of the peepul, that he might see Mowgli more clearly.

Mowgli snatched the basket full of sticky sap from the limb below him and, wiping off the insects from his hands as he took aim, let it fly at Ikki below.

The bomb of sap landed smack on the porcupine's back with a satisfying splat, spilling the sticky liquid all through Ikki's quills and down his tail.

"O! O! O!" the porcupine wailed and ran in three directions at once, trying to rid himself of his gummy burden.

Mowgli slid down the tree, slapping at his legs, and the two of them raced for the river, each cursing the other and trying to trip him up, splashing in up to their necks.

Finally, they hauled themselves out on the bank, glaring ruefully at each other.

"I have bites on top of bites," Mowgli scowled, examining his swollen toes.

"And every quill is sticking to another," Ikki fretted. "It will take me a solid moon to clean this mess off."

"*Ye* called for truce, lying Pig."

"And *ye* said ay, as I recall. All the time plotting revenge with a sneaky trick like the *Bandar-log*—sticky, nasty fingers—" and the porcupine bit at a mired quill.

"I've had much of games and little of laughter since I came to thy part of the woods," Mowgli said.

"And who asked ye to come, then, wolfling? Shall I dig *my* lair to your liking? Hmmmph," he grumbled. "You've been spoiled as a rotting plantain by your Bear and your precious Pack and—"

"Peace, peace, O Prickles," Mowgli sighed, scratching thoughtfully at the tender places between his fingers. "Let us birth a truce between us and make it live, eh? No more."

Ikki bent his head beneath his back legs, trying to reach his longest quills to clean them, and Mowgli could hear him muttering, his muzzle muffled in guard hairs. Finally, his grumbles subsided.

"Well, there is one piece of my forest you've not yet seen," Ikki mumbled. "I could show it to you, before you go back to your red-toothed masters. I'll not have it said that Ikki does not know how to treat a guest, even such a naked runtling as yourself." And the porcupine grinned up at the boy with what looked like grudging respect and the barest hint of a dare.

"Do the little Crawling People live there?" Mowgli asked, as he found a score of new bites behind his knees.

"The Crawling People?" Ikki chuckled lightly. "Nay, you needn't fear more bites, grubling. This place has no ants, only more rocks and hiding places than you have ever seen, and it is cool and pleasant in even the hottest suns. Perhaps a good place to know in coming seasons, eh?"

Mowgli reached for more mud to pat on his stings. "One look, then, and I will go. It is in my stomach that I have had enough of games."

"And it is in mine as well," Ikki said blandly, now scrupulously examining his backquills.

They reached the Place of Rocks as the sun was sliding below the upper branches of the trees. It was a huge hill of boulders which had long ago come to rest, one against the other, in a massive landslide of earth and stone. Now, the rocks reached the height of a small mountain, a jumble of cold slate and granite, fissured with cracks and holes and shadowed hiding-places. Huge roots and creepers had twisted among the boulders and then died for lack of water and nourishment, and the place seemed at first glance as unhospitable as a briar patch. But Mowgli could see that Ikki, and other animals who chose to burrow and nest, would find the Place of Rocks a likely refuge.

He clambered atop a boulder and drummed his heels against the cool stone. Ikki waddled up to him slowly, picking his way amongst the cracks and clefts of the rocks.

"This is a mighty fortress," Mowgli said, determined to be polite before he took his leave.

"Many think so," Ikki wheezed, panting as he climbed higher. "Above, there are caves taller than thy head, manling, which hold cool earth and water in even in the driest moons. Wilt thou see them?"

Mowgli noted the new courtesy and smiled. "If thou wouldst show me."

The two climbed higher still, picking their way up the maze of boulders and roots and fissures which grew deeper and darker as the sun fell. Occasionally, Mowgli stumbled on a loose stone and caught himself before he slid half-way down. Sometimes, he heard Ikki slip ahead of him, and the scrape of the porcupine's bristles against the rocks as he clawed for a foothold.

Mowgli came to a massive boulder in his path, and he began to edge around it cautiously. He felt the earth give under his feet, rocks slid, and he clutched for a root to hold him—but instead of slipping further, the rocks suddenly fell away, and he dropped, feet-first, into a deep, underground cavern.

Mowgli had been taught by Bagheera to fall, of course, so the drop did not hurt him as it would other boys of his size. He rolled the instant he felt his feet hit the earth, tucking his head in and his hands over his neck. Pebbles and dust rained down on his shoulders, and when it finally was quiet, he uncurled himself and looked around.

He was standing on a flat piece of earth, surrounded by jagged boulders and outcroppings of rock. Above him, higher than twice as far as he could leap, a small circle of light marked his only way out. He carefully felt himself all over, stretching first one arm and then the other, and as he leaned against the walls of the cave, he heard a chilling *hissss* shiver through the darkness.

He yanked his hand away from the stone, quickly gave the Snake's Call, "We be of one blood, ye and I," and moved into another corner.

The light at the top of the cavern was suddenly blotted out as Ikki's head appeared. "Are ye in there, manling? I cannot see ye. Speak out!"

"I am here!" Mowgli shouted and then lowered his voice when he remembered the hiss in the darkness. "I am *here,* Ikki, and I cannot get out!"

"Are ye broken?"

"Nay, I am whole, but I cannot reach the light!" And Mowgli jumped once, twice, stretching his arms up to Ikki that he might see.

Again, the low *hissss* came from the depths of the cavern, this time with many rustlings and whispers of scales. "Be thou ssstill, ye with dancing feet, or ye shall dance no more, Master Word or no," a cold voice said.

"I am still," Mowgli whispered, and he froze, giving the Call once again to be sure. He strained his eyes, trying to see into the darkness.

Now, as he adjusted to the shadows, he could dimly see scores of snakes at his feet. All around him, they were coiled on the outcroppings of cold rock: cobras, denned against the hot sun— huge black cobras, smaller mottled ones, and tens and tens of cobra-children, no longer than his forearm. Each had only to strike once, and Mowgli would never see the light again.

Ikki called from above. "Man-cub, man-cub! Are ye still there?"

Mowgli winced and said as loud as he dared, "I have no place to go, O Fool! This place crawls with Poison Folk! Curse ye and your rocks!"

Ikki sounded injured. "*I* did not know thou wouldst take into thy head to tread the belly of the place, grubling."

Mowgli turned to the mass of snakes, addressing what seemed to be the largest, fattest coils. "If it please thee, O Great One," he said as calmly as he could, "I would take leave of thee and thy lair."

"Mossst assuredly," a voice answered. "Be gone, then." As Mowgli watched, a huge cobra lifted his head above the lengths and curves of snakes. The cobra's yellow cat-eyes glimmered in the darkness and his hood was widened slightly in anger and threat, as though he could not help himself, despite his efforts to keep a courteous tone. His tongue slithered in and out thoughtfully.

"But whither is the way out?" Mowgli asked, keeping his eyes on the snake. "Is there some passage or tunnel through which I might crawl? Couldst thou—"

A smaller hiss interrupted him. "Strike and end it, O Hama. Who art thou to trade chatter with the *Bandar-log*?"

Hama is the name for Lord, or Highest, in Snake tongue, and so the boy knew he faced the King Cobra, the mightiest, most deadly snake in the jungle, who could grow to be eighteen feet or more and could strike with the speed of a blink.

Mowgli's hand strayed slowly to his knife, ready to fight what he knew would be a swift and painful fight to the death, should it come to that. But again, his voice was firm. "I am not of the *Bandar*-tribe, O Hooded One. My clumsy feet slipped on the rocks—for which trespass, I beg thy pardon. Is there a way out?"

"None for those with big legs and feet," the smaller cobra said as he twined closer to Mowgli. "Many small and precious tunnels, for they who know whither they lead, for those who can see in the shadows and move before thy heart can beat again. Truly thou should have thought of thy useless limbs when ye jumped among us." He slid closer still and his eyes glittered. "Not a *Bandar*, then? Art thou a naked weasel? Or perhaps some new form of hairless rat?"

Mowgli eased further away from the cobra, shuffling his feet uneasily. He shouted up to Ikki, "Go and fetch Baloo! Find Bagheera! On thy life, Ikki, or mine is forfeit, sure!"

"Can ye not climb?" Ikki called down in a weary whine. "It is a mighty trek to where thy masters hunt, and it soon approaches night!"

"On thy life, Ikki! Run quickly!" And Mowgli turned every attention to the restless snakes about him.

The moon was high when Ikki neared Baloo and Bagheera. The

51

Black Panther had killed and eaten at dusk, and so he was resting among the bamboo while Baloo browsed nearby for nightgrubs.

"I cannot believe the man-cub has not returned yet," Baloo said fretfully. "Thou shouldst never have sent him to Ikki, no matter that thy heart was angry. He is still unripe."

"And unused to madness," Bagheera said quietly, "but he was learning quickly to make madness of his own. I would he learn the *whole* lesson, and Ikki is just the one to teach it to him." The panther stretched out and crooned gently to himself, watching a cloud roll across the fat moon. "He likely hot-foots it home even as we speak. The boy likes to follow my trail on just this sort of—"

Ikki rattled through the bamboo, puffing and wheezing, his small piggy eyes watering with his efforts. "At last! At last! They said you were sleeping off your full bellies hither—"

"Who said—?" Bagheera began, rising quickly, but Baloo cut him off.

"The man-cub! Didst thou leave him in the jungle?"

Ikki threw himself down panting in the thicket, his quills heaving and clacking with each breath. "*I* did not leave him, O Teacher of the Law." He glared at Bagheera. "Neither did I *send* him, O Master of the Hunt." He pulled himself up with dignity. "And *I* did not tell him to go among the Poison People, either, but there he is and there he stays, lest ye hurry."

"The Poison People!" Bagheera snarled. "Ye have led him to his death with thy games?"

Every quill stood upright on Ikki's back, and he chattered angrily. "*My* games? He has his own games, that one, and a master at them he is, too. Truly, my tail will never be—"

Baloo stopped him, his voice calm, steady. "Whither have ye left him?"

Ikki hauled himself to his full height. "He has fallen into the Place of Rocks. Among the Poison People. He gave the Master Word, but he cannot get out." He scowled at them steadily. "And so I came, lest he die. But if he dies, it is not on *my* head."

Baloo turned without another word and crashed out of the thicket, Bagheera at his heels.

It was a long trek through the jungle to the Place of Rocks, but the two comrades moved swiftly, barely wasting breath to speak.

"Woof!" Baloo finally gasped, leaning for an instant against a tree. "If they strike, despite the Master Word, I shall seek out and stomp all Poison Folk I can find!"

Bagheera paused for a moment, his ribs flaring with his pants. "And Ikki feeds the kites before dawn. No matter if his mangy hide fills my jaws with a hundred quills—the boy can pull them out."

With the mention of Mowgli, bear and panther looked at one another in dismay and hurried off once more.

As soon as Ikki's head had withdrawn from the hole at the top of the cave, Mowgli quickly assessed his situation. It was growing dark swiftly now, and the moon's light did not yet reach into the pit. He could dimly see a foothold or two in the rocks up to the fading light, but the sides of the cavern were sheer, and if he fell back amongst the snakes—if he fell, O Mowgli! He would surely never rise again.

There was a hissing and a muttering in the darkness, and he guessed that some of the King Cobra's tribe were arguing about what to do with this great-footed creature among them. He knew he must think, must plan, must do *something*. What would Bagheera do? What would Baloo advise? He cast about for something which might divert the snakes from his bare legs, hands, and feet, which seemed the only things visible in the shadows.

"It is almost night," he began hesitantly. "Good Hunting go with thee, O Hama, as thou goest through thy jungle."

An evil chuckle came from the writhing mass of snakes, and the smaller cobra who had first threatened Mowgli moved forward, raising nearly one-third of his body off the rocks, hovering close, his hood spread wide.

"It will be a long night, yessss? For some, at least. Ample time for hunting. Thou art Man, is it ssso?"

"Some call me this," Mowgli answered. "But I was raised by the Pack, by the Free People, and bought with a Bull killed by Bagheera—"

"It is all one, ye hairless wolf of the Seeonee Pack," the cobra snapped. "Thou art Man. And we know a little of Man, yesss. A liar, a jackal, and Man were all hatched from the same egg. I have but to touch thee, and thy ribs will move no more. Look at me, Man!" And the snake fixed Mowgli with a yellow stare, his eyes like two glass moons, never blinking, swaying back and forth as a bamboo in the wind.

The King Cobra suddenly reared up, taller than the smaller snake, higher than Mowgli's head. He glared once at the younger cobra, who lowered his hood and slunk away.

"Which of us has taught thee the Master Word, boy? Though it saves thy life, it is not good that Man should speak it. Point out thy teacher." And the huge cobra froze the rest of the snakes with a chilling stare.

"None here, O Hama," Mowgli said quickly. "One of the jungle taught my tongue the Word. Rememberest thou great Kaa of the mighty coils? 'Twas he who gave it me."

"Thou art brother to Kaa?" The huge snake swayed slowly, thoughtfully, and Mowgli was close enough to count every scale on his wide and rippling throat.

"I count myself brother to many, O Hama," Mowgli said. "Some come, even now, to my aid."

"I said it! I said it, even ssso!" hissed the younger cobra sullenly. "Soon, there will be a hundred feet amongst us, and woe to this season's eggsss!"

"Hissst!" said the King Cobra, without turning away from Mowgli. "Dost thou speak truth? Man scarcely does."

Mowgli gathered his courage. "I am *not* Man, O Hama. I have said it many times over. I am of the Pack, of the Free People. And I speak the truth."

"He lies, he liesss!" hissed scores of voices, and two small cobras dropped to the floor of the cave and slithered towards Mowgli's feet.

"Sssilence!" The King Cobra spat the command through the cave, and all were still. "For the sake of Vishnu, silence! Boy, thou art more brave—or more foolish—than most who walk with thy feet and speak with thy tongue. We shall see. Thou shalt tell the Story."

"Yesss, the Story, the Story!" the snakes chorused.

Mowgli cast about in confusion, wondering what new madness

this was. "The Story?" And then he remembered. Baloo had once told him a tale about the Poison Folk, how they loved to hear the words of Men, were sometimes drawn to their villages in the night to listen to the croonings of the mothers over the cradles, and how they even were drawn to the herds of cattle, risking sure death by sharp hooves, to hear the songs of the herdboys.

"What sort of story wouldst thou hear?" he asked.

"What sort? What sort? Why, any sort at all, boy," a small cobra spoke up. "When the God Vishnu sleeps, he rests on the coils of the noble cobra Shesha, whose seven heads rise over him as shade for his sacred brow. Shesha tells Vishnu stories through the nights of cosmic rest, and thou must do the same for us." He looked up and grinned wickedly at his tribe. "Lest thou wouldst rather *we* tell the tale?"

A small evil glint came to the King Cobra's eyes, and Mowgli knew full well that he would never live to hear the end of such a tale, once it began.

"I shall tell thee a tale, then, O Hama," he began quickly, glancing once up at the hole above his head. Would they never come!

Mowgli began to chant a tale, a story he invented as he went along, and he swayed back and forth as he sang, mimicking the movements of the King Cobra. He talked of the seasons flowing one after the other, of the cool water in the summer, of the pleasures of the night wind during the Rains; he mimicked the calls of a score of wild birds and the hunting cries of the Jungle Folk. He repeated a few of the maxims of Hathi and Baloo and told his own versions of the stories he had heard in the wolf den when he was small. He chanted the tales one after the other, weaving them together with song, and each story was then retold with variations, for that is the Indian way.

All the while, the snakes listened, their heads cocked to one side, their eyes following his gestures, his movements. Still as stone they stood as he told the stories.

"Indeed," he thought to himself as he chanted, "these Poison People are mad to the bone and made foolish as the *Bandar-log* themselves by the weavings of words." And then he snapped back to attention, for several of the smaller snakes had slipped down close to his bare ankles, writhing perilously near in a sort of blind ecstasy, charmed by his swayings, by his song.

Meanwhile, Baloo and Bagheera had reached the Place of Rocks. They gazed up at the stony fortress in dismay.

"Somewhere, he is up there," Baloo said miserably.

Bagheera wasted no time with words but bounded up the boulders, sniffing the air for Mowgli's trail. "He has come this way!" the panther called. "Follow, O Baloo, swiftly, swiftly!"

The big brown bear lumbered up the rocks, panting painfully, for he could not leap as surely from height to height as the panther could. "Cry his trail!" he shouted to Bagheera, and pulled himself over a boulder.

Mowgli heard Bagheera's call and he froze. The King Cobra heard it as well, and he went rigid, fixing the boy with a malicious stare. "Ssso," he hissed. "They have come at last."

Mowgli backed away into the farthest corner of the cavern, watching where he put his feet. Suddenly, Bagheera's great black head blocked out the hole at the top of the cave.

"*Ohe*! Little Brother!" the panther called. "Art thou safe?"

"I am here, I am here!" Mowgli shouted, keeping his eyes on the masses of snakes. "The place is full of Poison Folk!"

"Strike now!" a young cobra hissed, "before we have them all upon usss!"

Bagheera's snarl echoed and re-echoed off the walls of the cave. "He who strikes the man-cub will know the shame of all the jungle, if Bagheera's claws let him live long enough to regret it! He carries the Master Word! Back away from him!"

"We take orders from no legged cat!" a cobra spat, and Mowgli saw that the King Cobra had moved closer to him. He glanced up to shout to Bagheera, but the Black Panther was gone.

Baloo reached the top of the Place of Rocks to find Bagheera wrapping his middle in long vines and creepers. The vines were coiled round his belly tightly and dragging behind him. The big cat was shuddering visibly as he bound himself.

"What—what—does he live?" Baloo panted, throwing himself on the ground.

"He lives," Bagheera snapped, grimacing as the creepers brushed against him. "The Poison Folk surround him like the

strands of a net. By the Broken Lock that freed me"—and the cat shivered—"to see those creeping, crawling—and then to wrap these about me—" but he set his jaw and kept on pulling the vines about his body.

Baloo stuck his head down the hole. "Auugrh, Little Frog, we come, we come! Keep back, O Poison People, lest we tread on thee!" He turned to Bagheera. "Thou didst not have to be the one. I could have wrapped myself and held the boy alone whilst he climbs."

Bagheera stopped, and his look silenced Baloo completely. "Think, my friend. It must be I who am bound, I who drop down low enough that the boy can catch the ropes, I who pull him forth, with thy help, if need be."

"Why?" Baloo asked fretfully. "Just because thy word sent him to Ikki does not mean thou must—"

But the panther turned away. "If I should slip—if I should fall—amongst them—" and here, he faltered for an instant. Then, he was Bagheera once more, and he went on. "If I should fail, it is still possible that thou couldst save him, even save us both. But if we bind thee and *thou* shouldst fall amongst them, I could do little. Now turn and brace thy feet, for I must take hold."

Mowgli had started up his chanting again, frantically trying to keep the snakes at bay. Some listened, but others rustled and hissed, angrily demanding the boy's death.

"Shame?" a cobra snapped. "The black one speaks of shame? Shame it will truly be when the jungle learns we have been tricked by a man-child! 'Little Frog,' the bear called him! Lulled by a naked *Bandar* who comes in the night and goes away with nary a scratch for his trespass!"

Mowgli chanted louder, glancing anxiously up the sheer walls of the cave, knowing he would rather leap and fall than die with no effort to save himself. He swayed rhythmically, his hand on his knife, shuffling his feet, still chanting the story-song.

A large mottled cobra slid off the rock ledge and twisted closer to Mowgli. He coiled within striking distance, reared up his hooded head, and hissed, "I have heard enough. 'Little Frog,' they called thee? Be it so. My stomach has known a few of such! If Hama will not give the command, I shall do so myssself!"

The mottled cobra lunged at Mowgli's dancing feet, missed, and drew back for the terrible second lunge in anger, but with a swift whisper of death, the King Cobra struck the mottled, coiled back, sending the smaller snake into writhing agony.

"He struck his own! He struck his own!" the mass of snakes hissed, and the King Cobra commanded, "Hisssst! If there is to be a killing, *my* tooth shall bring it!"

Mowgli looked up to see Bagheera backing slowly down into the hole, his tail hanging down into the darkness. From his back and his belly streamed scores of vines and creepers.

"Look into my eyes, boy," the King Cobra whispered, rising up with hood spread, swaying three feet above Mowgli's head. Mowgli turned his stare full into the cobra's cold opal-eyes, and he felt his stomach heave like a nest on the end of a bouncing twig—but he sensed the cobra hesitate, as though he, too, were hypnotised by the locking of stares.

The creepers suddenly fell down within Mowgli's reach.

"Jump! Jump, Little Brother!" Bagheera called, his voice strained by his efforts to hold himself low enough and yet steady for the boy's weight. Mowgli leaped as high up the creeper ropes as he could, and he felt the wind of the King Cobra's passing strike, as he yanked his heels out of the way.

"Missed! Missed! Missssed!" cried a hundred cold voices, and Mowgli pulled himself up the vines. Below him, the huge King Cobra gathered himself quickly for a final strike. The creepers suddenly sagged and gave, and Mowgli heard Baloo squeal in pain. Bagheera gave a single grunt of panic and frantically kicked with his back paws at empty air. Then, the vines tightened once more, and Mowgli shinnied up them, expecting to feel any moment the lightning stab of the huge snake's fangs. Higher, higher, he kicked and pulled, and brown hairy paws pulled him out into the clear night air, he felt solid ground beneath his heels, and he turned to stare down into the hole.

The King Cobra swayed below him, his gold eyes glinting. He had not tried a second strike. Something in him had made him strike once, something in his cold snake's soul which no stories or chantings or swayings could halt—but he had not struck again, even though Mowgli felt sure he could have hit home.

"Good Hunting," he called softly down to the huge snake in his own tongue. And then, he turned to his friends.

Bagheera was kicking his way loose of the vines, coughing and gagging as cats will do when they are disgusted. Baloo was bleeding badly down both flanks.

"Thou art hurt!" Mowgli said, going to him.

"The fault is mine," Bagheera answered faintly. "As I slipped, I grabbed for the strongest clawhold I could."

"It is nothing," Baloo said, wincing. "Thou art up from the pit, safe from death, and Bagheera, here, suffered worse wounds of the heart than any of mine."

The Black Panther dropped his silky head on the boy's shoulder and said softly, "I ask thy pardon, Little Brother. I sent thee to Ikki out of anger, not wisdom, though I clothed it in wisdom's hide. And wrath will not birth justice."

Mowgli ruffled Bagheera's coat and pulled Baloo close in a hug. "Nay, nay, thou wert right to send me. My heart was a little angry as well. But I have learned a true thing. Wit, like all else in the jungle, cannot live alone but must lair with judgement. When thou hast loosed a game, it is like a rock thrown in a pool, and the consequences spread, thou canst not tell how far."

"Ikki shall learn something of these consequences when I have met him once more. As shall all Poison Folk in my hunting grounds," Bagheera snarled quietly.

"'Twas not Ikki's fault that my foot slipped. 'Twas not the fault of the Poison Folk that I fell amongst them. Each followed the commands of his blood, and thou canst not kill those commands," Mowgli replied.

"And they said that teaching a man-cub the Law was one piece with teaching the peacock to sing! Thou hast learned wisdom this night, O Best of Little Frogs," Baloo said with pride. "But how is it that thou art still left with breath under thy ribs? Dost thou master the Middle Jungle as well as our hearts?"

The Middle Jungle was the hunting ground of the Crawling People, all things of the burrow, the cave, the tunnel, the earth.

"No," Mowgli said thoughtfully. "They would have killed me, Master Word or no, I think, save for their lord, great Hama, the king of their tribe. But"—and here, the boy gazed wonderingly at his friends—"for some reason which I cannot name, he would not strike. Not while I met his eyes and spoke and swayed, but only when I ran." Mowgli shook his head. "I do not know. It is an old and twisted trail we share, I think. Love and hate, water and mud, mixed in the same pool." He stared at his comrades. "Dost *thou* understand?"

Baloo and Bagheera dropped their eyes, as always, unable to meet Mowgli's stare for long.

"The jungle alone knows," Baloo said softly, "but it is in my heart that we, too, share such a trail." The bear stood and stretched one stiffening shoulder. "And now let us homeward, Little Brother, for we have a long way to go."

This is part of the story-song which Mowgli told the Poison People. He tried to recall most of it to tell Bagheera and Baloo later, once he was safe, but to his surprise, only this fragment would come back to his head.

Once, when all the stars were new,
Once, when Jungle Folk were few,
Once, ere even Hathi grew,
There hatched a single egg.
And from this egg, a cobra crept
And he crawled where a Man had stepped,
And he coiled where a Man had slept,
So Man was sore afraid.
Sing out the story-song! Sing out, both loud and long!
All heed the Jungle Law, with heart and tooth and claw!

Now, Cobra whispered in Man's ear,
Said he, "O Man, I see thy fear,
But ye have yonder knife and spear,
Whilst I have only tooth.
If thou wilt put up weapons fast,
Then friends we both will be at last."
The cobra dropped his eyes downcast
As though he told a truth.
Sing out the story-song! Sing out, both loud and long!
All heed the Jungle Law, with heart and tooth and claw!

So Man put up his spear and knife,
And trusted snake to end the strife,
But Cobra struck and took his life,
And thought the battle won.
Cried Man, "A Truce thou promised me!
But now I know that cannot be
Between my tribe and such as *thee*
But think not we are done!"
Sing out the story-song! Sing out, both loud and long!
All heed the Jungle Law, with heart and tooth and claw!

And now, the sons of Man and Snake
Revenge old deaths for each namesake,
Each kills the other when awake,
Each haunts the other's dreams.
Though Snake was old when life was young,
And Man's word is life's newest tongue,
Yet old and new, this song is sung
And each, their past redeems.
Sing out the story-song! Sing out, both loud and long!
All heed the Jungle Law, with heart and tooth and claw!

GARGADAN
THE GREAT RHINO

"Wash an ass as much as you like, you will never make a calf of him."

"The bullock looked at the drought plain and bellowed, 'This is vastly well! I must be fat since I have eaten all the grass!'"

"The rhino and the elephant are swept away, and the chital asks, 'Is it deep?'"

Favourite sayings of Gargadan

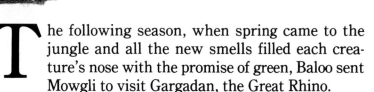

The following season, when spring came to the jungle and all the new smells filled each creature's nose with the promise of green, Baloo sent Mowgli to visit Gargadan, the Great Rhino.

Mowgli was more interested in fishing the deep pools, and he huffed a mighty sigh when the Brown Bear told him to follow the rhino's trail. But Baloo knew that a cub who learns the Law from only one master is like a bat with a bent wing: he can fly but he cannot balance. And when you come to think of it, you will see how this must be so.

Gargadan lived on the vast plain which stretched out from the feet of the jungle, as did many of the Eaters of Grass. Unlike the chital, the sambhur, and the nilghai, however, the great rhino roamed the grasslands alone, speaking to few, bellowing at all, and even running off most who trespassed into his feeding grounds.

"He is cunning, ill-tempered, and blind as a mole in daylight," Baloo told Mowgli when he sent him on his way. "But he knows the Law like few others in the jungle."

"I know enough of the Law," Mowgli sniffed. "And the spotted perch are just coming out of the deepest pools."

"Thou canst never know too much of the Law," Baloo rumbled, and there was no more to be said.

Mowgli was getting taller and stronger with each passing season, and though he grumbled to Baloo, once he began his journey, his feet ate up the long miles with pleasure, and he ran through the jungle for the sheer joy of moving.

He came to the top of a hill which overlooked the veld. Below him stretched a flat grassland dotted with herds, and the river coiled about the plains, shining in the sun. He stopped and listened.

In the distance, he heard the calls of the chital, the barks of the does and fawns calling to each other, and the bellows and stampings of the stags. The wild asses brayed, the nilghai snorted, the sambhur belled—but over them all, loudest and most lordly of all the noises of the plain, were the roars of Gargadan, the Great Rhino. He stood alone, feeding in the tall grass by the wild figs, and the other Eaters of Grass made a wide swath around his territory.

A well-etched path leading to the river marked the trail that Gargadan used, and deeply rutted wallows showed where he rolled in the dust. From this distance, the rhino looked gray and huge, his body armoured with hide, his tufted tail switching back and forth as he grazed the stubby brush.

Mowgli climbed a fig tree and gathered as many of the ripe fruit as he could carry. He carefully descended the hill, balancing the figs in his arms. As he approached, he called out to Gargadan the Master Word, for he knew the rhino would hear or smell him before he saw him.

But before he could draw close to Gargadan, he heard a small voice call out loudly, "Never fear, My Lord! It is only the man-cub from the Seeonee Pack!"

"Faugh! Man?" the rhino snorted, lifting his head in alarm. "Where? How many?"

And then Mowgli saw that the warning had come from a jungle mynah perched on Gargadan's head. The bird hopped higher up the rhino's skull and cocked its beady eye at Mowgli. "I have seen this one before, O Presence. Ye need pay him no mind."

Mowgli recognized the mynah as the same one who had, seasons ago, come to the bathing-pool and told Bagheera of the movement of the herds. "*Ohē,* Patwari!" he called loudly. "Good Hunting! Tell thy master, Mowgli comes!" Walking boldly up to the rhino, he laid the figs on the ground. "By thy leave, mighty Gargadan," he said, "it is I, Mowgli, of the Free People. Baloo has sent me to see thee."

The huge gray rhino looked around and sniffed cautiously at the ripe figs. There were none beneath the trees at his feet. Mowgli had rightly guessed that the rhino had eaten all within reach and would relish his offering.

Gargadan narrowed beady black eyes in the boy's direction and pricked his trumpet ears forward. "Bah!" he roared, ending with a testy snort. "The Free People? The Free People? Last moon, a pack of thy brethren lost their flea-bitten heads and mistook me for a bullock! Tried to bay me to the river like a yearling calf! But *I* quickly showed them the error of their ways. Not for nothing are they called 'the Free People'!"

The rhino moved closer to the figs, snuffling his terrible curved horn closer to the dust. "No manners, these young dogs, yapping and racing across the grasses with no thought for order, propriety, and the rightful time for things . . . the Law, boy, the Law!"

The mynah jumped about the rhino's head and shoulders crying, "The Law, wolfling! Tell him, My Lord!"

The rhino reached the figs and took one in his jaws, chewing lustily. "Too much mouth and not enough ears, these new ones," he grumbled half to the mynah, half to Mowgli. "No one wants to learn and listen. Listen and learn, boy! Ye say, Baloo sent thee? Uh-hmm. There's one who knows the Law, at least. Though what he thinks in sending a stripling cub to me—am I worth travelling ten miles over bad ground to look upon, boy?" And he settled down to eat all the figs, his ears twitching back and forth against the buzzing flies.

Mowgli sat in the grass and wondered which of all these questions, remarks, and grumbles he was to answer. Save for the *Bandar-log,* the Monkey People, he had never heard a creature say so little with so many words. But Gargadan was no beast to be reckoned lightly. He was nearly as long as a good-sized crocodile, taller at the shoulders than Mowgli's head, and on his snout rested an evil horn.

Finally, the boy ventured, "Baloo sent me, O Gargadan, to learn from thee the Law, but—" He hesitated, once again wondering what he was doing sitting on the veld before such a beast. "Perhaps it is a bad season for learning, and I should come another—"

"Come another! Come another!" screeched the mynah.

"Aurrr! Would ye, now!" the rhino bellowed. "Thou canst not escape so easily. Here thou wert sent, and here thou wilt stay! An order is an order till thou art strong enough to disobey. There is no bad season for learning, boy! And no good season for slackers, either." Gargadan finished the figs and moved into the shade of the trees, scratching himself contentedly on their smooth trunks, long polished by his rubbing.

He muttered, "I could tell thee tales, shocking tales of fuss and scandal. But they'd be cakes to an ass till thou hast learned the sense to winnow them out, boy. The Law, little badling, the Law is all!"

The rhino began to snort and grumble to himself, moving around the tree in a circle, rubbing his huge hindquarters back and forth, up and down, his little eyes closed in pleasure. Mowgli saw a quick movement in the grass at Gargadan's feet and froze.

A dusty brown snakeling, a karait, was snuggled down in the dust within swift striking distance of the rhino. One of the smallest snakes in India, it is also one of the most deadly, for it lies in the dust in the trail within easy reach of passing feet. Because few notice him or hear his tiny hiss, Karait is easily offended and usually eager for a fight, like the smallest rooster in a crowded chicken-yard.

Now, Karait was coiled in a tight, irritable ball, and he whispered, "Beware, O Big-Foot! I am Death!" But Gargadan's own voice was all that Gargadan heard, and he rubbed and shuffled closer to the snake.

Mowgli jumped up, grabbed a fallen fig limb, and leaped towards the rhino. He pinned Karait with the limb, and the snake struck viciously at the wood with his tiny fangs. Before Gargadan could flinch or trample, Mowgli slid the limb under the snake and flipped him far off into the veld, watching as he turned and twisted through the air and landed in distant scrub.

Gargadan blinked once and harrumphed, "Good work, boy, but wasted effort. That little worm could never pierce this hide." He set his foot down with a decided stamp. "Listen and learn, boy, listen and learn. Wasted work is no work at all!"

The mynah chuckled and rolled his eyes at Mowgli. "Time for thy patrol, My Lord."

The rhino consulted the angle of the sun hurriedly and snapped, "Quite so, quite so. Make haste, boy," and he turned and ambled down a worn path.

Gargadan led Mowgli to the river, pausing to point out the landmarks along the way. "Stay on the trail," he said as he trod the deeply rutted path. Mowgli glanced around and saw only a wide plain with no boundaries.

"Why dost thou walk such a narrow road?" he asked, gesturing around to the broad space about them.

"Because outlandish wanderings cause disorder!" the rhino said, swinging his head back and forth with each step. "What if each fat-headed fool on the veld went where he pleased, eh? Confusion! Chaos! There's nothing out there worth breaking line for, boy, and that's what thou art here to learn. To stand steady!"

It was nearly a mile to the river, and as they walked, Gargadan continued the lessons. There was a certain spot where he made his toilet every day and no other. It was a wide mound of dung, dried black in the sun, nearly as tall as Mowgli himself. The rhino approached it backwards, the better to waste no motion, always from the same angle, and always at the same time each day.

As he did so now, Mowgli said, "In the jungle, we do such things when the need comes, wherever we may be—but always off the trail, of course," he added quickly.

"And that is what is wrong with the jungle today!" Gargadan snorted contemptuously. "Mavericks and mutineers, making their own rules, breaking ranks whenever they please." He muttered and kicked his back heels through the dung. "We with the broad backs, we who are the Masters of the Law, we must set the example, boy. That is why Baloo sent thee to me, no doubt."

Mowgli scowled in confusion. "But Hathi is a lord of his piece of the jungle. And *he* goes where he pleases—"

"That four-toed, two-tailed bag of wind!"

Mowgli was startled by the rhino's vast and furious temper and shocked to hear the great elephant called such names. He glanced at Patwari, who only shook his head in warning.

"Hathi is my friend," the boy said quietly. "Indeed, he is friend to *all* in the jungle."

"The Silent One is no friend to my Lord!" Patwari said quickly.

Gargadan was blowing himself up larger and larger until his black eyes bulged.

The mynah glanced nervously down at the rhino's madly twitching ears and chattered, "Always, he takes the best shade, the widest wading places, the most tender grasses—'The Silent One,' phew! He tramples about in noisy herds, smashing the grass and muddying the water. He lets his squealing calves run under everybody's feet, he bends the Law to his own whims—"

The fuming volcano under Patwari finally exploded. "He works for Man! Betrays the Law for a bundle of sweet grass and a lullaby! Sells his back for a bottle of sour water! [The rhino meant the ale that the elephant trainers fed their captive charges to keep them docile.] All the jungle bows to that trumpeting fool, while I, *I* who am older—"

"And stronger!" Patwari clucked.

"And stronger. But he—"

"And wiser!" the mynah added.

But Gargadan's anger had blown itself out, and he twisted his great head back to glare at the bird. "Enough. This little badling claims Hathi as friend." He swung his head back to Mowgli and said, mustering patience, "I simply cannot stomach filthy bad management, and that is what Four-toes has done to the Law. But ye shall hear no more of it. Not from me." And he turned with slow dignity and continued down the trail.

Mowgli spent the better part of four suns with the great rhino, listening to his lessons and learning how he viewed the world. Gargadan had little patience for those who were "slackers" or "fools" or "ne'er-do-wells." He thought the chital unsavory and addled.

"They are in constant rut," the rhino confided to Mowgli. "Not a moment of peace but they're butting and bawling and herding their does hither and yon like barbarous rabbits! A time and a place for everything, boy."

He found the blackbuck frivolous. "Trust them to drivel if they get the chance, always blathering about like peacocks. A killer comes, and they stand about and bleat at each other as though that alone will save them. A word wasted is gone for good, boy."

And he thought the bullocks lazy and shockingly dull. "Mired in mud up to their chins all day. Sheer waste of breath to tell them a thing. The Law is for those who can understand it, boy!"

"And I thought it was for everyone," Mowgli said quietly under his breath, but Gargadan did not hear.

On the fourth day, the rhino took the boy to the edges of his territory—it was small quarters, which would have made any of the Hunting Folk feel confined—to teach Mowgli his most fearsome lesson.

In the middle of a narrow trail which led to a mudhole, a large cover of scrub and brush had been laid down. The bushes covered most of the path, yet no one had made any effort to drag them out of the way, as would have been the case if a tree had been felled by a storm.

"Pull up that branch there," Gargadan said quietly. "Careful now, and keep well back."

Mowgli pulled away a large palm frond and looked beneath to see a deep, dark pit. At the bottom, sharpened bamboo sticks had been sunk into the mud, their points like spears jutting upwards. Mowgli pulled back instinctively, sniffing the air for danger.

"Man?" he asked.

"Many of the little brown monkeys," Gargadan said. "But they are not here now. Thy nose does not tell thee this?"

Mowgli wet his finger and ran it over his nose and smelled all over the brush covering the pit. He stood and said, "Nay, my nose is not as wise as thine. But I can see the work of Man's hand well enough. Why have no Jungle People moved the brush so that others might see and not fall within?"

"Because all know it is here. And if we disturb it, Man will move it elsewhere, eh?" The rhino chuckled wryly. "We know Man in *this* piece of the jungle, boy. He always follows the same trails."

Mowgli sat down to reason this out. "Some little thing I know of Man," he said. "The son of Hathi told me there were as many kinds of Man as there are nuts on a palm. Which kind set this killing-pit?"

Gargadan glared at this mention of Hathi, and Patwari said quickly, "No kind that Four-toes knows. These are called the Gonds. Ko, the Crow, told me, and I told my Lord." He bobbed his head up and down. "Little black men with spears and rocks who live in the jungle in tribes like the *Bandar-log*. They were chased hence by the villagers, off their lands and away from the ploughed fields. Now, they put their hair atop their heads in a black knot, and they pray to the old gods."

"They live in the jungle? And I have not seen them?"

"O Thou of the Big Eyes Who Sees All," Gargadan grunted, "they are not *in* thy piece of jungle. *Many* things are not. Which is why Baloo sent thee to me, no doubt."

Mowgli turned and looked down at the sharp spears, and he shivered to imagine what they could do to even the toughest hide. "I wonder that no chital or blackbuck has fallen hither, chased by a hunting pack or even in play. Truly, this is a fearsome death."

Patwari fluffed himself up with pride. "My Lord found the thing and told it so that none might stumble there!"

"How didst thou know it was there?" Mowgli asked the rhino.

"My eyes may be dim, but my nose is wiser than most," Gargadan said gruffly. "And it is the Law, eh? To warn those who will listen, though some will not."

Mowgli stood and touched the rhino's shoulder. "That was a brave and true thing. I would go and see these Gonds. For if it is the Law to warn those who will listen, there are those in my piece of the jungle who should know of them as well. Shall I find thee by the fig trees when I have seen them?"

"Or close thereby," the rhino said. "*I* do not wander about aimlessly like others I might name."

Mowgli turned and slipped silently into the depths of the forest. He followed narrow deer trails, crossed a stream, and climbed a high banyan to look about, searching for traces of these strange brown men who lived in the woods. When the sun had moved behind his shoulders, he came to a thick grove of bamboo at the edge of the dried mud flats of a marsh. He bent and examined the mud carefully. There, among the tracks of pig and marsh bird, he found the larger footprints of Man.

"Oho," Mowgli thought to himself. "These *shikari* [hunters] trail their quarry boldly, making no efforts to conceal their own tracks. Bagheera would be most interested to see this." Mowgli knew, as did most other hunters in the jungle, that at any time, he who was the hunter could become the hunted. But these brown men knew no such fear. "So this is what it is to be Man."

He followed the tracks through the jungle, stopping to sniff the ground and the air frequently, his ears tuned to the slightest hint of the strangers. He began to catch the scent of smoke, and he dropped to his knees, moving closer. Finally, he came to a large

clearing in the woods. He climbed a tree and hid himself up in the thickest foliage, parting the branches with his hands.

Below him, clustered in the clearing, the Gond tribe had made camp. Mowgli quickly counted as many shelters as there were fingers on his hands. The brown men had made small huts of huge palm fronds, bracing them together with bamboo. Before several of the huts, fires burned. The tribe sat before their fires, and in the middle of the clearing, a large nilghai sprawled, its hide half-removed. Two hunters were cutting the carcass, and women waited to take the meat from their hands.

"It surely has been Good Hunting with these," Mowgli thought, "but how did they catch such a runner? Even the Pack, in full bay, cannot bring down a nilghai on the open plain, not unless it is weakened or a very young one—and this, this is a large bull in full horn." He remembered how Bagheera told him once that he had seen the White-Faces hunting the nilghai on horses, and even they had to gallop at full speed to turn the running herds.

But bring him down they had, and now as the boy watched, the tribe gathered round the bull and began to poke at the meat, laughing and telling tales among themselves. Mowgli could not understand their talk, of course, but he could sense that they were no more excited about this kill than Bagheera would have been over a rabbit. Clearly, they had had such success before.

Then Mowgli's eyes narrowed and he caught his breath. A young girl came close to his tree—the first one he had seen so near. Bagheera had often taken him to the ploughed fields to watch Man, had warned him of their traps, their arrows, their barking sticks, and Mowgli had seen the village huts and the people as they came and went, but always from a distance. Never before had he been close enough to a young woman to see the firelight dance on her dark skin, to catch the faint scent of her oiled hair.

She was quite short, like the rest of her brethren, and her face was rounded and plump, her eyes black as night. Mowgli's legs tensed against the branches, and he leaned slightly lower to sniff the air. She glanced up, as though sensing him near, and he froze. Her eyes wandered over the tree thoughtfully, and then she drew away. She had not seen him in the shadows. Mowgli let out his breath in a sigh.

A small group of hunters sat near the fire, doing something with their arrows. One stood and danced rapidly to the fallen nilghai, making short thrusting movements with his weapon. The women chanted and raised their voices in approval, and a hunting song filled the forest.

"This must be the killer," Mowgli thought, "But there is nothing magical about his arrow. Yet this man, a creature that Akela, my gray wolf brother, could squash with one paw, brought down a bull which would make even Bagheera's eyes gleam with pride." He thought for an instant. "Gargadan was right about one thing. If I can learn the secret of the Gonds, I should do so. There are many in the jungle—and there lies one such," he said to himself, glancing at the fallen nilghai "—who would have done better with such knowledge."

The Gonds began to drift quietly to their huts now, as the fires died to embers. A few lay down in the open on leaf mats; a child whimpered in sleep.

Mowgli waited in the tree, watching carefully to see what the hunters did. The one killer who had brought down the nilghai bent down and peered inside his hut. A woman called to him loudly from inside. He leaned his arrows against the bamboo frame and went in to the woman, and his comrades laughed quietly in the darkness. Soon, one by one, they too drifted to their beds, and silence came over the camp.

Mowgli waited still longer, thinking over all he had seen. "The secret must lie in the arrow," he whispered. "They are not runners; their legs are too short and fat to catch even me on the open plains. The bull was not pierced in many places, so they did not use their pits, nor did they rush him all in a group. No," he murmured, "if I would know how this death came about, I must see that arrow."

Finally, slowly, Mowgli crept down from his hiding-place. He slunk carefully to the edge of the clearing, watching the huts with wide eyes, crouched in the shadows. Once, a man cried out in his sleep, and Mowgli froze, his hand on his knife. But no one stirred from the huts; no head stuck out in the darkness to shout a warning. He edged past the nilghai carcass and towards the killer's hut. Moving so his shadow would not fall across the open door, he silently plucked an arrow from the bamboo frame and peered at it with wonder. He felt a cool moistness under his bare foot, and he glanced down. A few withered white flowers lay on the ground. He picked one up and sniffed it cautiously. He looked around and saw a bowl lying by the fire; in the bowl were three thorny fruit, prickly hard green pods set all round with spines. Now, had you been watching from within one of the shadowed huts, you would have seen Mowgli's eyes gleam with a sudden understanding. But no one was watching. And no one saw him take up the hunter's arrow and slide away once more into the jungle.

He reached Gargadan's particular patch of fig trees by the time the sun was coming up over the hills. Gargadan was leaning against his favourite tree, munching quietly on a thorn bush. As he drew closer, Mowgli heard Patwari once more warn the rhino, "The wolfling approaches, O Presence, and he brings something in his hand." The bird sat up and chirped nervously, "It is a Man's long tooth, My Lord!" And the rhino rumbled nervously to face the boy.

Mowgli dropped the arrow at Gargadan's feet and threw himself down wearily in the tall grass. "It was a long trek," he panted, "but I have seen the little men and I bring a new lesson."

Gargadan chewed thoughtfully and then kicked a great foot towards the arrow. "There is nothing new in this, badling. It is what they fling at the rabbits and birds, and perhaps a day-old fawn on staggering knees. Those who stand higher than a jackal pay it no mind."

"Unripe I may be, and foolish as well, but to *this* I would pay some little mind, O Gargadan," Mowgli said quietly, and he opened his fist to show the withered white *dhatura* flower. "The little men put it in their long tooth. I saw them do so. Perhaps it is time to move thy trails further from their camp."

The rhino chuckled wryly, and Patwari took up the laughter, bobbing his head up and down with glee. "And the flies will be bad this season as well, Your Honour. Perhaps thou shouldst cover thy head with palm and bleat like the chital at the injustice of life, eh?"

75

Mowgli glared at the mynah, but he held his temper in check. "Even the wisest heads in the jungle cannot understand Man and his ways," he said to the rhino, ignoring the bird's laughter. "It is in my heart that this is a new danger."

Gargadan stopped chuckling abruptly. "There is no *new* danger, man-cub, only those thou hast not seen. I have heard of these poison teeth before. The foolish deer talk of little else. The Gonds take the apple of death [*dhatura*] and smear it on their weapons, they say. Well, and what is that to me? I have always escaped them, and I always shall. And why? Because they are like the *Bandar-log,* boy, chattering monkeys with no sense of order and no leader among them. They fancy themselves great and powerful hunters, but they have never caught me yet. They chase me, and I run faster. They set their outlandish traps on the trails, and I smell their rank odours a mile before I reach them. They will do as they always do, and so shall I."

"But they brought down a nilghai! Shouldst thou not—"

Patwari interrupted the boy impatiently. "O fool, has he not told it a hundred times? The dog may bark, but the rhino moves on. Listen and learn! Learn and listen!"

Mowgli pulled himself up with angry dignity. "In the jungle, they say thou art blind, O Gargadan. When *we* move away from danger, we call it wisdom."

The rhino grunted and turned his back on the boy. "Ye are not in the jungle now, boy, ye are in *my* quarters. And where *I* live, we call it by an ugly name and we hear no more of it."

Mowgli turned on his heel and left the rhino leaning against the fig tree, Patwari's chuckles burning his ears as he walked away. He crossed the river and sat down in a thicket to think.

"Baloo was right," he told himself indignantly. "Gargadan has two piggy eyes and few manners. Any time he is questioned, his temper goes where the black crabs go, and there is only madness left!" He picked up a stick and poked at the ground over and over, thinking of all the things he should have said.

"Baloo would have left two suns ago," Mowgli thought sullenly. "And Bagheera would never have come at all! What is the rhino that I should sit at his feet like a fawn before a stag? Talk, talk,

talk! Gargadan is brother to the bird who rides his shoulder: Both beaks never shut."

But then Mowgli remembered the way the rhino had stopped his insults to Hathi when he knew the boy loved him. "Thou hast named him friend," the rhino had said, "and so I shall say no more." At least, he showed me that respect, Mowgli scowled.

And then he recalled how Gargadan had said, "The Law is to warn those who will listen, though some will not."

I *tried* to warn him, Mowgli told himself—and Baloo's voice came back to him in a low mind-rumble: "Thou canst never know too much of the Law."

Once, Mowgli stood and almost started back to the fig trees, determined to try once more to persuade Gargadan to leave the veld, at least until the Gonds moved their hunting grounds. But when he remembered the way Patwari cawed at him, "Listen and learn, boy!" over and over, his eyes narrowed in anger. Finally, he turned and started back to his piece of the jungle, vowing to keep from the rhino ever more.

The sun moved slowly as he walked, filtering down through the dense trees, dappling his feet as they moved silently over narrow trails, across rippling streams, and past rustling thickets of bamboo. The jungle seemed unusually quiet this day, as though even the winds waited, tensed and expectant. Mowgli rounded a huge banyan, intent on his own thoughts, and stumbled over the coils of a large python, waiting in the shadows for an unwary deer.

"Good Hunting," he said in the Snake Master Words, picking himself up carefully. It is not good to step quickly by a snake, and Mowgli never did. "What moves?"

But the python did not know him and barely responded to his courtesy. "Man moves," he threw over his shoulder, and the great snake slid into denser cover. Mowgli tensed then and eased behind the banyan, every sense tuned to the voices of the forest. Now, he heard it, faint and far away—the rustlings and mumblings of Man tracking in the jungle. He pulled himself up in the low branches of the banyan and waited, his breath still as the noon air.

From out of the clearing came a line of Gond hunters, nearly as many as the fingers on Mowgli's two hands, each walking in the footsteps of the other, each carrying a bow and a quiver of arrows on his shoulder. Though the natives would have easily surprised any other human in the woods, the creatures of the forest were well aware of their presence, and Mowgli felt a quick surge of shame that he had almost stumbled over the Gonds as well as the python, so distracted had he been.

The line of little black men moved quickly and determinedly down the trail Mowgli had just travelled. One was telling a quiet story to his comrade, and he put his thumb to his nose and grunted softly in a mimicry of the rhino. The other hunter grinned and slapped his bow.

"They go to the veld," Mowgli knew with a sudden swift knowledge. "They go to catch Gargadan at last."

He waited until they had disappeared into the jungle and then slid down the banyan, staring after them. There was every chance that soon, the rhino would be dead, perhaps even before Mowgli reached Baloo's side once more. He tried to picture Gargadan sprawled on the grassy plain, his tongue out, his great sides heaving in pain—and he turned his head away, his mouth twisted in despair. Whatever else the rhino was, he was not a coward, and he did not deserve such a death. Not a creature in the jungle did.

Mowgli recalled now, in an instant of vivid memory, how the rhino had responded when first he came across the veld towards him. "Faugh!" the great beast had snorted. "Man? Where? How many?"

"He was afraid," Mowgli said to himself suddenly. "As all are afraid of something, so Gargadan is afraid of Man. Yet, he does not let his fear master him." Under that gruff hide, behind his constant call for order, despite his pride which would not let it show, Mowgli realized that Gargadan feared Man as all the jungle fears Man. "Yet, he took me in, on Baloo's word alone." Mowgli dropped his head. "And I have left him to his fate at the hands of his enemy. I have listened to his words, but I have not heard his heart."

The boy knew that he had every right to turn and continue on his way home, back to Baloo and Bagheera, back to the safety of things well-known, back to the Pack. But he remembered, long ago, how Hathi had told him that hearts were like horses that go against the bit and spur. No matter how Mowgli might turn his feet away from the rhino, his heart kept looking back over his shoulder. He began to walk back to the plains whence he had come. And then, he began to walk faster, for he was afraid of what he might find.

Mowgli took a wide path around the Gonds, and by the time he reached the plains, he was running, his heart beating high and fast in his throat. He stopped at the top of the hill by the fig tree and scanned the veld. There, off in the distance, a few of the Gond hunters were bunched, hidden in the thick brush just on the far side of the river. "Where are the others?" Mowgli wondered to himself.

Gargadan was sprawled in one of his wallows, snorting and rolling, unaware of the danger so close at hand. As the boy watched, the great rhino suddenly stopped wallowing and froze in the dust. He stumbled to his feet, his nose in the air, his ears swivelled towards the Gonds' hiding place.

Mowgli raced down the hill, shouting a warning, but the rhino sensed the hunters at the same moment and turned to run. He bolted out of the mud wallow, down the trail out to the open plain, but as he galloped past the dung pile, two more Gond hunters jumped out in ambush and shot arrows at his flanks. Gargadan squealed in anger and swerved aside. To Mowgli's horror, the great beast ran across the open plain—with one Gond arrow sticking from his shoulder.

Mowgli ran with all his might towards the hunters, barking and snarling at them in a murderous wrath. "Leave him, leave him!" he shouted, clenching his fist and screaming. "This is not Good Hunting, but a *dog's* death ye bring! Aiyaaa!" The boy leaped into the middle of the hunters, scattering them in all directions. His eyes were flashing, his teeth bared in a snarl, and his long hair waved and whipped over his naked shoulders.

The little black hunters could understand nothing that Mowgli shouted in wolf-talk, of course, but there was no mistaking his killing rage.

"It is a godling," one cried in terror, "a jungle demon!" and he raised his trembling arm to loose a poison arrow. But Mowgli leaped at the hunter, his knife raised in a savage arc, and knocked the bow away.

With that, the Gonds scattered like leaves before a high wind and ran off, babbling in fear. Mowgli hesitated not an instant, but turned and ran after Gargadan, his eyes streaming with hot tears of fury and grief.

He trailed the rhino until the sun was low and finally found him at the edge of his territory, lying in the mud by the river. The great Gargadan had fallen with his head half-in, half-out of the water, his huge sides moving in and out in gasping breaths. Patwari huddled miserably by his ear, for once silent as stone. Mowgli sat down by the massive head and looked into the rhino's face.

Gargadan's eyes rolled open, and Mowgli could see the white cast of death already moving over them. "It was such a little tooth!" the rhino said feebly. "I knocked it off before I even put a mile between us!" He groaned once, a shallow, rusty half-roar of pain.

Mowgli willed his voice to calm. "Art thou thirsty?" he asked gently, but Gargadan only whispered, "This is a jackal's death, a feeble tooth to bring down a fawn!"

"Nay," Mowgli said quickly. "If such a tooth had bit Hathi himself, even he would lie as thou dost now."

"Truly?" the rhino asked.

"By the Bull that bought me," Mowgli nodded. "And all the jungle shall know of the might of Gargadan. It took a full pack of Gonds to bring thee down."

"A full pack," the rhino mumbled, "but only one tooth. Listen and learn, man-cub, listen and learn!" And the great beast's breath came out of him in a long, harsh sigh, rattling his huge sides to silence.

Mowgli stroked the dead rhino's ears softly. "We must live before we can learn," he murmured. "Thou hast taught me this lesson at least, O Gargadan."

The boy got to his feet and said to Patwari, the Mynah, "Sing his song well, Little Watcher, yet wait a little while before ye begin. Nothing was ever yet lost by silence, eh?" And Mowgli turned and walked back into the jungle.

This was the song which Mowgli heard Patwari sing before Chil, the Kite, circled down to see what had become of the mighty Gargadan.

Patwari's Death Chant

Watcher and warner am I,
High on his shoulders I sat,
Now, I must sing to the sky,
Gargadan's requiescat!
Law, Law, Law!
He lived and he died by the Law!
Record, Record, Record!
I sing of the death of my Lord!

I was his eyes and his ears,
Steadfast and faithful I stayed,
And when a new Lord appears,
I'll sing a new accolade!
Law, Law, Law!
He lived and he died by the Law!
Renown, Renown, Renown!
Until the Man's tooth brought him down!

No one was wiser than he,
He who was King among Kings!
Empty our hearts shall all be,
Till a new Lord walks under our wings!
Law, Law, Law!
He lived and he died by the Law!
I said, I said, I said!
The rhino, the rhino is dead!

IN THE CAVE
OF BADUR

Softly, softly, wings of skin,
Neither birds nor beasts are kin,
Therefore, let the Hunt begin,
Let fly the claws of night!

Tongues which whisper in the dark,
Hands which cling to smoothest bark,
Ears which always find their mark,
And teeth which well can bite!

Upside down, we sleep the day
Till it's time to find our prey,
Then together, wings away,
To quench our appetite!

Master Words, we heed to few,
Laws we have but only two,
Fly for home before the dew
And Good Hunting till the light!

Song of Badur, the Bat

Mowgli went hot-foot back to the Seeonee Hills with news of Gargadan's death. Bagheera was off hunting in other places, but Akela, the Great Gray Wolf, now white and grizzled with age, called the Pack together to Council Rock.

The wolves came from all directions to sit under the night-sky on a hilltop covered with stones and boulders where a hundred could hide. Akela stretched out on the Leader's Rock, as was his right, and Mowgli sat at the middle of the Pack circle with Baloo at his side.

"Listen well, O Wolves!" Akela bayed loudly. "A brother brings news."

A wolf-mother pulled her cubs closer and whined, "Ru-uroh! It best be news of some import, to take sucklings from the den on such a night."

"Speak, then, Little Brother," a black yearling snapped. "We have come far, and the night is short."

Mowgli stood up and threw his long hair over his shoulders, the better to see each wolf clearly. "Ye know me!" he shouted. "No longer am I the Little Frog ye once took into the Pack for the price of a bull. I have been to the plains among the Hooved Ones, and I bring grave news. Gargadan, the Great Rhino, is dead!"

An old wolf yawned hugely, stretching his paws out into the moonlight. "And for this, we left the herds running well?"

"It is not the death I speak of," Mowgli continued with a hard scowl at the old wolf, "but the *means* of that death. Ye have heard of the little hunters in another place of the jungle? The Gonds, they are called, and they are a piece with the Man-Pack. Always before, they took down only the Hooved Ones, the weak and the bud-horns, and none save the herds gave them mind. But now, they bring a new hunt into the jungle. They meddle with the apple of death!"

A rustle of snarls went round the wolf circle, and the she-wolves bared their teeth and pulled the cubs closer.

"The poison white flower!" a wolf barked. "It is against the Law!"

"Wu-owrr," growled Baloo. "Let thy Little Brother speak, O Free People. He knows the Law as well as thee."

"Man knows *not* this Law," Mowgli continued. "He takes the white flower and rubs it on the end of his long tooth, his spear."

"What of that?" another yearling asked. "The *dhatura* cannot kill unless it lodges in the belly, eh? Let the bud-horns fear such a small thing."

"With even such a small thing was Gargadan brought down," Mowgli said softly. "They have driven their own herds to the four winds, and now they seek new prey." The boy's eyes flashed with sudden anger, and every wolf's hackles rose. "I say, the rhino feeds the ants even now, and no wolf's hide is so strong as his. And I say more. These Gonds move their hunting grounds as often as Hathi's tribe. In one moon, perhaps two, they will bring their lawless poison to *our* trails!"

"Ye are so sure of this, Little Frog?" a wolf called. "Did these Gonds whisper in thy ear, Man to Man?"

Mowgli whirled on the wolf, his teeth bared in a growl. "I am thy *brother*, and I stand before ye to tell ye they are coming. Even now, their tracks lead past the Waingunga and to the feet of these very hills. Wouldst thou have my tooth alongside thine or not? Speak now, thou barking dog—" and Mowgli snatched his knife from round his neck and held its sharp edge to the wolf's throat.

Akela snapped, "Man or Wolf, we stand at Council, O Free People, and never has blood been shed on these rocks."

Mowgli relaxed his grip on the wolf's neck. Akela called to him, "Ye say they come, Little Brother. Why should the Pack fear this hunt? 'Tis the Hooved Ones who will be bitten by these poison teeth, eh? Surely there is plenty of game for all."

Mowgli shook his head. "This trail is not so simple. Who now runs the herds to and fro? Who takes more bud-horns than the tiger, the jackals, or even Bagheera? The Free People, my brothers. And who then takes the game back to the den to feed the cubs? The Free People, my brothers. And so, when the Man-Pack finds the herds scattered and reaped, who will they bite with their poison arrows instead? Whose cubs will die from poisoned meat left on the plains? Ourselves and our own."

The boy gestured with his finger round the circle of wolves. "Now, run down the trail the other way. Who among us could rid the jungle of these Gonds? Tabaqui, the Jackal, and his tribe? Hundar, the Hyena?" He fixed the wolves with a powerful gaze and asked, "Thinkest thou even Bagheera could do this thing alone? Nay. It is in my stomach that this fight lies with the Free People, more than any other. And if ye fail, there will be no new cubs at next season's Council."

"Aurrr-ou!" bayed a wolf. "We must kill them!"

"Kill them! Kill them! Kill them all!" cried the wolves in a sudden frenzy of fear and rage.

Mowgli held up his hands for silence, and all eyes turned to him. "Is this thine answer, then?"

And a chorus of barks answered him, "Ay!"

The boy glanced at Akela but could not read his glowing eyes in the shadows. "The Pack has spoken as one," he said finally. "Leave us now, whilst we plan this hunt. When we have done, we shall call Council once more. I say before the Rocks and the Moon, ye have my word on it." Mowgli stepped down from the speaking rock and watched while the wolves slipped away in the darkness. Now, only a few remained—Mother and Father Wolf, Mowgli's three den brothers, Baloo, and the Lone Wolf, Akela.

"O my Little Frog," Mother Wolf said, leaning against him tenderly, "ye speak with the tongue of a leader this night. Didst thou mark how they listened?"

Baloo rumbled, "He who brings such news will always prick ears, eh?" but his voice was gruff with pride.

"Thou hast promised them a great hunt," Father Wolf said quietly. "Hast thou a plan?"

Akela stretched and moved painfully down off his rock with stiffened legs. "They will remember the danger ye warned them of for only a moment," he said gravely, "but they will remember thy word each time they gather hence. They are ready enough to kill. But readiness alone will not bring down this buck. What wouldst thou have them do?"

Mowgli sat down cross-legged in the moonlight, his brow

wrinkled in thought. "I do not know. Truly, it is a hard nut. Thinkest thou the Pack could drive the Gonds as we drive the nilghai? Perhaps, if we sing them to sleep every night and follow their trails by day, they will go to another place."

"Perhaps. Or perhaps, as they tire of the singing, they will turn their long teeth to the nearest flanks, and the first wolf who ventures too close will die a dog's death," Akela said calmly. "I cannot lead them in such a hunt. Couldst thou?"

Mowgli leaned his chin on his knees and sighed. "It is good the Pack knows of this danger. But whether or not the Pack can turn it away is another tale."

"Perhaps . . . " Baloo said thoughtfully, half to himself, "perhaps, we must seek an ally in this fight." He sat up on his haunches as the thought struck him. "Perhaps we can set Man to trap Man."

Mowgli turned to the bear with amazement. "Does Man hunt Man?"

"Most assuredly," Baloo said gravely.

"I have heard, but never have I seen such madness." Mowgli shook his head in wonder. "Wolves do not hunt wolves; tigers do not hunt tigers; the foolish deer do not hunt each other, and even the hyena who eats all things will not hunt his own." He thought this over carefully. "But Man hunts Man. Hmmm. Patwari said Man drove the Gonds into the jungle from the ploughed fields. Perhaps we can set Man to drive the Gonds from the jungle elsewhere, eh?"

"Man hunts on the far plains, even now," Akela said thoughtfully. "The yearlings brought news of it two nights back. The White-Faces hunt the herds hither and yon, they said, but also they told of a strange thing. Thy brothers say that Man hunts there with a brace of *chita bagh.*"

"*Chita bagh,* the large cat that can outrace the fleetest hoof?" Baloo asked. "It is a long time since I have seen such a thing."

"Faster even than a nilghai? This, I myself would see," Mowgli said. "Let us go to the far plains. Perhaps we can lead the White-Faces here, that they may hunt the Gonds as well."

"Faugh!" snorted Mother Wolf. "From what I know of the

White-Faces, they will not be led hither or anywhere else. But thou hast given thy word, and so it is worth a try."

Akela led the trek, a journey of two days running. Though the Lone Wolf was almost white at the muzzle, he was still able to set a good pace. Baloo finally had to turn back, tired by the quick, loping gait of the wolves, but Mowgli ran on, Mother and Father Wolf at his side, until the four reached the wide stretch of grasslands across the hills which the jungle called "the far plains."

This was new territory for Mowgli, a hunting grounds far past the river and the hills which had bounded his world. Wide, dusty trails crossed the land at intervals, trails which Akela said were Man-Roads. The smell of smoke was ever-present in the air, and the sounds of the jungle fell behind them to a strange silence.

"Man lives just over that rise," Akela panted when they finally stopped at the edge of the forest. Before them lay the grasslands in a wide shimmer of heat. Few herds grazed; few trees offered shelter. "A large village," the wolf sniffed. "They come to and fro and gather wood for their fires."

Mowgli could see now why he had never been brought to this place. The smell of Man was everywhere, and only a small herd of nilghai browsed at the edge of the grass. It was a place for young wolves to practice at the hunt perhaps, but not a place for the Jungle People to frequent.

The boy crouched down in the brush, his nose searching the wind for scents. "Phew!" he coughed. "I cannot tell what is afoot with all this smoke in the air. A village breeds foulness like a dunghill breeds flies. No wonder only Man hunts here. It is *not* Good Hunting. Did the yearlings say when the White-Faces come?"

"They hunt only by day," Akela said.

"Good," Mother Wolf said, gazing back into the forest shadows with gleaming eyes. "Then we shall hunt by night. Wilt thou lead the kill, my Little Frog?"

But Mowgli was staring past the grasslands, past the nilghai, as though he could see over the next rise. "Nay," he said finally, "I shall hunt the ploughed fields tonight. I would see these Men in their lairs, before I see them at the hunt. Save me a mouthful, Mother." And he slipped away.

The village lay sprawled in a shallow, dusty valley, the largest collection of huts and fields that Mowgli had ever seen. For a moment, he hesitated, confused by the hundreds of strange odours and sounds. Light came from the thatched windows, and cooking smells mixed with smoke. Yellow pariah dogs barked at him fiercely as he slid close to the houses, but he snarled once at them, and they whimpered away. He crouched beneath the window of a clay hut and eased up on his knees to peer inside.

A baby cried within, and a woman hurried to the corner of the hut, making soothing sounds. Mowgli felt his stomach turn in his belly as it did when a branch broke beneath him and he had to scrabble for a handhold in a high tree. He looked quickly over his shoulder to see if danger was near, but it was only the sounds of the baby crying and the woman's lullaby which had made his heart lurch so. He stared, feeling a strange confusion, as the woman took the child from its bed and held it to her breast.

> Eye of the Moon, Eye of the Star,
> Lie here beside me, thy father's gone far,
> To find thee a spoon, to find thee a plate,
> That thou, little baby, might grow to be great

the woman sang softly, as she stroked the child's brow and rocked him back and forth.

Mowgli felt water rise in his eyes, and he quickly brushed it away, wondering what new pain this was in his heart. "It is nothing," he told himself. "Nothing but a Woman making a purr in her throat like Bagheera. Nothing to bring tears from a Hunter." Though he could not understand her words, yet, he could not pull himself away.

A footfall brushed behind him and Mowgli whirled, his hand on his knife. Two men approached the hut, their heads together in talk. The boy sank back further in the shadows, unseen.

"Even still," one said to the other, "I will be glad when the white *shikari* leave our village. Their horses have ruined our pastures, and the young girls grow more brazen with each night."

"We can buy four new pastures with what they have paid for their pleasure," the other replied, "and our daughters—well, and they are only daughters, eh? *Aiya,* never have I seen such rifles! Such riches!"

The men went inside the hut and Mowgli crept away, turning over in his head all he had seen and heard. When he returned to the edge of the forest, he found the wolves finishing a small muntjac, or barking deer. Mother Wolf had saved him a portion.

"The Man-Pack hunts this way tomorrow, I think," Mowgli muttered as he fed. "We shall wait and watch."

"What didst thou see there?" Father Wolf asked curiously.

"Nothing," Mowgli said quickly, for he could not explain his heart's unease. "Nothing worth telling."

Dawn came to the grasslands, and the four comrades waited in the brush. The sun rose high, and no White-Faces came. The heat waves shimmered over the plains and the browsing nilghai moved toward the few trees, and still, no *shikari* showed themselves.

"It is the hottest part of the day," Mother Wolf panted. "Even the White-Faces will not hunt now. Perhaps they come tomorrow."

"Hissst," Mowgli said. "Didst thou hear that?"

From across the plains, they could hear horses approaching: the stamp and beat of hooves, the jingle of bit and spur, an occasional whinny of impatience. The White-Faces were coming.

Now, Mowgli could see them faintly through the dust and the heat waves. Six hunters in strange white clothing with hats on their heads rode six prancing horses. The glint and flash of brass fittings on smooth-bore rifles was unmistakable, even from his position behind the scrub dhak trees, and he smelled fear ripple over the plains before the *shikari*. Behind the horses, two villagers walked, leading by thin ropes two long-legged cats. "These, then, are the *chita bagh,*" Mowgli whispered to himself: a brace of hunting cheetahs.

The nilghai had seen the approach of the hunters as well, and they clustered nervously together, eyeing the fringes of the forest. The dust cleared, and the horses were silent. Mowgli raised up on his knees to see the cheetahs more clearly.

They were long, lanky cats with small, dog-like heads. Tawny as the grasses, they were spotted all over, and their ribs were bigger round than those of Kaa. They strode out onto the plains with a bold arrogance, never troubling to hide themselves as most hunters would. Mowgli's mouth gaped as he saw the reason why.

Each cheetah was hooded with a white sash, and it followed behind its native keeper as a village dog followed its master. As Mowgli watched, one big cat was walked forward, and its hood was removed. Instantly, as though by command, the cheetah dropped into a stalking position. It hissed, a small sinister sound, and scanned the plains, focusing quickly on the nilghai.

One blue bull stepped from the centre of the herd and snorted a challenge, keeping the cows and calves well behind him. He stamped, once, twice; the cheetah was frozen, its eyes never leaving the bull. Suddenly, two cows broke from the herd in panic, instinctively running for the cover of the woods. With scarcely a glance at the bull, the cheetah broke into a full run, racing right towards one of the galloping cows. The cat sped over the grass, its long legs bunching and stretching in terrible speed. The nilghai cow screeched in terror and ran for her life, but just before she reached the safety of the trees, the cheetah caught her in a blink, leaped on her neck, and pulled her down. The cow bleated once; a cloud of dust enveloped the two, and when it cleared, the cheetah stood over the fallen nilghai, waiting calmly for the *shikari* to come to the kill.

It had happened so quickly, that had Mowgli taken his eyes from the scene, he might have missed the death. All in silence, the cheetah had stalked, outrun, and killed—and now, the nilghai were scattered over the plains.

"Never have I seen such a hunter," Mowgli breathed in awe. "Bagheera said even the fastest wolf could not bring down a nilghai in full gallop. And yet, this *chitah bagh,* as ye call him, scarcely pants at such a kill."

"See now what the White-Faces do," Akela whispered quickly. "The yearlings told of this as well." Mowgli and the wolves moved closer in the tall grass.

Two men got off their horses to approach the cheetah and the fallen cow. One knelt and slit open the nilghai's throat, while the other pulled the cat back from the kill. The cat accepted the white blindfold across its eyes and waited. The hunter took a bowl, filled it with the cow's blood, and set it before the cheetah, who began to lick from it, growling low, its tail switching from side to side.

"So," Mowgli whispered. "The *chita bagh* makes a mighty kill and must take only a bowl of blood from the man's hands, just as the ox pulls up the green grasses and yet must take the dried stuff at his driver's pleasure. This Man is a hard master. Will there be another kill?"

"No doubt," Mother Wolf snapped. "For these White-Faces, one death is scarcely enough."

The nilghai were now scattered over the grasses, but a lone sambhur had come to the edge of the forest and stood watching silently. He was in full rut, as Mowgli could see by the swell of his neck and the spread of his antlers. In any other season, the stag would never have approached the plains so boldly. But now, he was trailing a doe along this path, and his normal caution was smothered by his desire. He did not turn aside.

One White-Face spied the stag at the same moment and gave a quick command to the second cheetah. The big cat raised its head when the hood was removed. It looked up, took the stag's scent, and swiftly crouched into its spring position.

"By the Bull that bought me," Mowgli said, "that sambhur is so blinded by rut that he cannot even see his own death before him. I remember one such sambhur who pulled this frog from death a few seasons ago, when the herds would have had me." The boy raised his head above the grasses. "I gave a word then, as well."

Now, the cheetah moved closer, sliding silently through the brush. Still, the sambhur did not bolt. As though he could not smell, did not hear the great cat stalking, he stood tensed and waiting just outside the protection of the trees.

The cheetah flattened, bunched its haunches, and shifted its paws back and forth in preparation for its rush. With a loud yell, Mowgli jumped out of cover, running with all his strength to a place between the stag and the cat. He turned and faced the cheetah's charge, holding his knife well above his head, snarling angrily. The cat had leaped—but checked itself uncertainly. With a scrabble of claws, the cheetah stopped suddenly, flattened its ears, and returned Mowgli's snarl. The boy braced himself, but then the cat whirled and ran back to its masters in confusion. The stag, meanwhile, had bolted for cover.

Now, the White-Faces were shouting to one another and spurring their horses across the grasses. There was a rush of gray, a blur of snarls and snaps, and the wolves burst from the tall brush, ready to fight to the death. A horse screamed in fright and went high on its legs, pawing the air frantically. Men hollered, a single rifle shot roared out, and Mowgli and the wolves ran for the thicket, never looking back over their shoulders until they had reached the dark safety of the densest trees. When there was nothing behind them but the noise of the jungle, Mowgli sighed and sprawled in weary silence.

"Shall we still seek Man to hunt Man?" Akela asked dryly, licking at a twisted paw.

"They are surely a fearsome race," Mother Wolf whined. "And very noisy hunters. Dost thou think, my son, that thou canst drive them hither and yon like the marsh bullocks?"

"Nay," Mowgli said quietly. "Now I have seen them for myself, I would not bring them into the jungle, even if I could. They may well kill the Gonds, but how then would we drive them back out again? Thou art right, Mother, they are fearsome, indeed. And the less we run our tracks together, the better for all. Whew!" He shook his head in wonder. "Never have I seen death run on such swift legs, though. Truly, I think the *chitah bagh* could outrace the wind. And yet, he took the bowl meekly from the man's hand like a suckling kitten." He shivered as he remembered. "We shall have to find another way."

Akela raised a tired head and sniffed the breeze. "Then we must make haste. The stench of Man is moving closer. It was not here when we passed before."

The other wolves raised their heads quickly, and Mowgli imitated them, trying to read the odours on the winds.

"Far away," Father Wolf said dreamily as he closed his eyes and tasted the air. "They have passed this way, but now they are here no more and far away."

"Ay, but not for long," Mother Wolf said sharply. "And there is no jungle large enough for two Packs. Either the Gonds are driven forth or are we. A plan was promised."

"I have no more words to offer," Akela said gravely. "Perhaps the Teacher of the Law will know something else—"

Mowgli sat up, and his eyes gleamed with a new hope. "I shall go to see great Kaa," he said quickly. "He has seen all the jungle has to show, and some little he knows of Man as well. Perhaps Kaa can help us, my brothers."

"Those of the Middle Jungle do not follow our trails," Father Wolf said doubtfully. "Why should he bare a tooth for us?"

"It is for all, not only for us," Mowgli said. "And besides . . . he loves me, I think. Wait for me at Council, for I shall return before the moon rises twice." And he bounded away before Mother Wolf could speak again.

Kaa, the Rock Python, lived in the Black Marshes in the hot seasons, where he could bathe his scales in cool water and ease away the warm hours in muddy reeds. Even the evil mugger crocodiles kept from Kaa's places, for the massive snake was over thirty feet long and wide around as a barrel. Though his teeth did not carry death like his cousins, the Poison People, still, no creature had ever felt the crush of his powerful coils and lived.

Mowgli found Kaa basking beside a giant log, his huge head resting half-in, half-out of the water. "Good Hunting!" the boy called loudly, for the great snake was a trifle deaf and quick to strike at the slightest disturbance.

"Ah-sssh!" said the snake softly. "Here comes the Littlest Frog at last, come to see old Kaa, when finally he has grown tired of all his other friends. It has been six moons or more, man-cub. Thou hast grown, yea, even to *my* feeble eyes."

Mowgli chuckled and threw himself among Kaa's coils, for this was a game they often played. "Thine eyes are as sharp as Bagheera's, and as to my absence, it has been scarcely a fortnight, thou forgetful, old, wise, and most beautiful Kaa."

"It is not possible that any cub could have stretched so high in so short a time," Kaa said. "And so, I must truly be as slow and stupid with age as Ooloo, the Turtle." And the big snake tightened his coils imperceptibly about the boy, who lay lounged among them.

Mowgli felt the coils move closer, of course, and he grinned and braced his knees against Kaa's ribs. "Never slow, O mighty Kaa, and scarcely at all stupid"—and he pushed with his legs to keep the snake's coils from moving in against his chest.

"Ay, and thy *wit* has grown tall and wide as thy head, Little Brother," Kaa said smoothly, and tightened yet another coil, shifting and moving slightly so that Mowgli's knees could not hold him away.

"I—I think—*not!*" Mowgli gasped, finally wrenching free his pinned trunk and wrapping his legs about Kaa's nearest coil. He strained to hold down the slippery girth, crying, "Almost, O Gripper, almost do I have thee!" But Kaa easily twined himself, lapped another coil about Mowgli's shoulders, and the boy dissolved in helpless laughter, almost buried in the snake's mass. This was a familiar ritual they shared, and nothing sharpened Mowgli's senses more than a body and mind spar with Kaa.

When the laughter and the panting had ceased, Kaa asked lazily, "Ssso. What moves in thy piece of the jungle?"

"Thou hast not heard?" Mowgli asked in surprise, for usually, Kaa knew all forest business before most had heard the first alarms.

"I have heard some little thing or two," Kaa said calmly. "But I wait to hear it from thee."

"'Tis Man," Mowgli said darkly. "He has come into the jungle and broken the Law. It is not enough that he brings his long teeth and his pit-traps; now he puts the apple of death to work for him." The boy sighed deeply and pain blurred his eyes. "I saw great Gargadan fall, O Kaa," he said softly. "I would that I had not."

"The large deaths are no more painful than the small ones," Kaa murmured. "But they are . . . large, nonetheless. Yet what has this to do with thee?"

"The Gonds follow the trails of the Pack even now. When one, maybe two moons have passed, they will hunt our plains with their poison teeth and even to our most secret lairs, I think. We must drive them off, before they mark this jungle as theirs. So I come to ask counsel of the wisest, oldest, most steadfast heart. What should I do, O Kaa?"

The great snake looked deeply into the boy's eyes. "Do? It is not necessary that *thou* dost a thing. Thou art safe, eh? Thou needst not mix thy trails. The Pack may scatter before them like dead leaves before a high wind, but thou needst not fear, so long as there are other hunting grounds and feet to carry thee there."

"If the Pack is in danger, then so am I," Mowgli said staunchly. "Should I lie shaking in the jungle whilst the Gonds run the herds so far that every wolf's belly is empty? Shall I fly south like the birds to escape the Rains?" He dropped his head for an instant. "Besides, I have given my word on it."

"Kssh!" Kaa said shortly. "Thy mouth will lead thee to death yet, manling. It has happened to far wiser than thee."

"Still, it is done. I have promised my brothers a great plan. I had hoped to lead the White-Faces into the woods, that they might drive the Gonds before them."

"And so?"

Mowgli scowled. "Hast thou seen these White-Faces, Kaa?"

"Once or twice," the great snake said mildly. "Never have I hunted them. Even the Poison People turn from their feet when they can."

"So should we all. I have seen them at their hunting. It would not be good to lead such death into the jungle. Nay," said the boy, "we must find another to help us with this fight. Think, O Kaa. Is there a tribe whom the Gonds fear, some one People in the woods who would not fear the poison tooth, a hunter so mighty that the little black men would run away forever?"

"And one who would kill at thy bidding? Indeed, thou dost not ask much, O Dreamer. I know of no such master. For Master of the Jungle he would be, truly. If 'tis counsel ye seek, then hear me. Leave these trails for a time. I shall go with thee, if thou wish it. Let the Gonds do as they will; they will move on, as Man always does. The jungle will wait for thee."

"For how long?" Mowgli asked. "Ten moons? Tens of tens? The seasons are nothing to thee, O Flathead, but the life of a wolf is not so long."

"There speaks a man, truly," the snake said under his breath, "for Man can never let water find its own level." And then to Mowgli he said, "Be it so. If thou art determined to fight this fight, then let us think." He shifted his great coils and settled his chin on Mowgli's shoulder. "Ye mean to make war. And for this battle, ye need a powerful ally. The Poison People could drive this enemy off, but they will not do thy bidding. The Crawling People [Kaa meant the ants] will do thy bidding—indeed, they will do most anyone's—but Man will not run from them, at least, not for long. As for the biting flies, the stinging wasps, and the ill-tempered bees, they will never be driven by any save their own masters, and then not in any one direction.''

Mowgli heaved a sigh, and Kaa shifted his coils to make him more comfortable. The python continued, "The Hooved Ones are too weak, the apes are too stupid, and the rest of the forest folk are too small. Now, there are many great hunters in the jungle—Baloo, Bagheera, the hyena, the Lame Tiger, thine own Pack—yet none of these can stand against the poison teeth of the Gonds, even if they could be moved to fight.'' The great snake sighed hugely, his barrel-ribs moving in and out. "Keep still now, Little Frog, whilst I follow this root.''

Kaa began to murmur to himself, moving backwards in time and memory, recalling every creature he had ever touched in the jungle. From the smallest shrew to the largest tusker, he had known them all at one place or another—indeed, many had walked his throat over the long years—and his eyes were cold and still as he named them, one by one, in his head. He stiffened and hissed hugely now and again as he recalled many deaths, large and small. When he finally subsided, Mowgli put his hand on the snake's neck to bring him back to himself. He knew better than to speak, for every creature must come out of dreaming alone.

"There is one tribe . . . '' Kaa said at last, stretching his neck as though long asleep, "and only one who could, perhaps, help thee in thy battle.''

"It is not only *my* battle,'' Mowgli said indignantly. "All the jungle will suffer, if we fail.''

"That, thou must make them see. And, 'twill not be easy, for the tribe of which I speak is outcast of all Peoples and ever has been so. More even than the *Bandar-log*, they are shunned, for they are neither bird nor beast, and all Hunting People turn from their lairs and do not speak their name.''

Mowgli's eyes widened, and he whispered in horror. "I know only one who is as ye say. Badur, the Blood-Bat.'' He shivered as he remembered Baloo's warnings of this evil: Badur, the Vampire

Bat, who comes in the night and takes the blood-life from every creature, large and small. No sleeper is safe; no throat too powerful to withstand his silent bloody hunt. And sometimes, he leaves behind a sickness which the Jungle People fear above all others—rabies. "Many of Badur's brothers are as we," Baloo had told him. "They come by night, but they take only fruit and the flying creatures, and we leave them to their own trails. But Badur"—and here the old Bear had dropped his voice to a low growl—"Badur is sickness and shame and death. He is unclean, and we shall speak no more of his tribe."

Mowgli stared at Kaa and finally whispered, "But they are eaten with *dewanee* [madness], and all creatures they touch die an ugly death."

"Some of this is true," Kaa said patiently. "Some is only monkey-chatter. Few of Badur's tribe are mad, though some carry the madness in their bite. But think, Little Frog. *If* the bats will help thee, they could frighten off the Gonds as surely as a score of the most fearsome tigers. And Man's poison teeth would be nothing against Badur's hordes."

"Why should these outcasts help any of the jungle?" Mowgli shuddered convulsively and dropped his voice to a whisper. "None of my brethren will even go by their lairs."

"This is so. And perhaps, they will not. But they know Man well, I am thinking. They may listen to thee when they would listen to no other."

"Dost thou have truck with these Blood-Bats, O Kaa? Surely, thou hast never hunted such evil?"

"Nay, but I have come upon them gathered in the coolness of empty wells, caves, and the Cold Lairs. For some reason, they do not trouble those of us with scales. Unlike the rest of the Jungle People, they like to roost where Man has been and now is no more."

"Then, they do not fear Man?"

"Ye must ask them. Art thou game?"

Mowgli hesitated just an instant. "Is there no other way?"

"Ay, there is one other," Kaa said gravely, "and I have already given thee *that* counsel."

Mowgli sat silently, thinking over all his friend had said. The thought of going where the vampire bats roosted, into their cold, damp, dark places, perhaps to be bitten and made mad, and most surely to be shamed before all the Hunting People—it was a fearful, evil prospect. But try as he might, Mowgli could think of no other alternative. And he had, after all, promised a plan. If he could not drive the Gonds from the jungle, there would be a large killing ahead. Finally, he got up without another word and slowly followed Kaa where he led him into the jungle.

Kaa knew of a large cave on the edge of the forest, a great, ancient domed place of silence and darkness. There, he said, the tribe of Badur lived, as many as the bees in a hive, and from this cold cave they went forth, out into the night, to feed on the blood of those asleep and unwary.

"But out of so many, some will surely be mad," Mowgli muttered as he followed Kaa down unfamiliar trails.

"This is ssso," the snake said, pouring himself smoothly over the ground. "We must hope that their Old Ones are not."

"Perhaps they have no Old Ones," Mowgli said. "Perhaps the madness kills them before they are wise."

"And perhaps the moon may not rise tomorrow," Kaa said. "But shall we stop hunting tonight? Step lively, Little Brother, for the dawn comes soon, and then shall they all roost together."

They came to the solitary cave of Badur as the first light was just turning the blackness to gray. As they neared the great stone fortress, dark winged shadows flitted over their heads, darting and screaming in a frenzy of home-coming. The bats were back from the night's hunting, and inside the cave, the clamour of their arrival drowned out all other sounds of the jungle.

Mowgli shivered once more with instinctive dread. The foul stench which came from the cave would have been enough to keep off any intruders, without fear of the madness. And when the boy considered what might come of such a visit, he felt a cold fresh fear in his heart.

"Consider thisss," Kaa said quietly. "Inside, I cannot protect thee. And neither will thy knife stand between thee and death. Thou must use thy wits and thy tongue alone when dealing with Badur. But of these, thou hast plenty. A last time I ask thee: Wilt thou turn back?"

"To what?" Mowgli asked, angered at his own fear. "If there were another trail, I would surely follow it, but I cannot find it. And I have given a word."

He sat down on a huge rock before the cave and waited for the dawn to come and the sky to clear of bats. When the first light began to turn the gray to colours around him, he got up, stretched with a casualness he did not feel, and walked slowly into the cave, Kaa at his heels.

The lair of the bats was a huge hole in the side of a mountain, ringed by giant boulders and rubble. Long, slick columns of stone hung from the roof of the cave, and dark water dripped in pools at their feet. Hardened piles of bat dung crusted the floor of the cave, and Mowgli and Kaa moved gingerly inside its shadowed depths.

"Look up," Kaa whispered.

Mowgli turned his eyes to the roof of the cave and saw above them a black moving curtain, many hundreds of small dark bodies jostling and wriggling close together for sleeping space. Now, the stench of the bats was so strong that Mowgli's face wrinkled into a grimace. Unclean! his mind shouted, and all his instincts told him to run far and fast, but he thought of Gargadan's last words as he died: "A jackal's death, boy!"—and he went forward.

Kaa slithered now before him, thirty feet of silent power, over the limestone and the encrusted dung as though he felt nothing. He coiled slowly into a protective bundle with his back against a high, sloping wall of sheer granite. "Give the Master Word," he said softly to Mowgli.

"Which? These are neither bird nor beast," the boy whispered in horror, "and if they have their own Word, Baloo did not tell it to me."

"Give both, and we shall see."

Mowgli gave the Stranger's Call for Good Hunting and waited. Only angry squeals greeted his words, and the bats grew more restless above his head. He quickly gave the Master Word for the Birds, but again, there was no response. Now, he shouted the Word of the Hunting People, "We be of one blood, ye and I!" and he looked frantically back at Kaa, as one, two, three bats dropped from their roost and swooped low over his head. At any moment,

Mowgli expected to feel needle teeth in his neck, and he knew then he would run screaming from the cave forever.

Finally, a small, wizened voice called down through the darkness. "Enough, enough! We are not deaf, after all. Nor are we quite so stupid as ye of the jungle suppose. Come forward and be recognised!"

Mowgli slowly moved closer to the hovering blanket of bats. The morning light streamed into the cave's mouth, and even deep within as he was, the boy could faintly see about him. He called out, "Good Hunting, O Badur! It is I, Mowgli of the Wolf Pack, here with Kaa of the Middle Jungle. Might we trespass amongst ye?" And he squinted up into the darkness of the cave roof to see who returned his words.

"It seems ye have already done so," the voice said again, and Mowgli could see now who spoke. An ancient gray bat hung from one corner of the cave's roof. Upside down, he faced the boy, his huge mottled skin wings folded over his furry body. Claw tips spread his wings wide suddenly, and his face was visible—a wide-lipped fur mouth, a huge nose like a skin leaf, and giant naked ears. Mowgli shivered.

The bat chuckled wryly. "Ye find me good to look upon, boy? Ye have come this far—come closer."

Mowgli tried to smooth his face and block out the stench, but he could see only the bat's wide mouth and glittering eyes. Steadying himself, he walked forward. By climbing up on a huge spire of limestone, he was able to stand close enough to see the skinny leg- and arm-bones which held out the bat's wings, able to hear the scratching of the tiny claws on stone. The thinly-stretched skin of the bat's wings gleamed red with the daylight coming through them, red as his glowing eyes and wide lips. A small but fearsomely ugly creature, Mowgli thought swiftly, but he said aloud, "O Badur, art thou master here?"

"If master there be," the bat said quietly. "I am the Old One of this season's roost. Next season, there will be another. But ye of the jungle did not come here to talk of masters, surely. Ye never do." The bat glanced at Kaa, still coiled against the stone. "Art thou the mighty hunter the *Bandar-log* call 'the Night Death'?"

Kaa looked up in surprise. "The *Bandar* call me many things, O Badur. I had not heard this last."

"Nay," the bat chuckled. "Ye would not. The mother monkeys tell thy name to their sucklings to keep them still." He folded his wings about him once more and asked softly, "And so, we know who thou art. Why have ye come hither?"

The vast multitude of bats settled quietly now, as though by a silent signal, and every set of skin ears, large and small, old and young, twisted towards the intruders.

Mowgli took a deep breath and began. "In the jungle a new danger comes."

"We have heard it said," Badur replied courteously.

"Thou hast heard of the Gonds?" Mowgli gaped in surprise.

"We hear most all, man-cub," the bat said patiently, "and we have all the day to spread the news, each to the other. Our listeners, swooping in the night-shadows, knew ye were bought into the Seeonee Pack before Mao the Peacock could tell the word the next dawn. There is little which happens in the night that we do not hear. And little in the jungle which happens that does not give tongue in the night. So the Gonds come."

"They bring with them a new death." Mowgli gulped and went on. "Their teeth carry poison. It means a great killing, and no Good Hunting for many moons, and some say peace will never return to the jungle whilst they are here."

"This we have heard as well. But Man is no stranger to us, and we have no fight with his ways."

Mowgli glanced at Kaa for courage. The great snake shifted slightly, his tongue flickered, and his eyes glimmered like cold moon-stones in the shadows. "O Badur," the boy said finally, "we have come to ask ye for help. There is none in the jungle who can drive the Gonds as ye can. They fear thee as they fear no other. Wilt thou lead thy tribe against them?" He dropped his head and waited. He knew that the fate of many rested on the next few moments, on whatever words he might hear.

A great sigh murmured through the bats, and silence came to even the farthest edges of their roosting roof. "So," Badur said gently. "They send a boy to ask this. Why have they sent *thee*, boy?"

"No one has sent me," Mowgli said. "I gave a word to the Pack that I would drive the danger hence from the jungle. It is no boy, but Mowgli who stands before thee, who asks thy favour."

"It is no wolf who stands here, and yet no man. I see now why thou hast come. Ye, like us, are neither one thing nor the other. And truly, no other creature in the jungle would have come before the Badur as ye have. Have they not told ye of us, O Wolf in Man's skin, O Man with Wolf's tongue? We are *mlech* [unclean]."

Swiftly, Mowgli decided to speak the truth. "Ay, they have told me, O Badur," he said gently. "They have said ye are suckers of blood, bringers of madness, fouled in thy great numbers by the stench of death, and outcasts to be shunned by all in the jungle. But someone else told me, a wise old Bear who loves the Law more than most, that he who rebukes the world will be rebuked by the world."

The roosting bats shuffled nervously and a few high, angry squeals pierced the silence. Kaa stiffened behind Mowgli, ready to fight or flee, if need be. Gradually, the indignant rustles quieted, however, and Badur said, "So they say. But rebuked we were first."

"Does it matter?" Mowgli asked quietly. "And must it be for all seasons?"

Badur grimaced. "A Man's mouth with a Wolf's tongue and a Bear's wisdom. But tell me, do you see any madness before ye, O Brave Tongue?"

"Nay," Mowgli said softly. "I see only order. I hear only such courtesy as even the Teacher of the Law would praise. If there is madness here, I cannot find it." He cocked his head at the bat and moved closer, his fear gone. "Why does the jungle speak so of thee, O Badur?"

The bat heaved a weary sigh. "The jungle alone knows. There has been madness in every roost, to be sure. But no more than runs in thine own Pack. As to the blood, ay, we feed from those we can, but who does not? The Crawling People have more to fear from us than any of thine, for we hunt the moth, the fly, the frog, yea, even our own bat brothers more than we hunt any other. But some Peoples need an outcast, eh? And so, we are shunned. Ye are the first who have come hither. And now, ye come asking favour."

"I ask it for all the jungle," Mowgli said.

"And I say nay for all the jungle", Badur replied. "Thou art green and bold, but the jungle shall be wending its old trails when ye walk them no more." The bat appraised Mowgli keenly, noting with sharp eyes his dismay. A long pause. Finally he said, "Nay to the jungle, but for thee only, Little Frog—ay, I have heard them call ye that—for thee and thy friend, the Cold One, we shall fly."

Mowgli had all but given up hope, and now he gasped in grateful surprise. "Why? What words of mine—?"

"Because," Badur said "*thou* has asked it. And because ye stand before us unafraid. And perhaps because new winds may be coming, and we would ride those winds."

"New winds?"

"Do not question thy good fortune, man-cub," the bat said gently. "When favour has been asked and granted, there is no more to be said."

Mowgli crowed with excitement, "The jungle shall know thee as true friend! I shall make it so!"

"The jungle shall know us as always," the bat sighed, "as they would have us be. But a few, perhaps one or two, shall hear and wonder. Now, tell us what thou wouldst have us do, Little Brother Who Belongs Nowhere."

Mowgli began to tell Badur his plan, and the clusters of bats moved closer, as news moved quickly down the black, moving curtain of bodies. In a little while, the boy no longer noticed the stench and the squeals.

It was the darkest night of the following month, the night when the moon was less than a thin rind in the sky, when the jungle tribes assembled at the edge of the Gond camp. Mowgli's warning had proven true: they found the little black men only a few miles from the Waingunga, their dozen sleeping huts in a clearing of dhak trees.

Around the clearing the Hunting People and the Hooved Ones stood. They had come silently through the jungle, each moving into place in a careful and dangerous dance, while Mowgli watched and signalled them from the tallest tree. The Gonds slept on, unaware that around them in a tightening circle, Baloo,

Bagheera, the wolves, the elephants, and other tribes gathered, shoulder to shoulder, waiting for the battle to begin.

All was silent in the Gond huts. A single sentry dozed by a dwindling fire, deaf to the Jungle People's quiet trooping. Suddenly, Akela began the chorus around the edge of the clearing. A hundred wolves took up the cry, splitting the silence with barks and growls and wolf-threats which seemed to come from all corners of the forest at once. The Gond guard shouted a warning, and a woman wailed in fear. The hunters jumped from their huts, grabbing for their arrows.

The wolves bayed louder, more fiercely than for any hunt, their snarls finally dying away to a mournful sobbing which shivered through the forest.

As the song of the Pack dwindled, Bagheera began his battle cry. He had returned from the upcountry hunt in time to learn of Mowgli's plan, and now, he circled the Gond camp, melting invisibly into the darkest shadows, his voice terrible to hear in the night. Bagheera, when he wished to, could frighten the largest herds into stampede with his sing-song, raspy saw of a snarl. He roared with anger as he bounded from thicket to thicket, and Baloo was right behind him.

As Bagheera snarled and shrieked, the old Bear stretched high on his back paws and reached up each tree, shaking it mightily to and fro, rumbling his own war-cry. In the darkness it seemed that the whole forest, the trees themselves, were advancing on the Gond camp.

Now, the little men ran in circles about the clearing, shouting to each other in fear, their weapons to their shoulders ready to shoot—if they could only see a target.

Mowgli watched them from the low branches of the dhak tree, his eyes gleaming in delight. So far, his plan was working. He turned and shouted a command to the rest of the animals, and a chaos of noise came from the jungle. All around the Gonds, the elephants trumpeted, the sambhur groaned and barked, the wolves bayed, Bagheera and Baloo roared, and the bullocks bellowed. Each had come at Mowgli's bidding to stand together to save the jungle, and as the Gonds huddled before their huts, calling to the heavens for courage, the animals lifted their voices in angry battle cries.

One black man, the Gond leader, lifted his bow and arrow to the night-sky and began a chant to his gods, glancing over his shoulder nervously at the jungle behind and about him on all sides. The women took it up, and Mowgli saw the young girl he had seen before shivering next to her mother, her voice pleading with the others for protection.

Mowgli's heart was, for an instant, smote within him. For that moment, he felt her panic, tasted her fear, and he was saddened that this must be. But then, he remembered the way Gargadan had looked at his death and he lifted his hand to send in the Pack upon them.

The wolves raced into the clearing, Akela baying them on. The Gond hunters could at last see the enemy which plagued them, and they stood as one and fired their arrows into the running wolves. The women shrieked and ran for the huts; one, two, three wolves fell with anguished yelps, writhing and snapping at the arrows which stuck in their flanks and their necks. Here, a Gond was down on one knee, two wolves worrying his belly; there, another black man was face down in the dust, a wolf at his neck, snarling and bloodied. But most of the Pack ran out of the clearing as fast as they had run in, glancing over their shoulders at the panicked men who turned to see what next the jungle would unleash upon them.

It was Mowgli who appeared at the edge of the clearing now, shouting his own battle cry, a shrill shriek of anger and challenge. And then, the men heard the enraged grunts and bellows of the wild boars, as Mowgli drove them before him, a pack of tusked, red-eyed chargers who ran right for the hunters, bellowing defiance. There is little so mad as the enraged wild pig, as all in the jungle know, and this last charge scattered the hunters in all directions. The pigs rooted and stamped at the doors of the huts, and the women screamed in terror.

The men had loosed most all their arrows and had only spears and flaming torches for weapons, but they ran back to defend their people, shouting in panic. And then, as the boars ran off into the trees, an eerie silence fell over the night. No beast growled, no elephant stamped—and from far away, all ears heard the coming of a great roar, the sound of a thousand wings flapping, and finally, the squeals of hundreds of hungry voices.

The Gonds stood frozen in the center of the clearing, their eyes to the sky. One or two women screamed and broke for the forest—and then, they saw them: Badur, the Blood-Bat, and his hundreds, hurrying in a dark cloud towards them, swooping and darting down upon the clearing in a frenzy of wings, teeth, and shrill red mouths. This was the final stroke of battle, and with it, the fight was over. The Gonds ran as one pair of feet, deserting their huts, their broken arrows, their pots and cooking fires, leaving behind all traces of their camp in a mad rush down the trail away from the bats.

"Chase them across the Waingunga, my brothers!" Mowgli shouted as the bats went by, and a thousand wings turned the Gonds in that direction, flapping just over their heads; shrill voices squealed in their ears, and needle teeth nipped at their necks.

Now, Hathi led the elephants in on the camp, trudging the huts into the ground, scattering the weapons, and smashing the cooking pots. In a moment, there was only silent rubble where the Gond hunters had slept. The animals drifted away silently, back to their own hunting grounds over different trails.

Mowgli stood in the centre of the ruined clearing, looking quietly over the destruction.

"In one moon," Baloo said gruffly, "the creepers will cover all trails which led here."

"Some—some few," Akela said as he looked at four dead wolves, "will be covered as well."

"It was a grand battle," Bagheera purred. "Badur and his brethren shall have the jungle's gratitude. Never more will Man trouble this piece of the forest. What, no cheers, Little Brother? I have seen thee dance like Mao the Peacock for far less."

But Mowgli scowled and turned away from the sight of so much chaos and fear. "Ay, it was a grand battle. And I am glad the Man's poison tooth shall kill here no more. Yet, do I wish it could have been otherwise. It was not good to see their faces all twisted in fear. Indeed," he sighed, "I took no pleasure there."

"There speaks a man," Akela snapped. "I would we had opened their throats here and now. They broke the Law!"

Baloo rubbed gently against the boy's shoulder. "The jungle is large, Little Dreamer. They will find other places to hunt."

"Ay," Mowgli sighed, and stretched wearily. "Well, I go to make my thanks to Badur. Who will go thither with me?"

The three hunters hesitated, glancing nervously at one another. Finally, reluctantly, as they faced the boy's stare, each— Baloo, Bagheera, and Akela—fell in behind him. "It is good," Mowgli murmured as he walked the long trail to Badur's cave, "that something fine comes from such a fearsome night."

This is the song which the Gonds sang to muster their courage, as the jungle came in upon them.

Song to the Jungle Gods

Demons of the air and tree,
Gods and godlings, old and wise,
Hear our song, we pray to thee,
Keep us safe from jungle eyes!
From jungle teeth! From jungle claws!
From rhino horn and tiger jaws!
Hold the night outside our ring,
Make the wolf turn from our trail,
Hear us as we dance and sing,
Let our arrows never fail
'Gainst jungle teeth and jungle claws!
'Gainst rhino horn and tiger jaws!
We are masters of this land,
Second only unto thee,
O Jungle Gods, our mighty band
Shall stand as one and never flee
From jungle teeth! From jungle claws!
From rhino horn and tiger jaws!
We pray thee, stay thee by our side,
And through all danger, be our guide,
We sing to thee, we dance, we pray,
That ye will turn dark night to day!

BAGHEERA AND
THE SPRING HUNT

Move slowly and silent in cover; keep thy haunches and head
    to the grass,
There is no rush so swift, no claw so sure, that will bring back
    a chance which has passed.

Feed when thy belly is empty, but remember the fate of the swine.
Thy enemy may stalk behind thee, and his gorge is leaner than
    thine.

In silence go into the night-hunt; in silence bring down every
    kill,
Thy next deer will then browse unguarded, thy brothers will
    bear no ill-will.

When the cub whines that no game is moving, show him twice
    how the killing must go.
If he whines thrice more and would feed from thy kill, let him
    starve, or stumble, or grow.

When the time comes to hunt, be thou hunting; when the time
    comes to mate, thou wilt know.
These Laws are stronger than any; they were written in blood
    long ago.

Maxims of Bagheera

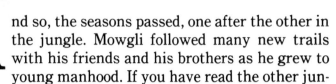

And so, the seasons passed, one after the other in the jungle. Mowgli followed many new trails with his friends and his brothers as he grew to young manhood. If you have read the other jungle stories, you know how Shere Khan, the Lame Tiger, came back to this piece of the forest to hunt Mowgli down. He had hated the boy since the first night he was brought into the Pack, and out of that hatred, Shere Khan swore to lay Mowgli's bones in the Waingunga. But Mowgli was warned by his Pack brothers, and he led the buffalo herds in a stampede, killing the great tiger. Thus, it was the skin of Shere Khan which Mowgli brought to Council Rock the night he claimed his manhood and left the Pack to visit the village of Man.

Also, if you have read, you will remember that in the village, Mowgli herded the cows and learned Man's talk. He came to know a village woman, Messua, who cared for him as a son. He came, too, to know the greed and the weakness of the village people but also to feel a strong bond with their tribe. When he again returned to the jungle, it was to lead his wolf brothers against the marauding Red Dogs who swept in from the Deccan and would have destroyed the Pack. In this great battle, Akela was killed, but not before every Red Dog lay dying as well. Mowgli sang a death song of honour and victory over the grizzled Lone Wolf, and then he returned once more to the jungle to walk the trails alone.

And now, Mowgli was nearly a man. He stood tall and straight as a young sambhur; his knife which he wore always round his neck was swift as a snake's strike. His eyes, however, were usually calm and cool, for he had been taught by Baloo and Bagheera never to show his temper. Though both of his teachers were growing old—Baloo was stiff in the joints and even Bagheera was slower at the spring—still, the three comrades turned aside for few in the forest. Together, they shared many adventures, and what follows is only one.

It was the end of the Rains, and Mowgli and Bagheera were

resting in the late afternoon shadows, hidden in the dense bamboo. Bagheera was sprawled on his belly, his tail switching lazily to and fro in the dappled sun. Mowgli dozed with his head on the panther's flank, his mind following old trails.

"Little Brother," Bagheera yawned, "hast thou ever seen the Place of the Black Mud? I cannot recall."

Now, it was far past the time when Baloo or Bagheera would send a young man-cub to learn this or that Law from Hathi or Gargadan, but when obedience is born from love, it never really dies, and so Mowgli opened his eyes and listened. He thought for a moment and then said, "The Place of the Black Mud. I remember the name, but I have never seen it, I think."

"If thou hadst, thou wouldst know," the cat replied. "It is an evil place, but there is Good Hunting, if one can find no easier kill. It is only as a last resort, but thou shouldst see it, nonetheless."

A dozen seasons past, Mowgli might have grumbled and stretched and tried to tell Bagheera that another day would do as well for such a trek. But he had learned the proper time for patience and the proper time for pursuit, and so he stood and asked, "Art thou rested?"

The panther chuckled wryly. "As much as these aged paws will ever rest, I think. Indeed, the time for a long sleep comes soon enough."

Mowgli patted his head fondly. "Oh, thou hast a score of springs left, my Best of Brothers."

"Even Hathi has not so many," Bagheera said dryly. "It is a strange thing how the seasons go by more swiftly these days. Never before did I count them, yet now I feel each in my bones. Youth is nothing but dried pith until ye try to hold it, and then it is all."

But Mowgli was standing and sniffing at the air. "Something comes," he said quietly. Bagheera moved fluidly to his feet, ready for friend or foe.

The bamboo rattled loudly, they heard the rustle of four scuffling paws, a muttered complaint, and Ikki the Porcupine waddled into their clearing.

"Ah, there ye be," he panted. "Good Hunting to ye both."

"Oho!" Mowgli said cheerfully. "It is the Pig with the Angry

Back! 'Tis many seasons past since ye favoured us, Prickles. Come ye hence to play more games?"

Bagheera grimaced in disgust, for he had still not forgiven Ikki for leading Mowgli into the lair of the Poison People, which you may perhaps recall.

"Ye remember my friend, 'the Creeping Shadow'?" Mowgli gestured politely to the Black Panther, recalling how impudent Ikki had been long ago.

But Ikki only snorted, for he feared neither boy nor cat, and in fact remembered Mowgli with a small grin, if he thought of him at all. "Naked grubling, your tongue is as busy as ever, I see," he said, rattling his quills. "I did not traipse all this long way to trade barbs with ye, but to bring news. I come from the Black Marshes. Ye know it?"

"We spoke of it just now," Mowgli said, unwilling to admit to the porcupine that there was any place in the jungle he had not seen. "What of it?"

"Gaur, the Bullock, is stuck in the Sucking Sands and bid me come for ye both. I told him it was a fool's errand, but he has sworn to bellow down the trees themselves if I did not hasten hence."

"Why does he send for us?" Mowgli asked.

"For the same reason he commanded yon pigeon-toed trickster," Bagheera snapped. "Because he thinks we owe him a favour, each of us. One of his tribe bought thee into the Pack, Little Brother, lest ye forget. And others of his brethren ran for thee when ye slayed Shere Khan. As for me, 'tis simply a little matter of an old honour, a small word given for a Little Frog seasons ago. What favour dost *thou* repay, O Bristle-Snout?"

Ikki snorted once more, this time with impatience. "He has pulled down a mango or two, but no matter. If ye stand here all the day wagging your tongues, ye might as well call in Chil the Kite and be done, for the Sucking Sands will not wait even for *ye* Lords of the Jungle. I have repaid *my* favour and brought the news." And he turned and waddled out of the bamboo again, in no particular hurry.

"He is an impudent pig, but he speaks the truth," Bagheera said quickly. "We must hasten, or Gaur is lost."

The two hurried away in the direction of the Black Marshes. The Black Marshes were sometimes called the Place of the Black Mud, or the Place of the Sucking Sands (for when the Jungle People are afraid of a thing, they give it many names). It lay north of the forest at the edge of the swamplands, a stretch of mud and shifting waters, a darkly shadowed region of mossy trees, thick reeds, and patches of quicksand. In times of drought, the herds clustered at its edges, for it often was the last place for mud wallows and untainted water. The Hunting People rarely went there, however, for a kill required great skill and an exact knowledge of where the shifting sands might be from season to season. The Black Marshes were several hours away from Mowgli's piece of the jungle, and Bagheera urged him to hurry, hurry.

"What was Gaur doing in such a place, anyway?" Mowgli asked with some irritation as he raced along beside the cat. "Surely there are better places to wallow after the Rains."

"I cannot say. Gaur is a hill beast, mostly. He does not seek the mud wallows like the bullock. Yet even the bud-horns know of the Sucking Sands, and so I cannot think why he ventured in."

Bagheera loped along at a swift pace, picking the trails most easily travelled, looking right and left as he went.

"Still and all," the cat muttered, "he must be sorely spent to call on such as we, favour or no favour. In another time, another place, I might take him down myself, for Bagheera owes no bullock a life." The two finally came to a flat place of dense trees and mangrove marsh. Moss hung from the brush, and stinging insects sang in their ears.

Mowgli slapped at a midge and said, "I see why I have never ventured hither. 'Tis full of tiny teeth—" and then they heard the bellow of Gaur, from the farthest corner of the marsh.

Bagheera splashed across the shallow water, shuddering in cat-like fashion as his paws slid in the mud. They forded the marsh and picked their way through low scrub, following always the bellows of the large bull. Finally they came to a sandy bank ringed by palms. Out in the middle of the mud, Gaur was stuck up to his shoulders, his hind flanks just visible above the Sucking Sands.

When he saw Mowgli and Bagheera, he shouted, "At last, ye have come! Get me out! Arumn-nph! Umnph-umnph! Get me out!"

"Look there," Bagheera whispered. On the far bank, watching Gaur's struggles, was a young cow. She had shied back in the brush when she saw the panther, but she did not run away. Her large eyes swivelled from Gaur to the cat and back again.

"Phaw! Now, I see what drove him hence," Mowgli said with no little disgust. "'Tis the season for chasing cows. *Ohē,* Gaur!" he called loudly. "We come! What would ye have us do?"

Gaur gave a mighty heave of his shoulders, twisting his horns angrily. "Stand about and shout, of course! I needed only someone to watch while I go under these—these cursed"—and here, he struggled again fiercely, slipping a little lower in the sands—"Get me OUT, man-cub! I need thy hands, not thy tongue!"

"Tell him to be still," Bagheera said. "Every move only makes the sands more hungry."

"O Gaur, keep thyself quiet," Mowgli called, "else ye slip deeper!" He turned to the panther. "Could we pull him out with creepers, thinkst thou? He is no spring calf."

"We could not alone," Bagheera said, glancing about at the ropes and vines which hung all over the marsh trees. "But our shoulders and his mate's *together* may save him." Gaur's cow, as though sensing Bagheera's glance, shivered back further in the shadows of the brush.

Mowgli quickly climbed a tree and cut a score of creeper vines with his knife. The ropes were thick and fleshy from the Rains, and he soon threw down more than thirty at Bagheera's feet. He climbed back down and said, "We shall have to move swiftly. The sands are swallowing more and more of him. But how do we get them about Gaur without being eaten ourselves?"

"Uhn-hn-hn!" bellowed the bull loudly. "About my horns, man-ling! Hurry!"

"Lay that log across the mud," Bagheera said. "But take care not to step into the sands, else thou wilt sleep by Gaur this night." The great cat spat in sudden anger. "This is a foolish quest! Better a hundred Gaurs sink to their death than thy foot dare the sucking mud. Let us go back to the jungle and leave him to his fate."

"We have come this far," Mowgli said calmly. "And a debt is owed. This will redeem it, I think," and he wove the creepers into nooses, tightening each with a knot. While Bagheera muttered in angry unease, Mowgli dragged the log out to the edge of the mud and then pushed it across the sands so that it rested half-in, half-out of the marsh. Fortunately, it slid easily once it hit the sands, making a bridge out to where Gaur waited.

"I come!" Mowgli called to the dismal bull, and he gathered the creepers in his arms. He trod carefully out the log, balancing the load of ropes and vines before him. When he reached the bull, he laced the ropes about his neck and horns, one after the other, layering Gaur with creeper vines.

"Pull them tight," the bullock panted, for the sands were sucking harder now at his belly. "Would that I had never *seen* that cow," he said, his voice low and frightened. "Unhn-hn-hn, man-cub, tighter!"

Mowgli finished tying Gaur and tripped back across the log to firm ground, trailing the creeper ends behind him. He wrapped them about a large tree and tied seven or eight about Bagheera's shoulders. He knotted ten more about his own waist, and then he called to the cow, "Come out and save thy master!" The cow lowed mournfully, eyed the great cat, and edged her flanks further into the trees.

"Come out, come out!" Gaur shouted angrily. "These are no foes of thine!"

Her soft voice wailed out from the shadows. "I dare not, My Lord! His claws! His teeth—!"

"—Shall surely break thy silly neck if thou dost not come forward at once!" Bagheera snarled. "O, that I had knocked Ikki clear to the next thicket!"

Gaur heaved once, twice, in desperate rage, trying once more to pull free, but the oozing sands only slipped a little higher on his flanks, edging now up his neck. "COME!" he bellowed to the cow, but she whirled in panic and fled back into the trees.

"Ouarr-rou, ye wretched female! COME BACK!" Gaur shrieked in helpless rage.

"There is no more time for this folly," Mowgli said to Bagheera in disgust. "We must save him together, thou and I, and would that Gaur remember this next time he chases a cow in blind heat."

Bagheera braced himself against the bank, muttering and snarling to himself, and Mowgli reached for the nearest tree.

"Now, pull!" he shouted to the cat, and together, they strained to loose the bull's shoulders.

"Hump-mp-mp! Are ye pulling?" Gaur bellowed, leaning into the ropes. "I can feel nothing!"

Mowgli gripped another tree and squeezed his eyes shut, trying with all his strength to yank the bull free. Bagheera panted beside him, groaning with his efforts, the creepers taut and straining. Like two cattle under the yoke, the boy and the cat pulled and moaned and worked. Mowgli looked back over his shoulder and saw that while Gaur's flanks were slightly higher in the sands, he was far from free.

Now, as the bull sensed that perhaps, indeed, he would perish in the sucking mud, he began to panic and thrash all the more, struggling for the bank.

"We need Hathi's shoulders," Mowgli wheezed as he braced his feet for another try.

"The creepers will not hold," Bagheera panted. "And neither—" he gasped and coughed "—neither will my neck!"

Gaur had begun his wordless bellow once more, lamenting his fate to the jungle at large, tossing his horns about in desperation.

"By the time we could get more help," Mowgli said, "Gaur will be naught but a scum on the water. And yet, there must be a way to free him!"

"There is a way, even ssso," said a quiet voice from the trees behind them.

Bagheera started, arched his back, and hissed. "Sptt! Thou frightened me, Kaa!"

"How long have ye watched?" Mowgli gasped, letting the vines loosen.

"Long enough," said the great snake as he slid out of the thicket into view, his mottled skin blending perfectly with the dappled shadows of the marsh. "I met Ikki on the deer trail, and he told me whither thou had come, manling. I thought this as fine a place for Good Hunting as any."

"Thou art the *only* one who would find it so," Bagheera said in disgust as he shook his paw free of the mud. "If I never see this black place again, I shall die happy."

Gaur snorted and bellowed and lowed, "More talk! More talk! Aruh-uh-uh, I am lost!"

"Ah-ssshh! Still thy great clamour," Kaa called to him calmly. "Must all the jungle know of thy madnessss?"

"OHR-RU-RU-RU, it is KAA! I am surely lost, indeed!" Well enough Gaur knew that Kaa had swallowed more of his tribe, especially the young and tender calves, than all of the sucking sands in India.

Kaa rolled his lidless eyes and nodded from side to side. "I said there is a way, but I cannot think why thou shouldst want to save such a wretch," he muttered to Mowgli.

"So have *I* said," Bagheera snapped. "But he will not be swayed."

"*Thou* wert the one who taught me of honour," Mowgli said to Bagheera mildly. "Indeed, I might not have come but ye reminded me of my debts. Now we are here; we cannot leave him, no matter that his howls bristle our neck-hairs. What is this way ye spoke of, Kaa? The sands move higher with each moment we waste."

"Will he die of fear, thinkest thou?" Kaa answered Mowgli's question with another question, which is a snake's way.

"Gaur? We could not be so fortunate," Bagheera said dryly.

"Then, I can pull him forth, I think, if ye can calm him."

Mowgli wasted no time. "Gaur!" he shouted. "Kaa means to pull thee out! Leave off thy thrashing, and ye will be saved!"

But Gaur threw a panicked glance over his shoulder at the great snake coiled on the bank and began to bellow all the louder. "Humph! Humph! Humph! 'Tis KAA!, O my horns, 'TIS KAA!" he shrieked, his eyes rolling white with terror as though he had only just now noticed him. His cries of alarm shivered the moss in the marsh trees, and Mowgli held his ears and winced.

"Do what thou wilt!" he shouted to the snake over the bull's roar. "He can surely suffer no more than this!"

Kaa wound his long tail round the nearest thick tree, lashing it tightly and tucking it under a heavy log for leverage. He flickered his tongue once and lunged, testing the soundness of the tree. With nary a splash, he slid into the mud. He held his head and neck higher over the marsh, slipping his girth on top of the suck-

ing quicksand, keeping the last six feet of his body firmly anchored on shore.

Gaur saw him coming and frantically tried to leap out of the deadly mud. In a desperate surge of panic, the bull actually freed his upper shoulders and part of his belly. Like a flash, Kaa was on him, wrapping his huge coils about Gaur's shoulders and neck, slipping one giant noose under his stomach, and heaving for the opposite shore. The terrified bull struggled, bawling piteously of his plight, but Kaa only squeezed tighter, his coils moving like liquid ropes, his ribs beating in and out, his neck and head stretched and straining with his efforts. Now, Gaur was half-in, half-out of the quicksand, his whole upper body engulfed by Kaa's coils. Only his wide-open mouth and rolling white eyes were visible above three laps of the snake's huge body. Kaa was stretched across the marsh like a length of India rubber; he gave a final, mighty heave, and Gaur left the sucking sands with a sound like a big boot being pulled out of ankle-deep mud. The python reached the opposite shore, dragging Gaur from the mire, and the two lay gasping for breath. As Mowgli and Bagheera met them, they could not tell where bull began and snake left off. Gaur's eyes were closed, and his tongue lolled out.

"Canst thou unloop thyself?" Mowgli asked Kaa, gently plucking at his head.

The great snake groaned. "Why not just let me finish the job? He is all but walking my throat."

Gaur's eyes opened wide and he began to bleat weakly, "'Tis Kaa! 'Tis Kaa!" And then he saw that he lay among the snake's coils, shrieked in new terror, and plunged and bucked to get free.

Kaa unloosed and slid away from him, coiling into a tight ball of disgust. "He has hooved me in a dozen places, Little Brother, and called me more evil names than even the black-tongued shrew knows. And for this, I have lengthened my ribs by more painful feet than I care to count?"

Gaur whirled on the snake and prepared to horn him viciously, blind in rage, shame, and lingering fear.

Mowgli smacked the screaming Gaur on the nose smartly and said, "Be still, thou Snorter, or debt or no, I feed thee to one of thy two enemies, here."

Bagheera sniffed in contempt. "I would not stomach such a thick-headed fool were I empty as a winter hive. Let us back to our own, O Kaa, before this Little Dreamer has us next rescue a troop of *Bandar* up a tree."

"Where is my cow?" Gaur panted, finally calming somewhat. "Which of ye ate her?"

"Thy memory is as short as thy temper," Mowgli answered him. "She ran into the woods when ye called her to shoulder the yoke. Next time ye chase a mate, keep thy head, eh? All debts are paid, each to each, and we will not be called hither—or else-where—again."

The three comrades turned and left Gaur pawing the ground and calling for his cow. When the sun was high overhead, it found them resting contentedly off in a steaming jungle glade. Mowgli was gathering fruit and yellow blossoms off the mohwa tree, while Kaa kept a half-closed eye on a deer trail.

"Ho!" Mowgli laughed suddenly as the thought struck him. "Gaur will have quite a tale to tell when he gets back to the herd: how he escaped the death-coils of the Great Kaa *and* the Sucking Sands, all in one day."

Bagheera opened one amber eye. "This is what comes of fa-vours in the jungle. Another time, I might have taken Gaur as he lay trapped, and made Good Hunting of him. Another time, too, he might have walked Kaa's throat. Instead, he goes to tell the herds that both Kaa and Bagheera are not so much to fear, after all. Before there was a man-cub in the Pack, none of the Jungle People spoke of favours. Now, there is a debt here, a debt there, and Good Hunting flees whilst we are yoked by them."

Mowgli sat down cross-legged by the great cat and stroked him gently, all the while mouthing the soft mohwa petals. "Ay, this is a true thing. But neither do we have Shere Khan to plague us, and neither do the Gonds hunt us down. These things, no one could do alone, and yet many find good of them."

"*I* asked for no such favours," Bagheera said silkily. "I walk where I would, and all things are alike to me. And yet, for love of thee, I share in thy debts. Is this fair?"

Kaa chuckled low in his long throat. "Speaking of what the man-cub brings which is new—now Bagheera speaks of fairness and the jungle in one breath. Does one look for a rat in a frog pond?"

Bagheera sighed and rested his chin on the boy's knee. "It is so. I am growing foolish as an old ape with white hair. Next, I shall try to reason with the Waingunga when it floods."

Mowgli was struck by another thought. "'Tis the first time I have seen such a thing in the jungle," he said wonderingly. "Something which would kill, even as a poison fang or an enemy's claws, but which is a piece of the woods, alone. Always, the jungle has been as mother to me. There was nothing in the trees, the sky, the water, which would harm me, and I walked all trails, never looking over my shoulder save as all do, lest I be taken by a stronger hunter. But in the Place of the Black Mud, the jungle is the hunter, eh? It is a hard thought. How does one do battle with the Sucking Sands?"

"Just as thou did," Kaa said calmly. "This day, thou hast won the battle, with a little help. Another day, the jungle may be the stronger. Even so, do we all take our lives from its hands."

Suddenly, a strange cry echoed through the forest, and all three comrades raised their heads and tensed.

"What was that?" Mowgli whispered.

Kaa glanced at Bagheera and his tongue flickered in and out, but he said nothing. The panther had half-raised up off his haunches, every bristle and hair quivering in the direction of the cry, his eyes black and open wide as though it were midnight.

"Bagheera, what was—"

But Kaa murmured, "Hissst," and the boy was still.

Then Bagheera did a frightening thing. He ran to the edge of the clearing, every muscle tensed, and he roared out into the stillness of the jungle. A dozen birds screeched alarms, a distant monkey troop whooped in fright, and the trees themselves seemed to ring with his roar. The silence of the midday was shattered, and the echoes of sound finally died away after a long moment to nervous rustlings in the trees above them as the birds settled back down to their normal roosts.

Mowgli's eyes were wide with wonder, for he had never before, in all his seasons in the jungle, heard Bagheera roar in the daylight. He went to the cat's side and touched him gingerly—but

Bagheera scarcely felt him. He flicked Mowgli's hand away as he might have shivered a fly off his ear.

Again, the distant call came, now a little closer. Mowgli recognised it this time: the scream of a panther. A strange cat prowled this part of the jungle, a panther Mowgli did not know, and he was struck by an unfamiliar wariness. The hairs on his arms lifted as though to scent the breeze for danger.

Bagheera never glanced at the boy but only bounded up the nearest tree, moving like liquid black silk up into the branches, his eyes gleaming with a private fire. When he was high above Mowgli's head, he called again, this time ending his scream with a long, wavering croon of restless power, kneading and ripping at the branch bark in a frenzy.

"What is it?" Mowgli asked Kaa in dismay. "He is mad as a boar in midday!"

"Thou hast never seen him so?" Kaa asked. "Yet thou hast lived through a dozen or more seasons of the New Talk."

Mowgli scowled as memory hit him. "O, ay, I have heard the New Talk, Kaa. Well enough I remember that each spring when the mohwa blooms, my brothers run away and leave me whilst they run foolish and yapping under the moon. But always has Bagheera hunted in new places for these times. Never have I seen *him* so possessed. Is this then what he is doing? Why does he not speak with me if he wants this New Talk so much?"

Kaa's tongue flickered out appraisingly as he eyed the panther high in the tree. "'Tis not thy words he seeks, Little Brother. Nor thy touch." The snake shook his head wisely. "It is the warm blood in him. My own tribe dances at such times, but we do not run quite so mad as *thy* brethren. Watch and learn."

The call of the strange panther was moving rapidly closer, and Bagheera hung way out of the tree to reply, his voice trilling and screeching and rebounding through the forest. Now, out of a thicket charged a spotted panther. It was a young female, her coat rippling like sun on water, her legs long and powerful as Bagheera's own. She came to a halt just out of the shadows, her tail switching from side to side angrily, her red mouth open in a snarl.

Mowgli instinctively ducked, his hand on his knife, but Kaa whispered, "Be ssstill, man-cub. Thou art in no danger."

Indeed, it was true. Not only did Bagheera never glance at the boy, but the spotted panther seemed not to notice his presence either. Her glimmering eyes flashed at the black cat in the tree, her roar shattered the woods once more, and then she turned her back and walked silently, deliberately, and with great dignity back into the thicket whence she had come.

Before Mowgli could move, Bagheera leaped from the tallest branch in a headlong race towards her disappearing shadow. It was a long jump, one which he would have taken in stages at another time, but now, the Black Panther jumped with no regard for the height, landed gracefully, and bounded away after her. Never once did he glance over his shoulder at Mowgli, who stared after him with his mouth agape.

"He is mad as Gaur!" Mowgli said finally in amazement. "And I only hope there are no sucking sands where he goes, for he is surely blind as well! Will he return, thinkest thou?"

"When the fever has left him," Kaa said softly. He cast a curious glance at the boy. "Hast thou never felt such a heat thyself?"

"Me?" Mowgli snorted, incredulous.

"I only ask it because I had heard that thy brethren are troubled by the spring madness more than any other."

"The Free People do their share of singing and racing with the moon, it is true," Mowgli said with injured dignity. "But never have I seen them quite so possessed as Bagheera."

"'Twas not that brethren I spoke of, Little Brother," Kaa said gently, "but the Man-Pack."

"What would I know of the Man-Pack?" Mowgli said with some irritation. "They are possessed in *all* seasons, and so it is all one with them."

Kaa chuckled, half to himself. "Even so. Come, man-cub, and we shall home again. He will return in time."

Mowgli picked himself up and strode down the trail, his jaw set indignantly. He followed Kaa back to familiar trails, but as he walked, his mind was uneasy. The birds in the dense trees sang their most beautiful and raucous spring songs, but he scarcely heard their joy. The green shoots burst up from the jungle floor with a wild swaying life; the scent of flowers was almost overpowering in the warm air—but Mowgli took no pleasure from these.

In other years, other springs, the time of New Talk was a season when he might have run miles through the day and night, returning to the woods with wreaths of fresh flowers round his head, panting and laughing with pleasure at the new smells and sounds all round him. But now, his limbs felt heavy and restless all at once, his face twisted into a scowl without a reason, and he finally threw himself down in the ferns, refusing to walk further.

"What is this?" Kaa asked in some surprise. "Art thou wearied already?"

"Faugh!" Mowgli said angrily, kicking at a tuft of moss. "I am wearied of it *all*. There is nothing to do and no one to do it with, everyone runs mad and foolish, and when they once more come begging Mowgli's favour, I shall send them off with a bad word and just such a—" and here he drew back his foot and sent the moss flying "—just such a kick!"

"Such a to-do," the python said calmly, for he could feel little of the tremors which spring brought to the warm-blooded Jungle People. "When thou hast found thyself again, O Lord of All Reason, thou mayest find Kaa as well." And he slithered away.

"A fine friend!" Mowgli shouted, now eaten up with temper. "Thou wilt call me 'Little Brother', coil thy fat self about my shoulders when thou wilt—'O, manling, my thoughts are all thee-ward'"—he mimicked Kaa in a high, mocking voice—"but when this same manling calls thee—!" But he stopped, for Kaa was gone.

"I shall go far away," Mowgli muttered to himself, slumping down again in the thicket. "And then, oho! shall they call and cry for naught! Bagheera can hunt me up and down every trail until he wheezes like old Hathi, but *I* shall not come to his call."

Up in the treetops, the macaques fought with the parrots over the ripening fruit, and the ants at Mowgli's feet went on with their busy foraging as though he were only another stump to go round. He had never felt so unimportant, so unnecessary to life at large, and he did not like this feeling at all. He planted a foot directly in the ants' trail, then took a twig and deliberately scattered them wildly in fright. Somehow, their chaos and confusion made his own feel small. He stood with a sigh and looked about him.

126

"Well," he said loudly, to no one in particular, "since the whole jungle is blind and deaf to me, I shall take myself elsewhere." That last sounded ridiculous, even to his own ears, and he remembered with a quick flush of shame how Baloo hated self-pity. He stood and stretched, loped down the trail, and then began to run, his long legs moving out in quick strides, heading over the rise towards the village of the Man-Pack.

He reached the village wall, a head-high fortress of mud baked by a thousand suns and built to keep out the jungle. It was dusk, the time Messua had called *go-dhuli* or cow-dust time, and the herds returned down the narrow path to be tethered and milked. He hid close by the village well, wondering even as he did so why he had come.

The people came and went down the rutted roads, from field to hut. The women carried water in their earthen jugs, balancing them on their heads, their ear-bobs and bracelets making a musical jangle in the gathering shadows. The cries of the herdboys mingled with the yelps of the yellow pariah dogs; the crows scolded as they fought for roosting space in the dhak trees, and from some distant sty, the village pigs squealed and the goats bleated and ran free. Two naked children raced down the path, yelling and slapping at each other's legs. A woman stepped from the sagging straw door of a hut and called to them softly. Inside, Mowgli knew he would find, if he were to go with them, a floor of dried dung and mud in a design to ward off evil, a few rags of bedding in a corner, an earthen pot in a carved niche in the mud wall, a slab stone for grinding spices, and little else.

The smell of cooking fires made Mowgli's nose twitch, and he crawled closer to the dusty path, ready almost to show himself just to see what the villagers might do. A holy man in orange robes went past, praying loudly and fervently, banging on his begging bowl and cleaning his teeth with a neem twig.

"These are such noisy creatures," Mowgli muttered to himself. "Always are their mouths moving, eating, or blowing smoke. *Hai!* Who comes?"

Behind him, a young girl had slipped off the path and walked silently towards the well. She had passed behind Mowgli without seeing him, but the soft clank of her ankle bracelets made him whirl and crouch lower.

Barefoot she came, with her large black eyes cast down, a fragment of whispered song on her lips. She wore a coarse bright cloth wrapped round her hips and her shoulders, and her dark hair fell down her back in a shimmering river.

Mowgli sat still as the shadow of a hawk on the fields. Every jungle instinct told him to stay hidden—but suddenly, he found himself rising slowly from cover and gazing boldly at the young girl. She sensed his presence and turned. She gasped, and her eyes widened in fear, one hand at her throat.

Mowgli stood before her, his every muscle tensed to flee. But to his surprise, his mouth moved almost of its own accord. "Do not be afraid," he said softly, never taking his eyes from hers.

She slowly set down her water jug, backing away from the well. "Art thou—art thou a . . . a godling?" she whispered, her eyes wide with wonder.

The restlessness, the anger, the despair and confusion which had led him here suddenly slipped from his heart, and he smiled. "I am Mowgli, of the jungle," he said gently. "Hast thou heard my name?"

She paused in confusion. "I have heard of a boy raised by wolves. But thou art—" she cast her eyes down "—thou art a man."

Mowgli frowned in bewilderment, and he looked down at his own body. When he looked up again, she was gone, running back towards the village, her hair streaming out behind her, her bare feet flashing in the dust. He ducked down, expecting at any moment to hear her alarm cries—but she reached the road and stopped. She stared at him for a long moment, smoothed her garments, and walked with dignity back up the dusty path.

Almost, did he follow her when he saw her glance back over one slender shoulder. But then he shook himself all over and slipped outside the village wall, wondering at the new feeling of peace which had settled over him. Whatever thorn had pricked his heart was now plucked away; whatever was wrong was now righted. The sounds of the jungle were a welcoming hum, and he followed a familiar path into the trees.

He heard a cough at his knee and said, "So, thou hast come at last." He turned and found Bagheera on his trail.

The Black Panther fawned and rubbed against him, purring loudly. "Forgive, Little Brother, for the New Talk led me a mad chase."

Mowgli bent and hugged the great cat round the neck. "It matters not," he replied. "Was it Good Hunting?"

Bagheera stiffened slightly and stared into his eyes. "Some things are better left unsaid, even though we are brothers, ye and I." His lips curved in a small smile as he changed the subject swiftly. "Ye come from the Man-Pack, eh? What pulled ye thither?"

Mowgli gazed through the trees to the distance, and his eyes were far away and private, as though he heard a silent voice, felt an unseen hand. "Ye are right, Brother," he said gently. "Some things are better left unsaid." He stood, and the panther followed him without question, into the deep stillness of the jungle night.

This is part of the song Bagheera sang as he chased his mate through the jungle. Mowgli heard snatches of it in the distance as it drifted away on the night-wind.

Bagheera's Spring Song

Now, when all the night is calling,
Breezes warm and clouds are crawling,
Now that darkness hides the jungle,
Now is time for song.
Soft as early bud-horn hide,
Spring is here and smells collide,
Of blooms and Blood and ripeness and
It will not last for long.
Sing the Spring Song to the sky,
Seeking, searching for another,
Who will answer back the cry,
Who will be this season's lover!
Call it long and call it proud,
Beasts on foot and birds on wing,
Now, when madness is allowed,
The woods will ring with Spring, with Spring!

THE MAD ELEPHANT
OF MANDLA

For the sake of the running,
My legs have grown long,
For the sake of the climbing,
My shoulders are strong,
I have laired with my Brothers
And shared in the kill,
And the jungle, the jungle!
It calls to me still!

For the sake of the hearing,
My ears have grown wide,
For the sake of the seeing,
I'm hawk- and owl-eyed,
I have walked with the Man-Pack
And stalked where I will,
But the jungle, the jungle!
It calls to me still!

Mowgli's Travelling Song

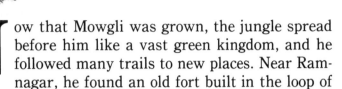

Now that Mowgli was grown, the jungle spread before him like a vast green kingdom, and he followed many trails to new places. Near Ramnagar, he found an old fort built in the loop of the river. The jungle was swallowing it on all sides but the towers, built long ago by the Gond kings, still stood out starkly against the trees. The *Bandar-log* had taken it over, of course, and the water tanks were alive with cobras, so he made his bed for the night in a spreading banyan outside its walls.

He was awakened in the darkness by distant cries, moving closer through the woods. An old memory flared instantly. Mowgli murmured, *"Shikari!"* and peered down through the banyan leaves to the forest below.

Now, he heard the approaching din of wooden clappers, the shouts and howls of men, the blasts of muskets—and the trumpeting of elephants. A khedda, a wild elephant roundup, was coming, and from his perch high in the safety of the trees, Mowgli saw the flicker of torches across the river. Suddenly, a small herd crashed through the brush and stopped at the bend of the river. Behind them came a troop of koonkies, trained elephants, who pressed them forward into the rushing water. The wild elephants screamed and trumpeted in terror as they surged into the river and across to the other side.

They ran directly under Mowgli's perch, a tumbling mass of gray mountains led by an old cow. Trunks waved in the air, white tusks flashed, but behind them, steady and firm, came the lines of the koonkies with brown men perched on their backs, waving and shouting commands. A pack of villagers followed, boys and men of all ages, banging furiously on drums, howling, whistling, and cheering.

Mowgli waited until they roared by, and then he slipped to the ground and ran behind the procession, all thoughts of sleep chased from his head. He followed the elephants to a stockade built in the middle of the jungle, large enough to hold a dozen wild elephants, all the koonkies, and half a village or more.

The elephant sentries shouldered the herd right up to the stockade gate—and there, the old cow who led the wild elephants balked. She turned to face the men, trumpeting in rage and stomping her withered feet in defiance.

The huge teak gate was held open by a rope. Men stood at each side of the elephants, shouting and waving their torches to force the herd inside. A large koonkie tusker charged the old cow, but she held her ground, refusing to lead her herd within the walls. The mahouts, the elephant-trainers, and their boy-helpers shrieked; the koonkies thrust their tusks hard into the broad backsides which stood stubbornly before them, and still, the herd would not budge.

Suddenly, a tiny calf, still covered with the auburn bristles of babyhood, broke from the herd and went running among the koonkies, dodging their massive legs, without the slightest thought of its danger. One wrinkled cow did not hesitate. Turning aside from the safety of the herd, she charged right at the *shikari*. Ignoring the waving torches and the screaming men, she shouldered her way to her calf, turned him in the right direction, and gently nudged him back to the milling feet of the herd.

The cow's courage angered the koonkie tusker, and he ran at the old leader with new rage. She dodged his blows, turning her shoulders this way and that, trumpeting in futile despair, while the herd plunged and stomped at her heels.

Behind her, a young cow began to scream a high, mournful cry, as though lamenting the fate which seemed now inevitable. The old leader turned and gazed at her sadly, and as she did, the tusker rushed in, and with a vicious twist of his head gored her side in a long, red slash. Finally, exhausted and bewildered by the din, the old cow turned and trudged slowly into the stockade. For an instant, the elephants hesitated—then one, two, three more wheeled and fell in line. A cheer went up from the crowd as the herd reluctantly followed her inside. A mahout slashed the rope that held up the gate and it came thundering down with a crash, trapping a dozen wild elephants within.

"*Ahi!*" Mowgli said to himself, "this is a large and dangerous hunting, indeed. Even Hathi could be taken by such a pack, jackals though they be."

Now, men surged up the walls of the stockade, clinging to the heavy teak posts and shouting encouragement to each other. Boys and men ringed the top of the enclosure, their shoulders crowding together, jostling for the best view. Mowgli shinnied quietly up a tall peepul tree which hung over the stockade and hid himself in the branches to see what would happen.

Inside the walls, the wild elephants clustered in a tight knot in one corner, the calves to the centre, the cows standing shoulder to shoulder in defence. A few mahouts spilled over the top of the stockade and approached the herd, waving torches and shouting to one another.

Behind them, the teak gate yawned open, and the koonkies rushed inside, their trainers riding high up on their heads for safety, turning to face the herd in a solid line of attack.

At a signal, three koonkies wheeled to one of the younger cows. With no calf to protect, she was on the fringe of the clustered herd. She glanced at the old leader nervously, wondering what she should do. The koonkies came closer and then quickly cut her away from her comrades, shoving her against the walls of the stockade. She trumpeted and tried to run, but they pushed her firmly against the wall. She swung her trunk wildly, trying to reach high up on a koonkie back to drag down the man-enemy, but the elephants pressed her even tighter. Finally subdued, she stood trembling helplessly, as a mahout jumped to the ground. Slipping around her stomping feet, avoiding her desperate kicks, he managed to slip a noose high up over her back legs. Mahouts atop the other koonkies threw a rope round her neck, and when the three guards pulled away, the cow was roped to a tree.

Now, teams of koonkies turned to the other cows, quickly moving them away from the herd and each other. In a short while, every wild elephant was tied to a separate tree. The calves were noosed to their mothers, who stood wearied, leaning against the walls. The young bull yearlings were noosed apart, and they fought the ropes the hardest, tearing away at their shackles, lashing out furiously at any mahout who ventured near, and sometimes rolling over and over on the ground in tantrums of rage. The older cows stood quietly and stolidly, watching with tiny angry eyes for any chance of escape or an opportunity for a swipe at their captors. The old cow leader lay down at the edge of the stockade, stretching her ropes as far as they would strain. No matter how the men shouted or the koonkies prodded her, she would not rise.

Now, the men brought in bushels of sugarcane and sweet plantains, laying them in piles at the elephants' feet. A few calves snatched at the fodder, but most of the herd turned away from this offering in weary disgust. Mowgli saw that many of the villagers were climbing down from the stockade walls and heading back through the jungle for their homes. He waited until the stockade was quiet except for the occasional wheezing and moaning of a captive. He crept closer in the darkness, still hidden by the overhanging branches of the trees, until he was just above an old cow.

"*Haimai*, Old Mother," he whispered in elephant tongue. "We be of one blood, ye and I. Look up!" He leaned out over the tethered captive.

A withered trunk shot up in the air, and Mowgli heard her snort in the darkness. "Who calls?"

"'Tis I, Mowgli of the Seeonee Pack," he said quietly. "I saw thee taken and hurried hither."

"Come out that I may see thee," the old cow said warily.

Mowgli leaned still further out of the tree and touched the questing trunk. The elephant started, snuffled in alarm, and the trunk dropped quickly away. "Thou art Man!"

"Nay, Old Mother," Mowgli said gently. "I am of the Free People. Hathi himself hath taught me thy tongue. Art thou wounded?"

The old cow leaned wearily against the wall and gurgled mournfully, "To the heart, Little Stranger, to the heart. Next season, I would have made the Trek to the Place of Bones. Now, I shall die among these stinking *Bandar* like a yoked bullock."

"Thou shalt not, whilst I have *this*," Mowgli whispered, holding up his knife so that the moonlight hit the shaft like cold fire. He leaned and swiftly cut the rope that bound the old cow to the tree. Sliding down the wall silently, he sawed at the cord round her back leg.

The elephant shivered to a new alertness, lifted her great foot out of the coiling rope, and laid her trunk on Mowgli's shoulder. "This is most wonderful," she said, "but what of the others?"

Mowgli said, "My knife is hungry enough to free all thy tribe. When Man opens the gates in the morning, ye can rush him all together. Whither are thy tuskers? Why art thou led by a grandmother?"

The old cow stiffened indignantly. "*We* need no tuskers, thumbling. *Maji Sahiba* [Respected Mother] has led this herd since I was no taller than thy scruffy head."

"And now, she lies yonder," Mowgli said quietly, "deaf to the world."

"Not so deaf I cannot hear the peepings of a frog," an ancient voice said suddenly, and the old leader of the elephant herd shambled as close as her nooses would allow. Mowgli went to her side and peered up at her rheumy white eyes.

"Cut me loose," she whispered. As Mowgli bent to saw away her cords, she asked, "Thou art the same manling who rode Hathi's back at the Dance, eh? I remember. How came thee here?"

"By chance, O Maji," Mowgli said, standing and pulling the cord from her foot.

"A lucky chance for us," she said. "Wilt thou free the others?"

Mowgli walked silently under her trunk from one captive to another, slicing through the ropes which held them apart, until one by one, they stood unbound. One cow started across the stockade to join a comrade, and the old cow hissed a command: "Stay where ye were pinioned. The Men will surely watch us through the night, and they must see us where they left us."

She turned to Mowgli and gurgled softly, "Thou hast done the herd a great boon, manling. When the gate lifts at dawn, we shall be ready for the rush. I would ask one more favour if thou wilt. Go and bite the heel-ropes of the koonkies with thy Man's tooth. Perhaps when the *shikari* wake, they will have no more armies to turn against us."

"Good Hunting, Old Mother," Mowgli murmured softly, and scaled the wall, disappearing into the shadows once more.

When the boy dropped silently on the other side of the stockade, he crouched down, his hand on his knife. Five campfires flickered in the night; each was ringed by dark mounds of sleeping men. A dozing guard sat before a fire, his musket on his knees. Mowgli edged cautiously past the hunters, moving low through the brush. He approached the line of koonkies, who were tethered just beyond the reach of the firelight. Six huge tuskers stood together, mumbling and swaying, their heels held fast by their ankle rings and picket stakes. Mowgli crept closer, his eyes on the guards, placing each foot as silently as he could.

Suddenly, an elephant's voice rumbled through the dark, "Halt! What moves?"

The boy froze and dropped to his belly. The closest guard did not even stir, so used to the elephants' night-noises was he. But the other tuskers stiffened in their traces, and their questing trunks sought out the scent of the intruder.

"Oh, it is only a mahout's boy," another said sleepily as he spied Mowgli.

"Why then does he come crawling like a tree-cat?" asked a tusker fretfully. "Boy, has thy master taught thee no more manners than this? Come and scratch my belly, since thou art up."

Of course, had Mowgli been any but Mowgli, he would not have been able to understand the elephants' talk—and well he knew that they would not speak so impudently if they thought he could. He walked boldly up to the closest tusker and whispered in his fan-ear in the Elephant speech, "I will do more than scratch thy belly, Big One. I shall cut thee loose to freedom."

The tusker turned as Mowgli's words startled him fully awake—and the boy gasped in surprise. It was no strange elephant who swayed above him, but Batha, son of Hathi.

"Batha!" Mowgli hissed, his eyes round with wonder. "What do ye here?"

"My job, of course, manling," the elephant muttered. "As do we all. What manner of mischief do ye bring to *this* piece of the jungle?"

"Mischief? Do ye call freedom mischief, then? I come to cut thee loose!" And he knelt to saw at Batha's heel-rope.

But to his surprise, the elephant's trunk cuffed him away lightly. "What do ye there? Get off, boy. Ye are taller, but no wiser,

138

I see. If my Man finds a broken rope on me come dawn, I shall wear two even tighter the next night." Batha yawned a huge yawn and scratched one foot with the other.

"The next night, ye shall walk the hills yonder with no rope at all," Mowgli said, and he bent once more to his task.

This time, Batha cuffed him away with more force. "Get off, I said! Else I call the guards!"

Mowgli sat up, his brows knitted together in confusion. "Has it been so many seasons, then? What do ye fear, Batha? The jungle? 'Tis as ye left it. Is it so fine here with the Man-Pack that ye forget?"

"I fear nothing," the elephant rumbled, "and neither do I forget. My name is Batha no more. They call me Vir Bare, the Bold One, and I am the most favoured of His Majesty's Service."

The rest of the tuskers had moved off in silence when they discovered that Mowgli had neither good things to eat nor any intention of scratching their ears. They browsed and mumbled together, scarcely glancing at the boy, as though nothing he said could be of any interest to them at all.

"The most favoured of his *slaves*, ye mean," Mowgli said with some heat, for when he did not understand a thing, he could not let it go. "I come to repay thee for my life—a small thing which perhaps ye do not recall—but I offer all the jungle for it now, O Son of Hathi. Thou and thy brethren could slip away into the night whilst the Man-Pack sleeps—"

"To what?" Batha asked with disgust. "To sweat in the sun and shiver in the Rains? To walk for miles to find the seasons' leavings? Here, we have all we need, and we eat it in comfort. My Man takes me to the cool waters, morning and evening. He scratches me all over as I command him, and he piles the sweetest grasses at my feet."

"And what must ye do for such bounty?" Mowgli asked dryly.

"Carry and lift, lift and carry," Batha said calmly, "and that is all."

"So ye sell thy back for a bundle of cane, and sometimes, ye must turn traitor to thy own."

Batha shook his head, almost amused. "Such venom from such an unripe mouth," he said lightly.

"Such folly from such an old one," Mowgli snapped back quickly. "I think thou art struck by *surrah* [sleeping sickness]. Thy father would hide his head in shame if he heard thee now."

Batha tensed and rumbled angrily, "My father knows only the jungle. There is far more in the world than the hills and the Waingunga. Someday, if thou art lucky, thou wilt know this truth thyself. Now, get away back to thy tiny pond, Little Frog. The world has business to do."

"An ugly business, to be sure." Mowgli dropped his voice to a gentle pleading. "Batha, come away. There is a pleasant wind in the cedars, and the streams are bright with snow-water. Bagheera told me long ago, better a bone in freedom than a banquet in slavery."

The elephant only chuckled and turned away in dismissal. "Much he knows of bones, but little else."

Mowgli set his jaw and rose to his feet. He said under his breath, "Well, and we shall see what *ye* know, O Wise One, come the morrow and the mutiny."

But Batha heard him and snorted, "What? What did ye say? What have ye done! Guard! Guard! An intruder!"

Batha's trumpets woke the sleeping hunters, and they leaped from their beds, grabbing their weapons. Mowgli bolted for the cover of the trees, but a *shikari* caught him fast, hollering for his fellows. They surrounded the picket line before Mowgli could escape. One grabbed his shoulder and thrust a torch in his face.

" 'Tis a jungle boy!" the guard shouted. "Ye have heard of him! Raised by wolves, the villagers say, and just as devious as his brethren!"

"Bind him!" commanded the hunter leader. "The Maharajah will find him amusing, no doubt. This jungle cur will think another time before he tries to steal the elephants of the King!"

Mowgli struggled and kicked and fought with silent fury, but the guards overwhelmed him and tied him fast to a tree. Though he could understand most of what the hunters said, he could not find the words to make them let him go. He gave a Stranger's Call for help, but received no answer from the jungle shadows. He was too far from familiar trails to expect rescue, he knew. With rope bound all round his chest, he stood, glaring into the night, while the camp fell slowly back into silence.

His knife was still round his neck. In the darkness, the hunters had not thought to take it from him, but they had tied his hands down to his sides, and he could not reach his weapon. He shrugged his shoulders, trying to work the ropes loose, but he finally stopped, exhausted. He fought to keep his eyes open, but they gradually dropped lower and lower.

Just before he dozed, he heard Batha murmur softly, "It is not such a bad fate, manling. Thou wilt see. Soon, ye shall ride high on the shoulders of thine own elephant, a mahout of the first rank, and ye shall look down on all thy brethren below ye. Indeed, there are worse trails to follow."

Dawn crept into the hunters' camp, and Mowgli woke with a start, lunging into the ropes with newly-aroused rage. For an instant, he had hoped it was all a dream, and he would awake with his shoulders on Bagheera's soft flanks. Instead, his back was chafed and sore, and his legs were stiff with standing all night.

The camp was silent; the stockade beyond was quiet as well. Behind the captives, the koonkies slept undisturbed. The rose-headed parakeets screeched somewhere near in the forest, and a grumble of disturbance moved through the guards. One stood and stretched noisily, and the camp began to come awake.

A mahout passed by Mowgli, ignoring him, and went to Batha's side. "*Salaam*, O my Largest of All Pearls!" he greeted the elephant loudly. "My profoundest apologies for the disturbance to thy rest last night." He slid under Batha's chin and scratched his left ear lovingly. "It is not enough thou must manage the most mighty burdens in the jungle, not enough that thou hast the staunchest heart, my king. Now, thee must needs listen to a jungle brat's prattle half the night and suffer him under thy feet all the day."

Batha nodded his head in rhythm to the man's crooning, and Mowgli rolled his eyes in disgust. The mahout moved back to the elephant's tail and began to scratch him all over with a rough-scaled stick. Batha swayed side to side, his eyes half-closed in pleasure, his ears pricked back to catch the man's words.

"And I am afraid I have more bad news, O Mighty Thunder,"

the mahout went on in a wheedling tone. "Today, thou must stay back of the brigade and guard this most infamous nothing of a woods-cub. The *shikari* say they would trust no other to bring him safely to His Majesty's cages." Now the mahout came full circle round the elephant, ducked, and slid a piece of sweet sugarcane in Batha's waiting mouth. "Wilt thou suffer their nonsense for my sake, O Chiefest of All Tuskers?"

Batha gurgled foolishly from somewhere up at the top of his trunk and reached in his mahout's pocket for more cane. As Mowgli watched in amazement, Batha and the other elephants were fed and fussed over, watered and bathed and cajoled, and finally fit with their trappings. Some wore giant howdahs, fit for the *shikari* to ride in elevated splendour. Others wore only rush halters and crude pads, that their mahouts might ride them into the stockade. Batha was fitted with the most beautiful of all the elephant howdahs, and his mahout carried a giant ivory *ankus*—an elephant goad.

A mahout's boy brought Mowgli water and *chapattis*—dry, coarse cakes made of wheat and buffalo butter. He put a cake in Mowgli's mouth, impatiently waiting for him to chew and swallow. Not realizing that Mowgli could understand his speech, he carried on a running complaint against his masters.

"It is not enough I must clean between the Big One's toes, now I must stand and feed this wolf-boy, too. Paugh! For this, did my mother raise me? For this, did my father pay the priest a sum twice what that fool, Rani, collects in his dirty heathen hand every week? To play *ayah* to a jungle brat? I, *I* could be the best mahout in all the King's service!"

Mowgli, vexed by the boy's insolence, gave him his most piercing jungle stare and from out his throat came a perfect imitation of Bagheera's snarl. The helper backed off hurriedly, his eyes wide with terror, and ran stumbling back to the elephants' picket line.

Now, the fires were doused, the elephants at attention, the camp ready to move. Batha's mahout sauntered over to where Mowgli still stood, tied to the tree. His eyes stared the boy up and down, and he said, "So this is the infamous wolf-boy, eh? I think ye have no more use for this—" and he snatched the knife from Mowgli's neck. "'Twill serve to amuse my little son, and His

142

Majesty will not miss such a trifle. O Bold One, keep a watchful eye on this monkey. I go to help herd the Wild Ones."

The mahout hurried off, chuckling to himself and fingering the knife in his pocket. Mowgli swallowed his anger and asked Batha, "What will happen next?"

"Nothing thou needst know," Batha said shortly.

Mowgli thought swiftly and changed his tone to one of respect. "Thou hast been on many of these kheddas, then?"

Batha sighed hugely. "Enough to know I need not answer to *thy* proddings, manling. Indeed, there are few men the Bold One must heed at all. Without these shoulders, even *my* mahout would be as a calf against the Wild Ones."

"And yet, ye are picketed hither," Mowgli said quietly, watching Batha under his lashes.

"I am not," Batha said with annoyance, lifting his great feet to show that he was untied. "I stay, as a favour only, to guard thee, frogling. And when the Wild Ones are tied, one to the other following the calves, I shall lead them as always into Mandla."

So, Mowgli thought to himself quickly, they lead the calves before, and the cows will then follow behind. Aloud, he asked, "What of the Old One? And the young tuskers?"

Batha shrugged. "They will stay or go, it does not matter which. It is the cows and their calves which the *shikari* take on this khedda. The tuskers are too hard to train, and the Old One is of no use to anyone. *I* shall lead the herd to Mandla."

"I can see now why thou didst not care to be freed," Mowgli said politely, "and if thou wilt extend to me thy gracious understanding, I give my word I will not run. These ropes bind me fiercely. Surely, His Majesty would not wish his captive wounded?"

Batha shot the boy a suspicious glance. "Ye will run."

Mowgli scowled. "Is my word less than that of the Bold One? I shall not, I say. And thy master will see that thou canst guard a captive with only thy will. Loose these ropes, Batha, and I follow behind thee all the way to Mandla. Keep me bound, and I shall fight these ropes to the death."

Batha looked first one way and then the other, as though seeking advice. He swayed nervously, eyeing the ropes looped across

Mowgli's chest. Finally, he reached behind him and plucked lightly at a knot. "'Tis too tight, manling. I cannot free thee anyhow."

"The Bold One who lifts and carries the mightiest burdens cannot loose a baby's twine? Try again."

Once more, the trunk snaked behind Mowgli's back, and Batha tugged at the knot, pulling it down to the boy's hands. "There," the elephant said with some relief. "Now, thou canst loose thyself."

Mowgli quickly fumbled with the rope, pulling the cords out and around, forcing his chest away from the tree until he felt the ropes loosen. Now, he wriggled and jerked his shoulders, working the cords down to his belly. He inched his hands around and pulled them all the way off—and stepped away from the tree.

"Remember thy word," Batha said, looming above him. "If ye stir a step, I crush thee here and now."

"My word has gone from me," Mowgli said with dignity, "not my honour."

Batha relaxed visibly and said, "If thou wilt be still, thou wilt perhaps see quite a thing. Soon, the koonkies will lead the Wild Ones forth. It has been quiet, so they must have given little trouble—"

As Batha spoke, there was a thunderous crash, and the gate to the stockade broke open, splintering bamboo to the ground. The Old One was half-in, half-out of the gate, her trunk lashing wildly; her trumpeting ripped through the silence. Behind her, Mowgli could see the rest of the cows, pushing and screaming to get through. He jumped to his feet, but Batha stepped before him quickly.

"Stay back!" he shouted. "The koonkies will stop her!"

To Mowgli's dismay, Batha was right. As though they had seen a dozen such escape attempts and had calmed a hundred wild cows before, the koonkies forcefully shoved the herd back from the ruined gate. The mahouts prodded and pushed and shouted above the din.

A few young tuskers rushed the guards, but the koonkies only turned them aside as men would a pack of small and furious boys, dodging their inexpert blows, easily parrying their thrusts, and finally moving them to one side as though they did not matter at all. At last, only the Old One still rammed the sagging gate, battering repeatedly at the broken bamboo, calling over her shoulder again and again for her herd to follow.

As she saw that no one was behind her, she turned with a new rage and rushed at the splintered gate, trampling it into the dust. Once outside the stockade, she looked around bewildered, as if she suddenly could not make up her mind which direction to go. Two koonkies rushed at her and then stopped a few paces away. She trumpeted a last fierce and desperate cry, but there was no answer. She sagged, and her trunk dropped to the ground.

The koonkies stepped back to let her pass. Slowly, the Old One walked out of the camp, away from the herd. She turned towards the river, moving through the brush like smoke as only an elephant can, leaving scarcely a rippling leaf behind her, never once looking back.

In the stockade, the captive elephants stood silently. Though they could not see her departure, each knew she was gone. They clumped together slowly, awaiting new heel-ropes.

Mowgli let out his pent-up breath in a long sigh. "So it is over?" he asked Batha.

"Nay," the great elephant said patiently. "It is only beginning."

And so, the caravan of koonkies, mahouts, captives and *shikari* made its way north to the great city of Mandla. Mowgli traipsed behind Batha as he had promised, and he slept at his feet at night with no other tether holding him save his word.

As Batha had predicted, he led the parade: first, a line of koonkies, then the calves, the captives, and the guards. Petted and cajoled with sugarcane by the mahouts and tugged along by the great tuskers, the calves soon learned to follow at a good pace. The cows plodded after, staunch ropes at their necks and heels. Mowgli wondered if even these bindings were necessary, for the cows never took their eyes off the calves. In such a way, the caravan travelled for three days without incident, getting closer and closer to His Majesty's city.

At night, the mahout brought sweet grasses to Batha and rubbed him all over with damp leaves. He scratched the great elephant in all of his favourite places, crooning a lullaby as he moved unconcernedly under Batha's belly. And when the great beast was all groomed and soothed, the mahout brought him a bowl of *todi*, the powerful liquor made from palm sap, and then Batha stood and mumbled and swayed half the night away, his eyes half-closed in pleasure.

Mowgli recalled the great trumpeting rage Batha had shown when he was first captured on the night of the Dance and the Gleaning, and he could scarcely recognise that memory in the elephant which stood before him now. The mahout's son, Tamil, a small brown cub of a boy, ran fearlessly to and fro before the great elephant, tugging at his trunk, whispering love-croonings into the lower folds of his ear, and tickling his toes for fun. Batha only gurgled foolishly, trailed his trunk over the boy's shoulder, and felt him all over for hidden sugarcane.

After four days of travel, the captives were no longer fighting their ropes, and in fact, were no longer called Wild Ones at all. "They are raw recruits of the worst sort," Batha said mildly one night as he chewed his cane. "But we'll soon right them out."

When the caravan rested, Mowgli sat at the edge of the fire-light, listening to the mahouts sing their camp songs. Into one ear came the speech of the Man-Pack; in the other, he could hear the koonkies gossiping over their fodder. The men considered him another jungle captive, too frightened to run away. The elephants considered him just another mahout's helper, and so paid him little mind. He was neither one thing nor another, and his heart felt hollow and queer.

When he tried to speak with Batha, he found no comfort there. Once Mowgli said, "Thy father and I have spoken together with naked hearts. Our tongues have tasted the same water, and he has been to me as a brother. And yet, I cannot understand thee, his son. What dost thou take from this Man-Pack that the jungle cannot give thee?"

But Batha only shrugged and turned away.

Mowgli noticed that while the koonkies bullied and prodded the members of the herd, trumpeting at them to keep pace and stay in ranks, the mahouts spoke with the gentlest of voices, their hands always full of soft plantains and sweet cane. The elephants, like the dogs, seemed to develop a puzzling affection for the noises and antics of men. Soon, the cows were beginning to wait for their baths as impatiently as the koonkies, and so long as each had her calf by her at night, she was quieted.

By day, the caravan travelled slowly at the edge of the jungle, never trailing far from the river. Sometimes, they passed a small village, and all the people hurried from their huts and their fields to stare at the mighty hunters and the mahouts. They stood in a line along the dusty road in silence, bowing to the elephants as they strode by, their hands together as though in prayer. Only after the caravan passed did they erupt in excited chatter, and the children chased behind in gleeful capers.

Soon, Mowgli came to know all of the koonkies in the Maharaja's service. Besides Batha, there were seven huge tuskers, two young recruits new to the hunt, and three old sergeants who had been kept on more for sentiment than actual usefulness. The working elephants tended to be more clannish than their wild brethren. The young recruits kept off from the old veterans, and the largest tuskers clustered together away from them both. The koonkies ordered Mowgli about, wheedled him for scratchings and cane, and after a few nights under their great heels, with the sounds of men all about him, the jungle began to seem far away, indeed.

One great tusker, almost as large at the shoulder as Batha, was particularly feisty and difficult to approach. Mowgli had tried to speak to Kala Raj twice, and each time, the big male glared at him with a suspicious white eye and snorted with contempt.

"Pay him no mind," Batha said. "He's riddled with musth and looking for a fight. Were we back at the compound, he'd be off his picket to roam the jungle for a night or two and get it out of his system. But duty calls, and so all must answer. There's no place for musth when His Majesty's silver moves."

"What is silver?" Mowgli asked. Though he had seen an ancient coin or two in the village, he had no conception of wealth.

"'Tis a cold white stuff which men hold dear to their hearts," Batha said, "and His Majesty has more than anyone in the land. It has no legs and so must be carried hither and yon. We shall guard it as it moves to Mandla."

"Guard it? From whom?"

"From everyone, for all men seek it. Now, no more questions, boy, for the night is too hot for speeches."

In two more days, they reached the village of Ramnagar, only a day's travel from Mandla. There, they were joined by a procession of bullocks who pulled great carts piled high with teak boxes—all full of silver, Batha said. Now, the mood of the elephants changed. No longer did they stand about idly exchanging gossip and swaying to and fro. Each new turn of the road was warily inspected for possible ambush; each crack of a twig at night snapped them to alert attention, for the King's silver was moving, and it was their duty to see it safely home. They left the river and turned into the jungle, where the road turned to a narrow path through the brush. Tempers became taut away from the cool water.

The sun rose that morning with an ominous glow, and before it was half-way up the peepul trees, the heat began to build. The jungle crept close to the path, dank and steamy and thick in the shadows. Vines twined around stumps as though to smother them in green; orchids sprouted out of the dead logs. Some of the trees bore enormous blossoms bigger than Mowgli's head, and the leaves of the trees themselves were streaked in red and gold. The thick heat seemed to press at his throat, and the black flies hovered insultingly at his ears, sticking to his lips no matter how often he brushed them away. Still, he walked behind Batha, thinking surely the caravan must stop and rest when the sun was high.

Suddenly, from the back of the column came the sound of rage and a thundering disturbance. Mowgli turned and saw that Kala Raj had jerked himself out of line. His howdah was askew, and his mahout was dangling half-off his back, shouting at him to stand.

"The musth!" Batha whispered in horror, and his mahout shouted the command to halt. But the command was fruitless—Kala Raj, in a mindless rage, was stampeding down the caravan line now, scattering bullocks and carts before him as though they were no more than blossoms in the wind. He crashed against a bullock who could not move from his path, and the beast went to its knees, bellowing in pain. The yoke twisted, snapped, and the cart spilled broken teak and scattered silver all through the brush.

"*Mai! Mai!* Hit him!" a mahout shouted, and the man atop Kala

Raj tried to wrest him under control. "Hit him on the head, fool! Thy goad! Thy goad!" But Kala Raj whirled so fast, that the mahout could do little but hang desperately onto his howdah.

Before anyone could move, the man fell from Kala Raj's back with a crash. The enraged elephant turned on his master and squealed a mad peal of vengeance, kicking at him viciously. The mahout scrambled to escape the plunging feet, but he was too slow. Kala Raj caught him at the knees, smashed both his legs, and went careening up the line. Now, the mahout's screams mingled with Kala Raj's trumpets, the shouts and the bellows of the oxen, the roiling dust and the cries of the frightened peacocks. Over the din, Mowgli shouted to Batha, "Ye must turn him to the trees!"

But Batha seemed frozen with indecision. His mahout gave him first one command, then another, turning him this way and that, shouting, "Stand! Nay, back, back! *So malo!* Careful!" as though the sight of Kala Raj's rampage had robbed him of his mind.

Now, the enraged elephant bolted towards a cart which carried not only six boxes of silver, but also the young boy, Tamil, son of Batha's mahout. To the back of the cart were tied four young calves, and they cowered together, squealing in terror. Kala Raj roared down upon the cart, bent on its destruction, for in his rage it suddenly seemed the engine of all his woe. When he hit the cart broadside, it splintered, knocking Tamil to the ground, where he lay gasping. The silver went flying, and a piece of the yoke struck the elephant smartly in his softest rear parts. Now, his squeals grew more piercing, and he whirled on the cart, scattering the calves in all directions. Tamil tried to scuttle to safety under the wreckage of the cart, but he was pinned by a teak box. He screamed in fright as Kala Raj reared above him, mad with blind fury.

Mowgli raced towards the bull elephant shouting, "Get off! Get off! Ye will kill him!" He snatched up a piece of splintered wood to use as a weapon and whirled it high over his head, prepared to beat Kala Raj away if he must. But a mighty flank shoved him aside, tossing him into the dust, and he looked up to see Batha rushing towards the bull elephant, his tusks raised and ready for war. The mahout was urging him forward with shouts and beatings with his goad, but Batha quickly reached up with his trunk, encircled him by the waist, and gently put him to the ground. Then, the mighty tusker turned on Kala Raj, and the two bull elephants came together with a thundering crash.

The captive cows broke free in a rush of panic and stampeded towards the calves, who had streaked for the trees. The men shouted and tried to pull the koonkies into position; they waved their goads and threatened and yanked on halters, but no koonkie would come near Batha and Kala Raj, who continued to crash shoulders and flanks and tusks at each other, slashing and roaring and stomping the ground.

"Batha!" Mowgli screamed, running to the fighting elephants with the snarl of a wolf. He barked fiercely at Kala Raj, trying to drive his feet further away from the cowering boy. He bent to Tamil, snatched his own knife from the boy's chest, and whirled to face Kala Raj. The bull elephant turned on him savagely, but before he could lower his flashing tusks towards Mowgli, Batha gored him from behind, raking him across his flanks, exposing blood and muscle.

Kala Raj stopped, screamed terribly, and ran for the trees. He crashed through the brake like a runaway locomotive, puffing and snorting madly. Batha wasted not a moment. He plucked Mowgli off the ground and set him on his broad shoulders.

"Ye bleed!" Mowgli cried, for blood and foam streaked Batha's body from his back to his knees.

"I feel nothing," the elephant replied, and turned to the captives huddled by the trees. He gave a long, wild trumpet and strode quickly into the forest. Mowgli looked back and saw the cows fall in line behind him, herding the calves before them. Not a koonkie moved, despite the kicks and urgings of the mahouts. Batha's own mahout was so busy cradling his son, that by the time he looked up, his Bold One was gone. In moments, Batha led them across the river, into the safety of the densest woods, where even the bravest *shikari* would not follow.

When they had run so far that the scent of man was no longer on the wind, Batha stopped to let the calves rest. Mowgli fell panting to the soft grass and stared up at Batha in wonder. "What changed thy mind?" he finally asked the elephant.

Batha looked down at him gently and then gazed over the browsing herd. "Who says my mind was changed at all?"

"But, ye said—"

"Who is to say, this was not always my plan?"

Mowgli followed his eyes to the herd, the grazing cows, the fat calves nuzzling them in peace, and he laughed suddenly, hugging his knees with delight. "Oho! What a salt tale is this, O Best of All Pearls!"

"Well, and we shall say no more, then," Batha chuckled, far up his trunk, "except thy debt is paid, manling. Ye may take my greetings to my father. And say I am well."

Mowgli stood and grasped Batha's trunk, patting him fondly. He looked over his shoulder as he strode into the forest and called, "I shall tell him, indeed! Good Hunting go with ye, O Bold One!"

"And with thee, Little Brother," Batha murmured. And then he turned to his herd.

This is one of the songs which Mowgli heard the mahouts sing round the campfires at night.

Song of the Mahouts

There is only a little light before the darkness comes,
Only the smallest space, only the driest crumbs.
There is only the briefest shade, for the sun is large and hot,
And hotter still and briefer is our end at the burning *ghat*.

There is only a little love, then the bed grows cold and hard,
Little there is that is safe, less that is unmarred,
We share scarcely a few delights, of only the meanest stuff,
But O my heart and my soul, it is enough, enough!

JACALA
TYRANT OF THE
MARSH

Come, my children, to the edge
Of shadowed water, where I rule.
Ye who swim or race or fly
Where the river's deep and cool.
Life waits here for ye to take,
Drink ye deep with head a-bent;
Death waits, too, upon my back,
And *my* jaws bring his sacrament.

The Song of Jacala

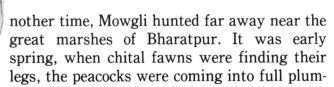

Another time, Mowgli hunted far away near the great marshes of Bharatpur. It was early spring, when chital fawns were finding their legs, the peacocks were coming into full plumage, and the wild boar was in rut.

At Bharatpur, there is a vast swampland of rivers and lakes where waterfowl blacken the air with their comings and goings, and their cries and jostling can be heard for miles around. Storks, spoonbills, white ibis, cormorants, herons, and egrets crowd in the lush acacia trees so densely that the tree limbs droop. Geese and ducks, greylags, pintails, and mallards come from the north to squabble for space around the edges of the lakes in the brush, and pelicans dive from great heights to pull out beakfuls of flopping fish. They fly in dark clouds, passing low with the whisper of beating wings, and their voices fill the air with an incredible din of cries, cackles, and croaks.

Mowgli had heard that a singular visitor came to the marshes in the season of nesting and dancing, a visitor from the northern places of ice and snow. And so, when the new ferns began to push up from the earth, he travelled to the Place of Low Waters, as the Jungle People called the marshlands, to meet this sojourner.

As he approached the marsh, he heard the din of the drongos and babblers, the sentry birds, far before his feet touched water. He gave the Stranger's Call for hunting, and a young dabchick scolded from the brush, "We do no hunting here, Bigfoot! Lest ye stamp on our nestlings, keep off! Keep off!"

"I also do no hunting, Winged Brother," Mowgli said quietly, mindful of the nesting birds all round him. "I come searching for the Sojourner. Where might I find him?"

The dabchick flitted onto a low branch at Mowgli's nose, his bright eye cocked this way and that. "By my pintails, ye art Man, I think! Man! 'Tis Man!"

Before the bird could sound the alarm and rouse a thousand fowl, Mowgli snatched him quickly off the branch and held him gently cupped in his hands. "Be still, Little Shouter. We be of one blood, ye and I," and he gave the Kite's call with a long, low whistle.

The dabchick opened his eyes wide with wonder, hopped to Mowgli's thumb, and then up to his shoulder. He pecked cautiously at the boy's ear, muttering, "'Tis the largest Winged One I have ever seen, to be sure." He drew back and chirped, "Art thou a crane from the High Country, O Ye of Long Legs?"

Mowgli chuckled and put him back on his branch. "I am of the jungle, and no foe of thine. Now again, where is this Sojourner thy people tell of, for news of his arrival has gone far before him."

"Even so! Even so!" the bird screeched, flitting about in excitement. "Garuda sits there under the sacred bo tree," he said, cocking his head towards the broad expanse of marsh. "I said the low and the mighty would come to sit at our pandit's feet! I said it, I said it!"

Mowgli left the bird bobbing up and down on the branch and walked silently through the thicket until it opened up on a vast marsh. All about him, as far as he could see, the water lay still and warm. Ringed by trees and mud and brush, the lakes and rivers spread out like a tapestry of silver. One pond flowed into another, which birthed several meandering streams, which finally came together to make a lake, which once again ran away to river. In between, the grassy knolls of mud and scrub were crowded with roosting birds of all kinds, and the thunder and clap of their calls, the deafening din of their meetings and greetings, made Mowgli wince.

For an instant, he almost turned to go back to the relative silence of the jungle, but then he spied a spreading tree which hung over a shadowed pond. Beneath the tree sat a large white crane and at his feet, a flock of black rooks clustered before him, like a committee of the devout offering fervent prayers to a *sadhu,* or holy man.

It was Garuda, the Sojourner, an old Siberian crane who flew to Bharatpur each season, more than a month in flight from the northern wilds of China and over the Himalayas, to rest beneath the bo tree and counsel the flocks. The crane was long-legged and long-necked, taller than Mowgli at the head, and whiter than the beach sand with a brilliant red brow. His broad wings were tucked trimly, like a man who stood with his hands behind his back, and his black beady eyes moved from one bird to the next with a silent alertness. He listened as the rooks argued among themselves, watching patiently as they stalked back and forth on their black stick-legs.

"Ye know our ways, O *Hare* [Lord]," one large raven called raucously. "We will not suffer a traitor in our midst!"

The rest of the ravens began to crow and caw together, leaping about and batting their wings in a frenzy. Mowgli's mouth twisted, but he sat down to watch, apart from the wrathful flock.

Rooks, in India, are birds of low esteem. The Jungle People call a dishonest creature "thievish as a nesting rook." If one badger steals another's burrow, his comrades say, "He is like a rook, whose neighbor's twigs always look better than those on the ground." It is said that rooks swagger like swans, forgetting their blackness. They make a great fuss before they settle to rest, as though each bird must recount the day's doings, all talking at once. Mowgli avoided rooks on principle. And yet, the Sojourner sat before them patiently as they squawked and spat their complaints.

Finally, the crane said, "Ay, I know thy ways. Ye would set upon him, though he is one of thine own, and kill him altogether. But think, O Ravens of the Wood. How better may he serve thee alive? Do not be as the cock-sparrow who fights his reflection to the death."

One large rook, evidently the leader of the flock, listened carefully to Garuda, cocking his head back and forth. Then he interrupted angrily, "He has led the Ravens of the Fields to our nests for a row of parched corn! He has betrayed his rookery for a full crop, and the dead eyes of a hundred hatchlings stare up from the ground. Yet, ye would have us spare him?"

The crane nodded slowly. "If ye would. If ye would not, then cry to the heavens. But all thy fury is only a scratch against the sky, and his death will not bring back thy nestlings nor appease thy mates. Alive, he may serve thee yet."

The rook leader thought this over for a moment until the rooks around him began to scuffle and argue with impatience. "Let us go!" one young rookling called. "There is nothing for us here but last season's seeds. We must kill the traitor! Garuda is only an ancient—"

But an older bird cuffed the rookling to silence. The leader of the rooks turned to his comrades. "And what if we take this counsel?" He glanced at Garuda and then away. "What if we pin the traitor to the ground, just at the edge of the forest where our lands *meet* those of our enemy, eh?" He smiled a crooked raven smile. "What then, O Brothers of the Wood?"

The rooks began to crow and jump about, pecking at each other in excitement as they understood their leader's plan all at once. "The Rooks of the Fields will come to kill him!" they called. "They will not be able to resist a pinioned stranger! He will die! He will die!"

"And who will be waiting just beyond the rows?" the rook leader cawed triumphantly.

"The Rooks of the Wood! It is war! It is war!" And all in a jumble of black wings and gaping beaks, they flew off to begin their private battle.

The Sojourner was suddenly left alone under the bo tree. He sagged slightly and sighed. Mowgli stood up and came closer. He cleared a place and sat quietly at the crane's feet.

"Good advice to such as those is as a flower in a monkey's hand," Mowgli said politely in bird speech. "Good Hunting, O Garuda."

The crane looked up, mildly startled. "Good Hunting," he answered with courtesy. "And who is this new *chela* [disciple] who greets the Sojourner with the mouth of Man and the tongue of the kite?"

"In the jungle, I am called Mowgli, and the Free People are my brothers."

"Uhmm. Those of the jungle do not come here often. Indeed—" and here, the crane scratched at his head with a long, horny claw "—indeed, I can recall no other Grounder [for that is what the birds call creatures who cannot fly] before thee." He rearranged his wings and raised his voice. "Ye have come for counsel, then?"

Mowgli shook his head. "I come to hear thy tales of the northern places of ice and snow. In the jungle, they say thine eyes have seen the highest places in all the land and many lands beyond."

The crane smiled quietly. "They say true." He looked up as a flamingo flew into the clearing and hurried over to the bo tree.

"O Baba, the committee comes!" The gawky, ruffled bird looked breathlessly over his shoulder at a flock of flamingos who were advancing with stately dignity upon the bo tree.

"Have them wait," Garuda said calmly.

"Wait? Oh! But—" and the flamingo backed away, unsure what to do.

"Or they may take their rest, if they prefer. But another comes before them."

The flamingo noticed Mowgli then, blushed a furious pink, and hurried off to delay the flock committee.

"Thou needst not send them off," the boy said, a bit uncomfortable.

"I did not," Garuda replied, undisturbed. "Now, what wouldst thou know of the high places and the lands beyond?"

Mowgli hunkered closer and said eagerly, "Everything."

The crane laughed gently. "It is ever so with the young wings. But I did not know those of the jungle had such restless hearts as well." He mused for a moment. "But perhaps they do not, for thou art the first." He opened his wings expansively and his eyes took on a faraway look. "The mountains are ever so high, Grounder, and colder than the oldest egg. The air is thin, so thin that feathers cannot churn it. The sun is not yellow like this stuff which warms us now, but white. White and old and weak. The moon comes out at day and spars with the sun until neither are strong enough to melt the ice."

"What is ice?" Mowgli asked, for of course, he had never seen it.

"It is water which has died, cold and white as stone. Think of all the water ye have ever seen rush past thy feet. Hast thou ever wondered whither it runs?"

Mowgli nodded, his eyes wide.

"It goes to the water burial place, the highest mountains, where the ice is taller than a thousand cedars, and there, it gives birth to new waters. And the lands beyond, the lands beyond, O, I could tell thee—" but there, the crane stopped, as though wearied by all he had recalled.

Mowgli waited respectfully for him to regain his strength. Finally, he asked, "And is the flight hard, O Sojourner?"

Garuda lifted his head and pierced the boy with a stare. "Harder than death, Grounder. A full moon of beating against the wind and the cold, with only the thin white stars to lead the way."

"Why, then, do ye come?"

Garuda shrugged, an ancient wearied movement of his wings. "Ah. Life is *maya,* eh? An illusion. And the flocks await my coming. So, I fly." He brightened. "Hast thou heard my most recent parable? No?" He chuckled with satisfaction. "Listen well, *chela.* Three animals argued as to who was the oldest, and therefore most deserving of veneration. As a test, they asked each to recall how he first remembered the banyan tree which they sat under. Ye have not heard this one before?"

Mowgli shook his head patiently.

"Well and so. The elephant said that he remembered the banyan first as a bush. When he walked over it, it tickled his belly. The monkey said he remembered the banyan first as a seedling, for he ate of its first leaves. And what did the partridge say, my son?"

Once more, Mowgli shook his head, wondering at the old crane's glee.

"The partridge said, 'I left its seed in my droppings—and so not only do I remember the banyan before it was a banyan, but *I* gave it birth!'" The crane watched him intently for his response.

Mowgli smiled politely, somehow certain that in different places, others told the same tale with a different hero. It is the same with the old of all tribes, he thought, be they bird, beast, or Man.

"Perhaps the beasts are the best tale-tellers after all," the crane finally said softly, as though he had read Mowgli's thoughts. "For they must lay their ears to the ground every night, eh?" He cleared his throat and assumed a dignified stance. "And so tell me, *chela.* Why exactly hast thou come to the Place of Low Waters?"

Mowgli thought this over for a moment. "There is much here to learn and to see, and I am weary of the same trails in my piece of the jungle. Wilt thou give me leave to trespass amongst thy brethren for a time?"

The crane glanced over at the flamingos who waited impatiently for an audience. "Ay, thou art welcome, Grounder. Mind thy feet in the rushes, for the nestlings are many this season. Only keep away from the far lake, and thou wilt be safe."

"The far lake? What danger dwells there?"

"Two kinds. One of the heart and one of the flesh." He dismissed the boy with a gentle wave of his wing. "Ye may come another time, if ye wish."

"Many thanks and Good Hunting, O Sojourner," Mowgli said. And he took himself away from the bo tree, wondering what it all meant.

He walked the edge of the marsh, watching the many waterfowl go about their business, nesting, courting, feeding, fighting—and finally, he came to the edge of a large lake where the birds were far fewer. Those who nested by this water stayed high in the acacia trees; those who fed in its shallows looked nervously about them, bobbing their heads up and down in anxious fits and starts. As he approached, a small flock of grebes started up from the rushes and flew over his head calling, "Beware! Beware! Beware!"

In the far corner of the lake, he saw two dark forms diving in and out of the water, splashing froth high into the sun. He crouched down, his hand on his knife, and crept quietly closer. At the edge of the lake, he moved through the brush until he could peer over a bank of lantana. There, he saw two large otters swimming and diving together in a swirl of energy, nipping at each other and mewing excitedly as they played.

Mowgli grinned and relaxed. He had never seen large lake otters before, but he had heard Baloo speak of them often. "Crazed, they are, with more wriggles than a trout in shallow water," the old Bear had said. "They live only to play and feed, with never a thought for next season's belly." Baloo came from a long line of hibernators, and even though he did not sleep in the cold season—for it was never cold in the jungle—still, he fed heavily during the monsoons as though he feared he would never have enough. According to Baloo, any Jungle People who did not plan for scarcity deserved to starve.

But these creatures were sleek and fat with brown fur that shed water like a hot stone, thick muscular tails, huge paddle-feet, and a bristling array of rigid whiskers. Their teeth were many and sharp, and they could crack through a fresh-water clam as quickly as Bagheera could snap a rib. While Mowgli watched, they squealed and tossed a fish between them, mock-fighting for the best half. When the fish had been almost torn to shreds, they stopped, dove down once to clean their faces, and then popped up with two twin gasps onto the beach.

They spied Mowgli at once and waddled over to him unhesitatingly, their backs humping up and down like Kaa's when he moved over rocky ground.

"*Hai!* See, Ud, 'tis a man! I told you so!" The female sniffed Mowgli's foot and wriggled all over with excitement.

"I shall bite him!" the male otter cried, running at Mowgli with a fierce face. But when he got close, the boy gave a single sharp snarl of warning, and the two otters tumbled all over each other in startled confusion, racing back to the water.

Mowgli stood and called out, "Come back! I am Mowgli of the Free People!"

Two brown heads popped up again out of the brush. They dropped down like a shot. The reeds rustled, two furry backs wriggled and humped, and then the otters peered out at the boy from a closer vantage point.

"Well, and is he Man or Wolf," the male asked the female with some vexation, "Ye Who Knows All and Says More? Almost did I lose my tail, thanks to your moss-talk and froth and I—"

"Hist!" cried the female. "He listens! See how his head moves!" She moved closer. "*Hai!* Ye with the wolf mouth! *I* say ye art Man!"

Mowgli chuckled gently.

"He laughs!" the female said triumphantly, cuffing her mate. "None but Man laughs so." And she bounded towards Mowgli with renewed courage.

"Thou dost not fear Man, then?" Mowgli asked with wonder.

"Nay," the male said, running up and sniffing curiously at the boy's hair. "We fear nothing! How came ye hither, Man?"

"I came over the hills, to see the Sojourner. He has given me leave to lair amongst thee for a time. But he said I was to take care in the far lake. Is this the far lake?"

Ludra, the female otter, chuckled delightedly, her belly jiggling and her whiskers bristling. "He still warns strangers away from us, Ud! 'Beware, beware,'" she moaned, in a mockery of the crane's solemn speech.

"He said that here there was danger of losing the heart and the flesh. What did he mean?"

Ud, the male otter, turned a quick somersault, knocking Ludra off her feet. They rolled over and over each other, tumbling into the water. "He means us! He means us!" the otters cried, and then there was a terrific splash.

Mowgli ran to the edge of the water and saw the two cavorting and ducking each other. The day was hot, the water looked inviting, and soon, the boy could not resist joining the two otters at play. He dove in, swam under Ludra, and boosted her out of the waves. She squealed and swirled round him like a small cyclone, while Ud hopped on his shoulders and tugged his hair. Together, the three frolicked and churned up the water for half the day. They had contests to see who could swim the fastest, dive the deepest, hold his breath the longest, and make the biggest splash by rolling up in a ball and hitting the water from a great height. They herded minnows into the shallows and then tried to catch them, ambushed ducks from underneath, and made a mud slide into a deep pool, taking it belly-down over and over. They pushed two logs together to make a raft and then fought over its possession, ducking each other in a frenzy. Finally, Mowgli dragged himself out on the shore, panting for breath. Ud and Ludra plopped down beside him, scarcely wearied at all.

"Now I know why Garuda warned me of my heart," Mowgli said, gasping, "for mine will surely burst!"

"Ay, Man has the spirit for play, right enough, but lacks the strength—though ye did better than most," Ludra said as she combed out her backhairs.

At the sound of her voice, a series of small squeaks and mews and cries came from somewhere close by in the mud bank. Mowgli rose up on one elbow and looked about in confusion. Ud bounded off in the direction of a half-submerged log while Ludra sprawled unconcerned.

"Hast thou a nest nearby?" Mowgli asked.

She sighed hugely and flopped on her belly. "A half-dozen water rats this season. They're stashed in the holt till I'm ready to be mauled again. They're nothing but bellies and teeth now, but they'll be beauties before long. Ours always are."

Ud emerged from the sunken log with a trail of otter kits behind him, six small bundles of brown fur with large black eyes. When they saw Ludra their squealing grew more frenzied, and they ran to her and rolled her over to nurse, upon her like a pack of fleas.

She sighed again and let herself be handled, their six snouts worrying her bellyfur, their six sets of eyes closed in ecstasy as they found her teats.

"Never have more than three," she said to Mowgli over her shoulder. "They wear ye so!"

Mowgli grinned, watching the kits in their frantic suckling. Ud stood by proudly, prodding one kit into place, shoving another kit aside when it grew too greedy.

"So," Mowgli asked finally as they subsided, "what other danger is it that lives in this water? Garuda spoke of a danger of the flesh?"

Ud shuddered convulsively and turned away. Ludra patted a kit fondly and did not answer.

"Well?" Mowgli asked again after a long moment of silence. "Thou wouldst have me stumble into its jaws unwarned?"

"Ye *have* been warned," Ludra said softly.

"To hear is one thing," Mowgli said. "To know is another."

"We do not speak of the Big One."

"No one *does* by name," Mowgli said impatiently. "Ye only cry 'beware' and take flight. But surely, the sound of its name does not bring it hither. What do ye fear?"

Ludra looked over her shoulder and finally, "Jacala," she whispered. "The Belly That Runs on Four Feet."

"Hist!" Ud cried in horror. "He will come!"

"He will come, no matter," Ludra snapped. "And soon now."

"A mugger?" Mowgli asked, his eyes widening. "'Tis he who haunts these waters?"

"He is the Tyrant of the Marsh," Ud said reluctantly, looking over his shoulder. "And he knows all."

A mugger is the Indian crocodile, feared by all river people for his strength and his cunning. He will eat anything which crosses his path: fowl, fish, animals as large as a buffalo and as swift as— an otter. He has been known to grab and drown horses crossing a shallow stream, pulling them under and then dismembering them with voracious appetite. He crawls into marshy fields at night, lying in wait for the unsuspecting traveller who thinks to take a shortcut to his village. He can grow to be near twenty-five feet long, over a ton in weight, and with luck, can live to be as old as Hathi. And on a warm spring night, the thunder of his mating roars splits the jungle sky.

Mowgli had had only one meeting with a mugger—that night long ago when he'd almost been knocked into the river by a flashing tail—but he had not forgotten the swiftness of the attack and the terror he had felt.

"Ye say he comes soon?" he asked. "Why do ye not move thy holt to another lake?"

"All waters are the same to Jacala," Ludra said mournfully. "He rules them all, and in none can we escape."

"And so, ye simply wait for him to come and kill?" Mowgli asked in disbelief.

"We wait," Ud said resignedly. "And we play."

Mowgli fell silent as he watched the kits trundle back to the burrow, following Ud in a single file, their bellies now rounded, their eyes half-closed in sleep.

"How do ye know he comes?" Mowgli asked finally, his voice low as though the mugger himself listened.

"He always does," Ludra sighed. "He takes three, maybe four of each season's nest and leaves the rest for other waters. We have tried hiding them; we have tried moving them—still, he takes them."

"Have ye tried fighting him?" Mowgli asked softly.

Ludra snorted in contempt. "Nay, and we have not tried to spar with the sun for shining too hot." She rolled over, her eyes hidden under her paw. "He does not take them all. He cannot catch us,

I think, for we are too swift. And . . . he does not take them all. And so, the seasons come again."

Mowgli shook his head in scorn. "There must be something ye can do."

Ludra said quietly, "*Man* always thinks so."

Ud waddled back, eager to frolic again. He had already forgotten the mugger, and he jumped on Ludra, nipping her neck and tugging at her tail. They rolled off into the water, and Mowgli could see them writhing and twisting, their bodies flashing to and fro in a frenzy of play.

For a day or two, Mowgli lounged by the far lake, swimming with the otter family, fishing and dozing in the sun. The rhythms of the marsh were different from those of the jungle. Food was so plentiful, he had but to dive into the water and swim to the far side to catch enough fish to feed himself for the day. When the sun was too strong, he lolled in the shallows. At night, he slept in the burrow which Ludra had enlarged so that he could enter, a warm otter on either side. There was no need to stalk his food; no need to climb or dig or even think, for everything was at hand. And so, though he had been told of danger, it was easy to push the warning from his mind and enjoy the ease which the far lake offered.

The otter kits were becoming expert in the water. Ludra and Ud paddled them from one side of the lake to the other, teaching them powerful diving techniques, the art of twisting and turning swiftly after an elusive fish, and how to keep their coats in good condition. The kits did not need to be taught to play, for this instinct was as natural to them as breathing. When their daily lessons were over, they spent the rest of the afternoon chasing each other in and out of the water, sliding down the muddy bank, and blowing bubbles.

One day, Mowgli was following them in single file, sliding through the ripples they left behind like another otter in the procession. An early rain had left the lake muddier than usual, and the sun felt good on his back. He stopped to rest on a log, panting with his eyes closed, when the log moved under him with a shudder and shot forward towards the swimming otters. He caught a glimpse of two yellow slanted eyes, a gaping set of teeth, and then the last two otters in line disappeared in a froth of silent waves. Mowgli snarled and leaped on the scaly back, his knife raised high. The mugger thrashed, snatched two more otter kits and sank, throwing the boy off his back with a single whip-like roll of his tail. The final kit taken had an instant to squeal before the water filled his mouth, and Ludra turned in time to see her family down to two remaining kits, scattering in panic for the shore.

Now, the crocodile twisted underwater and came up under Mowgli, his wide jaws open for a final wrenching horror. The boy saw ten feet of armoured death launching upward at him, snaggle teeth open, wide white mouth hissing, the eyes covered with their reptile lid, winking and leering, and he stabbed with his knife down with all his strength at the place where the monster's head met his body. To his horror, the knife snapped off at the hilt, and he was left with only the nub in his shaking hand. He kicked backwards, frantically trying to get a grip on a log, the reeds, anything with which he could defend himself.

The mugger writhed once, twice, trying to rid himself of the knife, no more wounded than a buffalo with a determined blowfly at his ears. He bellowed in rage and shot through the water, hitting Mowgli sideways and knocking the air from his belly with a whoosh. Mowgli's groping hand reached a stick of driftwood, and he brought it up over his head, smacking the crocodile across the snout. He turned the stick suddenly and stuck it solidly between the gaping jaws which twisted now for a fatal bite. The mugger roared again, snapped the stick like a dry leg-bone and lunged, but Mowgli scrabbled out of the water with the crocodile right behind him. Up the bank, Ludra, Ud, and the two remaining kits were disappearing into the holt, squealing in terror.

Mowgli threw himself into the burrow head-first, kicking and twisting to escape the snapping jaws behind him. The mugger was slower on land, just slow enough to let Mowgli's feet slide into the damp darkness ahead of his teeth. The long ugly snout shoved into the earth and then stopped—the opening was so narrow, he could go no farther and still open his jaws.

Now, an otter's burrow is narrow at the opening but wide at the end. It enters the earth, takes a sharp turn to the side, and then dips down to where the mud is cool and damp. Above the main tunnel are usually several smaller tunnels, with roomy dry compartments for relatives. Mowgli shoved himself as far into the earth as he could go, his shoulders and head bent almost down to his chest. Ahead of him, he heard Ludra trying to quiet a whimpering kit. The mugger gave a final furious bellow, and all outside the holt was suddenly still.

Mowgli waited an instant for his eyes to adjust to the blackness, hearing his heart pound in his throat. When he could breathe again, he whispered, "Are ye all here?"

Ud wailed mournfully, "Those of us who are left!"

Ludra, who had a more practical mother's heart, asked swiftly, "Are ye hurt, Little Brother?"

"Nay," Mowgli said, examining himself all over quickly. "But I do not know why. He has a most evil set of teeth."

"And now, they wait outside, all in a row!" Ud wailed again.

Ludra cuffed him to silence. "Be still!" she hissed. "There are others still to think of here." And she pulled the two remaining kits closer to her belly.

A loud growl suddenly came from outside the burrow, a rumbling threat which died off slowly to a hoarse cry. Mowgli stiffened, and every hair rose on the back of his arms.

"O ye brown *Bandar* who seeks refuge among my children!" the mugger called angrily. "Come forth! Come forth, or I dig ye out!"

Ludra whispered in the darkness, her shining eyes huge and round with terror, "The Tyrant of the Marsh calls ye, Little Brother! Jacala speaks!"

"I can hear him well enough," Mowgli muttered, "but I think he cannot shove his great jaws into the belly of the earth itself. Let him call."

There was a pause, as though the crocodile listened. He finally spoke again, his voice now more gentle. "Come out, manling, if that is what thou art. Indeed and yes, I know much of Man. Once, I was kept in the temple pond and fed by the holy Brahmins. They put honey and gold in my mouth with their own hands, and never did I offer to bite. Wouldst thou see the riches I carry in my jaws? Ay, I have swum the *Ganga Ma* [the Mother Ganges], and well I know of Man. Come out, manling, and we shall speak of great

kingdoms and rebirth and the Wheel of Life, as Man likes to do. Come out and meet Jacala."

Mowgli scowled fiercely and shouted back, "I have met thee once, O Scaled One, and my knife speaks with thee even now! Go, I tell thee! Go and leave us in peace!"

The crocodile growled angrily, and they could hear his huge webbed claws digging at the mouth of the burrow, digging with powerful strokes which made the roof of the holt shake and tremble.

"Perhaps ye should go and see what he wants," Ud said, casting his eyes about nervously. "Perhaps now he knows ye are Man, he will not—"

"Be still!" Ludra snapped. "Were it not for his Man's tooth, we would have no kits left at all!"

"And surely ye *shall* have none," Jacala bellowed hoarsely, "if I must come in and drag thee out! Send the manling to me!"

"O! O!" whimpered Ud, pulling himself into the smallest possible ball of fur in the back of the burrow. "He means killing, Jacala does!"

"As do I," Mowgli snarled, looking all about him with a cold rage. "Is there no other way out?"

Ludra nodded, pushing the kits into their father's arms. "There is, Little Brother, but thou couldst never get through it. It opens on the meadow above. We closed it off in the spring rains, but I could open it up, I think."

"Couldst thou push the kits and thyselves to safety?"

"Ay," she whispered, watching him intently, "if Jacala will give us time."

"Do it, then, whilst I hold him here."

"But what will ye do when he—?"

"Just do it," Mowgli said, "and quickly. Before he guesses what thou art at."

Ludra turned without another word and shoved her shoulders up to the topmost narrow part of the burrow. She wriggled and grunted and squirmed, digging silently with her front claws, until she had almost disappeared upwards into the earth. The dirt rained down on Mowgli; he heard Ud frantically herding the kits upwards after their mother, but his full attention was focused on the scrapings and clawings which came from the front of the burrow. Jacala was getting closer all the while.

"*Ohe,* Mugger," Mowgli called loudly to cover the sounds of the digging behind him, "there are a thousand fish in thy lake, plenty to fill thy jaws a hundred times over. Why dost thou stand and bellow for this small *Bandar?*"

"Thou art NOT a *Bandar,*" Jacala grunted, now pushing heavily at a boulder in his path. He shouldered it aside and moved further inside the holt, the edges crumbling down upon him. "Thou art Man! I hate Man to the marrow of my bones, and I will not suffer him to live!"

Mowgli glanced over his shoulder and saw that now the two kits had climbed up, mewing and wriggling, after their mother. Behind them, Ud nosed them desperately, his back legs straining for purchase.

"What has Man ever done to thee, O Jacala?" Mowgli called out again, trying to divert the monster from his determined digging. "Thou art lord of all these waters!"

"And I mean to *stay* so!" the mugger bellowed. With a final burst of rage, the crocodile poked his snout round the bend of the tunnel. He had worked himself far enough into the holt that though much of his body was still outside on the bank, his snapping teeth were less than a jaw's length from Mowgli's leg.

The boy whirled and saw Ud's tail disappearing through the upper tunnel. They were safe! He turned to face the monster before him.

Jacala's yellow eyes glinted in the darkness, and he growled, his voice like muffled thunder. "Ye have set my children against me, I see." A strange smile wrinkled his bony snout, a smile in which seven teeth still showed on the outside of his jaws. "Never mind. *Thou* art still for the taking. Though . . . a man is a very little thing in the belly of Jacala." He leered an ugly grin.

Mowgli had squeezed himself back as far as he could go, bent almost double at the waist in the narrow black passageway. He looked around frantically for a rock, a branch, any sort of weapon.

"We be of one blood, ye and I!" he said desperately. "Remember the Law!"

"Here, *I* am the Law!" the crocodile snorted, and then chuckled evilly. "And *thou* art one blood with none here!" He moved his head back and forth slowly, as Kaa did while he was following a deer track. Each nod widened the space around his jaws, as though the earth itself fell away before his might.

Baloo's voice drummed in Mowgli's head, and an old memory came to him swiftly. Long ago, the Bear had told him, "Use thy head and thy tongue, manling, for these are thy strongest weapons. Among the Jungle People, thou art weak and small—but thy tongue will stop even the tiger's charge. Think, man-cub . . . think and live!"

Think! he told himself in a fever, while the yellow eyes watched his every move. His tongue began to prattle of its own accord. "I am a guest here in thy waters, and soon I will be gone. But if I do not return to my jungle, there are many who will seek me hither, many who will come to thy lake—"

"Let them come," Jacala crooned, his grin wider still. "My belly has ample room for all."

"Let me go, then, O Mugger, and I will come no more!"

"Nay, nay, manling, that would never do," the crocodile said, opening his mouth an inch or two. Another few inches and he would be able to open it wide enough to grab Mowgli's leg. "Thou hast already fretted my children overmuch, I think. They will begin to think their lord no more to fear than the lizards in the sun. Always, does Man bring such disorder. Such"—and here, the great crocodile lunged forward with lightning speed to within inches of Mowgli's leg—"DISRESPECT!"

Jacala twisted his huge head sideways, the better to grasp Mowgli's ankle. The boy kicked and shrieked—and suddenly the mugger stopped, his eyes widened, and his jaws closed shut with a snap. He made as though to turn his head to look behind him, but of course, he could not turn.

Mowgli heard a noise as though a small dry branch had broken somewhere near, and Jacala flinched. Snap! again, and once more, the mugger winced. Now, Jacala tried to back out of the tunnel, but Ludra called desperately from right outside.

"Hold him, manling! Hold him fast! We whittle him down, we two!"

In a flash, Mowgli was on the mugger, his arms wrapped round his snout. Had he been ready with gaping jaws, Jacala would have had the advantage, but Mowgli moved too quickly for him to recover. The crocodile tried to wriggle free, but his shoulders were cramped by the earth. Meanwhile, the snap! snap! snap! went on, faster and faster.

"What—" Mowgli panted as he squeezed tightly, trying to hold the crocodile still, "—what are ye doing?"

"We—*snap!*—save—*snap!*—thee—*snap!*" Ludra called, her voice coming in jerky gasps interrupted by cracking noises.

"We—*snap!*—bite!" Ud added.

Jacala now began to thrash more wildly, pulling and pushing himself out of the earth. He tried to bellow, but with his jaws clamped shut, only a hoarse cry rumbled through the darkness. Snap! snap! snap! went on, louder and faster now, and the crocodile's eyes rolled back in yellow panic. Mowgli braced his feet against the walls of the burrow and pulled with all his might. He could not budge the crocodile, but at least, he stopped his thrashing for an instant—and all the while, snap! snap! snap!

Now, the mugger gave a final, convulsive heave, and erupted out of the burrow, Mowgli close behind him. Blinking in the sunlight, the boy scrabbled from the earth in time to see Jacala staggering to the water. His neck was bleeding badly on both sides, bitten nearly to the bone. He did not even try to catch Ludra or Ud, who had scampered to the top of the bank when he pulled forth, but only slid slowly into the lake and then sank like a stone beneath the surface. Mowgli ran to see. The blood bubbled up in an oily slick on the water, and Jacala did not rise again. Mowgli sat down cross-legged on the muddy bank and waited, Ludra and Ud at his side. After a few long moments, the minnows swirled through the blood, hunting for bits of Jacala's flesh. But the mugger was gone.

Ludra coughed and spat suddenly. "Phah! Jacala tastes of rotten fish and old snails!"

Mowgli fell back on the bank, hugging his knees with relief, while the otter kits swarmed over his chest, squealing and mewing with delight.

"Thou hast saved my life," Mowgli said to Ludra and Ud, rumpling their fur and relishing the feel of the sun on his shoulders. He felt like rolling in the mud for the sheer joy of it.

"Against we two, Jacala can never stand!" Ud crowed in triumph. "For we fear nothing!"

Ludra chuckled low as she pulled the kits off the boy. "Against we two, Jacala stood well enough. But against Man's hands, nothing can stand. Not even the Tyrant of the Marsh. And now, whither wilt thou go?" she asked, glancing at Mowgli.

Ud frowned in confusion. "He will not go!" the otter cried, and the two kits took up the chorus.

But Mowgli remembered with a swift sure knowledge that he was wishing for nothing else but escape when the mugger's snout was reaching for his leg—escape from what had at first seemed a paradise. For here in the marsh, where life was effortless compared to the jungle, one paid the price with fear.

"I shall go back to my own places," he said, standing suddenly. "And now is as good a time as any other."

"But why?" lamented Ud loudly. "We have many more games to play!"

But Mowgli looked at Ludra, who only smiled gently. "And that is well enough," he said, returning her smile. "But ye can play them without another frog in thy pond." He turned and walked up the bank. When he looked back, the otters had hurled themselves into the water and were in a mock-frenzy over a notched stick, battling for its possession as though it were the only one for miles.

He went back to take his leave of Garuda, the Sojourner, for that was the courteous thing to do. He found the old crane still under his sacred bo tree, and he looked up as Mowgli approached, his beady eye wise and quiet.

"So. Thou hast returned. I see thy flesh is whole. Is thy heart?"

When Mowgli said nothing, the bird continued, his eyes up to the sky in thought. "Hast thou heard about the cuckoo, *chela*?" he asked softly.

Mowgli sat before him cross-legged and shook his head.

"The pied-crested cuckoo is a clever soul," he said slowly—and then with a wink, "much like Man. He deposits his eggs in the nest of the babbler and then flies far away to fill his crop with the season's best. Meanwhile, the babbler feeds and cares for the cuckoo hatchling, starving even his own chicks to fill that strange and wonderful beak. And when the cuckoo gets larger and stronger than his nest-brothers, he pitches them to the ground to die." The crane cocked his head and eyed the boy curiously.

"I have heard this one before," Mowgli said quietly.

"And do ye know how it ends?" the crane asked gently.

"Ay," Mowgli scowled, catching a glimpse of the crane's trail. "The cuckoo feeds off the babbler from season to season, and the babbler builds no more nests. What is thy point?"

"I think ye see it, *chela*. Thou art like the cuckoo nestling, eh? For the jungle has reared thee, ay, even to its own destruction. But Fate is all. And like the cuckoo, ye will fly to thine own in time."

"Many have told me this before, Sojourner. I have been to the villages of Man, and I have come back again to the jungle. Ye say that Fate is all—and yet, no one knows what will happen by chance. If thy gods knew where the tiger would strike next, then he must strike there and then, eh? And the deer would be struck down, no matter what he would do. But yet, the deer sometimes twists and breaks free, chance *does* walk the jungle, and all know it to be true." He gestured with his hands, as he was wont to do. "There are, therefore, no gods which know all which will happen, no Fate which puts my feet on this trail or that, and *none* can say what I may or may not do!" His voice had grown more commanding as he reasoned it out, and finally, he stared back at the crane in open defiance, for he was weary with this talk which he had heard so many times before.

"There indeed speaks Man," the crane said softly. "For only Man believes that the mould of his fortune lies in his own hands."

Mowgli stood impatiently and dusted off his legs. "Well, and I shall leave thee to thy gods, O Garuda," he said with a distant politeness. "Thy kingdom is fine, to be sure, but I belong to another place."

"Now, thou speakest a truth indeed," the Sojourner said.

Mowgli walked away, leaving the crane under the shade of his bo tree. As he left the Place of Low Waters, a vast flock of chattering parrots flew overhead, dipping and crying with crazy abandon, fighting to roost all on one limb so that half fell fluttering to lower branches.

Mowgli shook his head. "When the masters are mad," he muttered to himself, "what shall the servants do? It is time to turn back to familiar trails . . . where at least the madness runs on four good legs!"

This is one of the songs which Mowgli heard the otters sing.
There were many more, of course, but this one was his favourite.

Here we go in a daring dive,
Faster than any fish alive!
Hands as clever as Man have we,
This is so and we all agree!
Let the others lament their woe,
Sweat and starve and run to and fro,
The water's cool and the day is long,
Come, let us sing the Otter Song!

Will aught we do halt the waterfall?
Will worry hurry the season's crawl?
Will River heed what we do or say?
No! And so we might as well play!
The mud is slick on the water slide,
Here, I'll go down with you astride,
Catch my tail, and I'll do the same,
Come, let us play the Otter Game!

THE GHOST TIGER

O eyes of night that loom so bright,
Where few can see to flee.
O fangs so swift, the killing gift
I bring relentlessly.
There's none to stay my dark foray
For loosed till dawn am I.
These reddened claws, these sovereign jaws,
Deem who shall live or die.

Nightsong of the Tiger

The Rains came and went again, and the jungle went forward, as all things must. Mowgli returned to his old trails to tell Bagheera and Baloo of his visit to the Sojourner. When he spoke of the killing of Jacala, however, Baloo shook his head sadly. The Bear was almost deaf and certainly blind in one eye, so Mowgli sat at his knee, that his old teacher might share in the tale.

"Why dost thou turn down thy mouth?" Mowgli asked. "Wouldst thou have Jacala kill and kill again? He was the Tyrant of the Marsh, and now his bones feed the minnows." He glanced at Bagheera, but the big cat was looking off into the jungle, his thoughts in another place, as they often were these days.

Baloo leaned back heavily and snuffed the wind. "Soon, there will be no more minnows to feed on those bones," he said quietly, "or on any others. For with Jacala gone, the otters will fill the Low Waters with more young mouths than he had teeth. He was their tyrant, ay, but he was also their god."

"Paugh!" Mowgli snorted impatiently. "More talk of gods. Thou and Garuda could while away many a moon, ye two old heads, untangling such cobwebs. There was a killing to be done, and I did it."

Bagheera swung his head back round. "So ye have said. And since it is so, let us speak of other things. Ye remember the letting in of the jungle, when ye gave a Master Word to Hathi?"

Mowgli thought for an instant. Well he recalled the time, two Rains past, when he had called upon the elephant and his sons to destroy the village, that the Man-Pack would go elsewhere.

If you have read the other Mowgli stories, you will remember that he saved Messua and her husband from the villagers—villagers who would have burned the pair for having given refuge to a "jungle devil child"—and then in a fury of cold despair, the boy sent the beasts in to trample the fields. When the ground was churned under their hooves and the villagers had fled, Mowgli then asked Hathi and his sons to tear down the very walls. Now, where once a village stood, the jungle grass grew tall and rank.

"I remember," Mowgli said. "I reminded him of the Sack of the Fields of Bhurtpore, and at such a word, he came and the walls tumbled."

"At *thy* word," Bagheera said. "Now, it is in my stomach that he needs that favour back again."

"This is not Good Hunting," Baloo rumbled darkly. "Ye speak not of killing but of war. Let each take care of his own, as we have always done. There is a time for this and for that, and the Law says—"

"—Much that is good and seemly," Bagheera interrupted smoothly. "But the Law says nothing of debts owed and paid, eh? Yet these things are among us since Man came to the jungle."

Mowgli scowled. "Ye chatter over my head like a flock of rooks. If there is something I needs must know, tell it quickly."

Bagheera appraised the boy keenly. "By the Broken Lock that freed me, thou art all of a man."

"Thou hast told me. Now, what of Hathi and a killing?"

Baloo struggled to his feet, his old bones groaning and creaking. "If thou wilt no longer heed this old head, I shall take it elsewhere. But I ask a favour, Little Brother"—and with a dark glance at Bagheera—"not a killing favour, as some may."

"Ask, and it is thine," Mowgli said gently, for over all, he loved the old Bear.

"Kill, if thou must, but only for thyself. To lift thy knife for what some may call justice, is the way of Man. There is no 'justice' in the jungle, at least not by Man's reckoning. The Law says that each pack looks to its own. The tiger does not kill, that the jackal may feed."

"And yet," Mowgli said, "am I not brother to many in the jungle? Ye said not a word when I lifted my knife against the Red Dogs for the good of the Pack. Or when I brought Badur and his brethren against the Gonds. Why should I not do the same for Hathi and his tribe?"

"I have asked my favour," the Bear said.

"But ye have told me, again and again, I am one blood with so many, and Hathi taught me my first Master Word."

"I have asked my favour," the Bear repeated patiently.

Mowgli sighed hugely. "And so, I grant it. But indeed and truly, I do not understand."

"As always," the Bear said gently, "it is not necessary that ye understand. It is only necessary that ye obey." And he turned and disappeared into the forest.

"So what is this killing ye speak of?" Mowgli asked Bagheera finally.

"Already, it has started," the Black Panther replied. "Twice and thrice in as many nights have three young calves been taken from Hathi's herd. Almost right out from under the feet of their dams. In the morning light, there are only a few tracks . . . and a few drops of elephant blood."

Mowgli held his breath, for he guessed the answer even as he asked the next question. "What sort of tracks?"

Bagheera stretched out one paw, and steel-blue claws leaped into the light. "Tiger. A large rogue, by every best guess."

Mowgli frowned and thought quickly. He knew, as every creature in the jungle knew, that tigers do not stray far from their own piece of the forest. They do not hunt in packs, as does the wolf; nor in mated pairs, as the lion or the leopard sometimes will. Alone, they stalk the night; alone, they take down the unwary, and until they are killed or driven away, they are masters of whatever jungle they roam. This rogue had been driven hither, no doubt, by a female who would not share her territory, for only another tiger—or Man—could drive out the most dangerous killer in the jungle. There would be no peace for the hunting folk, nor, indeed, for any Jungle People, while the tiger was among them.

"How could he take the calves from within the safety of the herd?" Mowgli asked. "Never have I heard such a thing."

"Nor have I," Bagheera said thoughtfully. "They have named him the Ghost Tiger, and all the jungle whispers in fear now when night falls."

Mowgli picked up a stone and began turning it over and over in his hands. "And Hathi has called for me?"

"Hathi calls for no one," Bagheera said. "Ye know as much."

Mowgli picked up another stone and struck it against the first one, sharpening the end to a fine cutting edge. He struck it again and again, turning it expertly until he had made himself a weapon. He held the new knife up in the sun so that it flashed like a sudden fire. Bagheera put his ears back flat to his head. "And no one has seen this Ghost Tiger?" Mowgli asked, testing the blade of stone against his thumb.

"Three," the panther said quietly. "Calves all. And his secret died with them."

Mowgli stood and rubbed the blade against the palm tree, dulling the hub that he might hold it easily. "Where is Hathi now?"

"The herd rests by the White Caves, for the wild cardamom is in fruit there," Bagheera said, rising slowly. He shook himself all over as if ridding his flanks of an old, bad memory. "Come. I shall take thee." He turned fluidly and bounded out to the trail. Then he stopped and looked back at the boy, as if momentarily doubtful of what he had begun. "Truly, thou dost not *need* to come. Hathi does not expect it."

Mowgli shrugged and followed him. "Well, and I would see these tracks, at any rate. A Ghost Tiger! More jungle mouthings and moonbeams, I am thinking."

Hathi had brought his herd to a wide place by the river to browse the ripe fruit trees. The white beach spread out on both sides of the water, far up the bank before the jungle scrub began. On one side of the river, the caverns which those in the jungle called the White Caves pocked the hillside. They were formed of solid white basalt, their crevices and spires glistening in the sun like dusky snow. It was said that at one time, the river rose higher than the trees, plunging and bucking past the hillside, carving out the narrow caves. Now, the water was low and narrow between the sandy beaches, and the abandoned basalt spires stood like sentries before the cool labyrinth of caverns.

Mowgli and Bagheera found the herd grazing in the trees, plucking the cardamoms from the branches. Hathi stood off to one side, flanked by his sons. An old memory tugged at Mowgli's heart as he remembered the first time he had come to the elephants to learn the ways of the jungle. He grinned.

"He is older," he murmured to Bagheera.

"So are we all," the panther said. Bagheera stayed back within the shelter of the bamboo, for even at this distance, the elephant mothers eyed him warily. They knew that he would never attack in broad daylight; knew, too, that the panther preferred other game; and guessed, finally, that the presence of the boy with him guaranteed his harmlessness. Yet, there were half a dozen small calves darting to and fro, running between the legs of their elders, squealing in play—and so, the mothers kept their bodies between Bagheera and their young ones, watching his every move.

Hathi lifted his trunk in salute when he spied Mowgli, beckoning to him. "Bring thy friend forward as well," he called.

Bagheera rose from the shade of the thicket, following Mowgli to where Hathi waited. The herd parted before the great cat in a wide swath, and he walked forward slowly, looking neither to the left nor to the right.

"Good Hunting, O Hathi," Bagheera said courteously, his voice a low rumble.

"Good Hunting," Hathi replied. "Thou wilt forgive, I hope, my people's silence. These have been hard nights." He turned to Mowgli with an appraising smile. "And so, ye come at last, Little Frog. Grown near to my tusk, art thou, and twice as wide. The tales of thee have run before thy shadow, ay, even to these old ears."

"Tales of thee run to my ears as well, O Hathi," Mowgli said.

"And ye have come to see if what thou hast heard is true?" the elephant asked. Hathi's sons began to sway nervously, but the old leader stood still as stone.

"Ay," Mowgli said softly, glancing at Bagheera, who said nothing. "For I have heard another name, one which I do not understand. What is this Ghost Tiger, O Largest of My Brothers?"

Hathi's trunk stiffened. "There is no such thing. 'Tis only the frightened chatter of the mothers. There is a tiger, ay, and he has taken three calves in as many nights. But he will take no more."

"Why do they call him the Ghost Tiger?"

"Because they have not seen him."

"Surely, *someone* has seen him," Mowgli said, and his voice betrayed a bit of youthful scorn. "A tiger cannot come and go without a single bird, a single winged thing giving the alarm, eh?"

Bagheera interrupted him smoothly, his eyes half-lidded. "Ye say he will take no more, Hathi?"

"I say it," the elephant said, his eyes somber.

Mowgli thought for a moment silently. Finally he asked, "Wilt thou show me the tracks?"

"There are none," Hathi said. "The beach sand is soft and the dew smoothes them. By the time the sun is high, there is no sign at all." He shuffled restlessly. "And what is this to thee, Little Frog? And to thee, Bagheera? We will keep watch, my people and I."

"Listen now," Mowgli said softly. "Once, there was a wolf, my mother, and a wolf, my father, and an old elephant who was my brother. He is perhaps deaf and near blind, but not so ancient he cannot recall that it is I, Mowgli, who brought Shere Khan's skin to the Council Rock. No Striped One shall kill in my jungle, nay, not among *my* brethren shall he steal in the night. Ye say he shall come no more. Well, and here is another tooth to stand beside thine." He took the new knife, keen and flashing as a wet trout, and flung it into the sand where it stuck, quivering like a live thing. He smiled up at the elephant. "By thy leave, O Hathi."

Hathi glanced over to the herd. Several of the old aunties, elephant cows who helped look after the young ones, watched and listened carefully. One ancient mother took a trunkful of dust and squirted a calf's shoulders tenderly, as though to remind the leader what was at risk should their vigil fail.

Hathi sighed hugely. "Thou art welcome, of course," he said at last. "Though what ye can do that we cannot, I do not know. Bagheera, I must ask thee to stay well back from those who would fear thee."

The great cat nodded solemnly. "This is the boy's hunt. It matters not to me if one or a dozen tigers stalk these woods."

Mowgli glanced at Bagheera curiously, for in fact, the cat had brought him here, but the adventure ahead swept his mind of caution, and he took his leave of Hathi, already planning where he would ambush the stalking tiger when night came.

As dusk fell, the herd gathered closer and closer to the river. In another time, the elephants would have splashed happily together, hosing each other's backs and rolling in the cool water. Now, two large males stood sentry at the edge of the forest, watching the shadows of the thicket carefully. Once, when Bagheera strode quietly out of the trees, a guard sounded a startled alarm,

and two mothers almost trampled each other, trying to snatch their calves out of the shallows to safety before they saw the panther's black hide and subsided, muttering nervously.

In another time, too, the herd would have spread out on the grassy bank to rest, each elephant finding his own place to roll and sprawl or stand and sway, with little fear of what might approach in the night. Now, Hathi and his sons stood at the top of the bank, facing the forest in a half-ring. Behind them stood a line of nervous aunties, their trunks shifting back and forth, scenting the night wind. Down the beach, closer to the water, the mothers with calves lay quietly—and behind them, within inches of the river and buffered by layers of sentry elephants, sprawled the sleeping calves.

Mowgli lay along the length of a thick branch, low in a paw-paw tree. Above him, Bagheera rested his chin on his paws, his black tail dropped down among the leaves.

"Surely," Mowgli said, "no tiger, ghost or otherwise, can sneak through that line of guards. Nothing can come out of that brush without being spotted. Hathi says the first calf was taken unawares, while its mother browsed apart. This, I can understand. The second calf was stolen off the grassy bank—and the third . . . well, and I do *not* understand how the Striped One took a third calf at all. And no one saw him?"

Bagheera yawned hugely. "Uhmnn. So they say."

"Hathi could move the herd elsewhere."

"And well he might. But there are those among them who mutter that another should lead, and if he cannot rid them of this killer, those voices will grow more strong."

Mowgli thought this over for a moment, watching the sky. "'Twill be a dark moon tonight. A night for Good Hunting. Yet, if this tiger has taken three calves in three nights, he surely will not feed again so soon."

"A tiger of flesh and bone would not, if he hunts for his belly alone. But a Ghost Tiger. . . ?"

Mowgli chuckled lightly, turning over on his branch as if to dismiss such an idea. But in his heart, he felt a quiver of quiet fear, for somewhere out in the gathering darkness was a killer which he did not understand. And what he did not understand, he could not accept, he could not let alone . . . he could not let live.

The night grew deeper and darker, and the rustlings, shiftings, and stumblings from the herd ceased. Mowgli could see an occasional white eye flash as the guards continued to watch the woods. A dark form moved slowly from one vantage point to another, as the sentries shifted position, murmuring to each other. Behind them, the aunties stood, some already dozing on their feet, a few still alert. And on the ground, in the last line farthest from the trees, the mothers lay with the calves. A trunk lifted now and again from their ranks, testing the air, but all was still.

The hours of the night crept by, and now the only sound was the flow of the river; the only light came from the distant stars. Mowgli's eyes closed once, twice, and he jerked himself awake again, tensing first one leg, then another, to keep from falling asleep. Above him, he heard Bagheera shifting as well, and he knew the cat watched the scrub at the top of the beach, waiting for the intruder to come.

Bagheera sniffed the air cautiously and whispered, "Nothing moves."

Mowgli gazed across the river at the white basalt hills, at the huge boulders which marked the entrance to the caverns. "Hast thou ever been inside the caves?" he whispered lazily. "Perhaps, when we have killed this Striped One, we might see what lies within, eh?"

The panther sniffed. "*Thou* mayest walk the belly of the earth, if ye like. Bagheera need not go where Badur and the Poison People lair."

But Mowgli stopped him with a quiet hiss, his eyes wide. "Something moves. Over against the hills." And he rose slowly up on his elbow to see more clearly.

He stared into the darkness, squinting. Bagheera was silent as stone above him. Across the river, against the white rocks, Mowgli thought he saw a movement, ever so slight, a shifting of light and shadow—a sliding of white. And now, it was gone.

"Didst thou see it?" the boy whispered, for Bagheera's eyes were much better than his own in darkness.

"By the Broken Lock that freed me," the panther murmured, "in all my seasons, I have never seen—"

"What?" Mowgli hissed. "What do ye see?" And then, he saw the movement again, this time on the beach leading down to the river. Something crept silently into the water, crouched low, and began to swim towards the sleeping calves.

Mowgli slid quickly down the branch. When he hit the ground, Bagheera landed quietly beside him. "Do not shout the alarm," the cat whispered. "'Twill do no good to scare him off if we do not kill him as well." The two moved swiftly through the sentries, slipping between their ranks like two shadows. One guard bleated a startled snort, and then saw it was only the boy and the cat and resumed his watch, facing the woods.

Mowgli and the panther reached the edge of the river, up from the sleeping herd, just in time to see a large head slide up out of the water and into the shadows. A calf lay just feet from the river, his mother dozing nearby.

Bagheera hissed and flattened himself to the ground. The head moved closer, and Mowgli could see clearly, now that the killer was silhouetted against the darker water: A white tiger, white as the sands themselves, crept up the beach.

Mowgli shouted an alarm, snatched his knife aloft, and raced among the startled elephants. Mothers leaped to their feet; calves bleated in alarm; sentries snorted and whirled to the attack; and in the confusion, the tiger grabbed the nearest calf round the throat, throttling its cry in a smothered gurgle. The huge killer was back in the water before the calf's mother could scarcely react, but she threw herself in the river, trumpeting in rage.

The tiger wasted no time with stealth but thrashed through the shallow river, carrying the struggling calf easily in his jaws. Now, against the blacker river they could see him clearly—a huge male, over ten feet in length, sheer white with pale shadows of stripes, white as his fangs, white as death.

He leaped gracefully to the other side, holding the now-limp calf out of the water. He stood and watched the herd for an instant, as if daring someone to follow. The sentries trumpeted wildly, and Mowgli could hear Hathi calling for order over the chaos, but only the wailing mother followed the tiger into the river. When he saw that she would keep coming he turned, snarled a threat, and bounded up the beach. Against the sand, he was almost invisible; only the calf in his jaws made his progress apparent. In a moment, he had disappeared into the white caves like a flowing phantom. Mowgli blinked. He could scarcely tell which cavern hid him, they looked so alike and he so a part of them all.

Bagheera appeared now at the boy's side, a slinking shadow. "Hathi was wrong," he said quietly. "There *is* such a thing. And this Ghost Tiger has struck again, for all his sentries."

Mowgli bared his teeth in an angry grimace, for the hair was standing up on the back of his neck, and he hated such a feeling. "Never have I seen such a tiger," he said finally, his voice still quivering with sorrow and rage.

"Nor have I," Bagheera said. "But when I was in the cages at the king's palace at Oodeypore, I heard the men talk of the White Ones—one or two only, had they seen—which sometimes stalked the higher mountains. This Ghost Tiger is far from his forest."

Mowgli ran his hand down the panther's back to smooth it, for the hair along his spine was all raised, his tail stiff and full as the bottlebrush. The boy knew that if it came down to a killing fight between the two cats, the panther would surely die, and badly, for the tiger was larger, stronger, and carried fewer years in his jaws. "It is not a Ghost Tiger," he said firmly, turning to go to Hathi. "It is but a Striped One with a bleached hide, and it is in my stomach that I know a little of Striped Ones. This one will bleed and die, just like Shere Khan, or I shall leave these trails, for he and I cannot share the jungle."

Bagheera followed Mowgli up the bank silently, his tail lashing, switch-switch, switch-switch. Neither boy nor cat had to say it, but it was so: Just as Mowgli could not suffer the tiger to live, neither could the panther, for only one could be master hunter in the jungle.

Hathi and the sentries stood to one side, their heads together, discussing this new raid. The elephant aunties clustered in a tight knot, shocked and silent, gazing across the river towards the caves. Only the grieving mother echoed her lament over and over, lashing at the grass, the sand, the water itself in her rage and sorrow, as though even the jungle had betrayed her.

Mowgli stepped under Hathi's trunk and waited until all eyes turned towards him.

"So. Now, we know," he said quietly. "Wilt thou take the herd to other places? For certainly, the white *billi* [Mowgli used the word for cat, with a scornful twisting of his mouth] shall come again and again."

"And if we do?" one of Hathi's sons snorted. "He has the taste of our young in his mouth now. He will follow until he is sated."

"Or he is killed," Bagheera said from behind the group. The elephants' ears pricked in his direction. "Ye could lay a trap for him."

"What sort of trap?" an auntie called loudly, anguish in her voice. "And baited with what flesh? We have but a few calves left!" The females huddled together, and all eyes turned now to Hathi.

"Bagheera is right," Mowgli said. "We could dig a trap as the Gonds use, a large hole filled with pointed sticks, and drive him forward to his death."

"And who will do this driving, Little Brother?" Hathi asked solemnly. "There are no cattle here to do thy bidding." All the jungle knew how Mowgli had herded Gaur and his brethren to trample Shere Khan, and some had whispered that it was a man's trick to turn one beast against the other.

Mowgli thought for a moment. "We could starve him out. He cannot stay within the caves forever. Station thy sentries at the cavern's mouth to keep him from water and the hunt. When he finally comes forth, weakened with hunger, I shall kill him myself." And he raised his knife in a slashing gesture of triumph.

"There are others here also who may strike a blow or two in such a battle," Bagheera said, showing his fangs.

Hathi glanced around the circle of listening elephants and saw hope on a few faces. "Ay," he said finally, "this plan could work. The fruit hangs heavy in the trees and the grass is good, enough for seven suns or more. The herd could mount such a vigil." He raised his trunk and lifted his voice over the heads of the sentries. "What say ye to such a hunt, eh?"

Mowgli gaped in astonishment. Never before had he seen the old leader ask his charges what they thought of this or that command. Always before, he gave the word, and they followed. Such questions would have been considered a sign of weakness in the Pack. But the she-elephants responded with one voice, trumpeting with fury all together, "We say, AY!"

The night was still long ahead, but having decided, Hathi would not wait for the light. He led the herd across the river, the sleepy calves trundling alongside the restless mothers. Few elephants spoke now that a plan of battle was at hand. When they reached the mouth of the white caves, the she-elephants could scarcely be stopped from rushing to the front of the sentries to roll boulders and trumpet a challenge to the killer within.

Mowgli and Bagheera crouched down among the rocks and waited. Now that the herd was in place, the guards facing the cavern's black holes, their tusks at the ready, Mowgli felt the futility of their plan. "'Twill be a long watching," he said impatiently. "Doubtless, he has water within the caves, else the herd would have seen him drink at midday. After four calves in as many nights, he will not feed again soon."

"Perhaps," Bagheera said thoughtfully. "Perhaps not. But thou said as much before he took the fourth, remember. It is in my belly that this is no ordinary tiger. Thou couldst hurry his fate, whatever it shall be."

"How?" Mowgli asked, glancing at the panther quickly.

"Call to him. Thy voice alone may bring him forth to thy knife."

"And if it does not?"

Bagheera shrugged. "His belly will plague him sooner or later, whether he knows ye wait or not."

Mowgli could not read Bagheera's eyes, for they were closed to half-slits as the cat mulled their position. For a swift half-second, he wondered that they had come so far together. There was a time, long ago, when Bagheera fought to protect a small man-cub and gave his all to keep him from danger. Now, this same Bagheera told this same cub to call out the tiger to his knife. *Ah mai!*, Mowgli sighed to himself. Such it is when the seasons pass, and we all grow older. I am a cub no more, but Master of the Jungle, and Bagheera . . . Bagheera looks now to *me*. A boy grows to manhood and his father grows from man back to boyhood, he thought, and they each know a secret sorrow for that which has passed. So it is in the Man-Pack, and so, even a little, is it here in the jungle.

But then his attention was drawn abruptly back to the mouth of the cave, for a strange, deep-throated chuckling came from within. It was the sobbing, snarling, singsong whine of the tiger, a sound full of insult and defiance.

"*Howahii!*" the beast called out into the darkness. "*Ohe,* thou great gray pigs, ye have come at last, with wet bellies and dripping trunks, to sit at my feet!"

The tiger's voice rumbled and echoed out of the caverns, around the white basalt spires, and out into the night, filled with power and malice. Bagheera growled deep in his throat, every hair on edge. Instinctively, he looked over his shoulder, for the tiger's whine seemed to come from all directions, bouncing off this stone and another. Mowgli clutched his knife and stood up, facing the caves.

Hathi silenced the outrage of the she-elephants with a scowl. He lifted his trunk and called to the tiger within. "We have come not to sit at thy feet but to trample thee beneath our own." His voice was quiet but steady. "The days shall be long and the nights longer, and thou shalt die with an empty belly. On this, ye have my word, O ye bleached and sneaking jackal!"

Once more, the tiger's chuckle shivered through the silence. "Hathi's word. The windy word of a wrinkled bullock, yoked to a beggar's brat!"

Mowgli's eyes widened in amazement. To kill was one thing; to hurl insults was another injury altogether, and rarely practised among the hunting folk.

The tiger went on, "Bring him forward! For I know he is among thee! Come out, ye naked, thieving, cowardly MAN!"

Mowgli's eyes flashed with a cold rage, and he walked out among the elephants, out to a clearing of stone before the caves, and he faced the blackness and the killer's snarl. For he suddenly knew that the white tiger had wanted *him* all along. And he wanted him within the cave walls.

"I am here," Mowgli said, his voice as ominous as the tiger's. "I await thee, thou white worm."

The tiger's voice descended to a loud purring rumble. "Ahh. I thought thou wouldst come. I await thy pleasure, O Master of All Things. Man cannot keep his muzzle out of the business of others."

"Any business of Hathi's is mine own," Mowgli said. "For we are brothers."

The tiger chuckled again, his voice rising in a painful whine. "Brothers! Ye are brother to nothing, ye false whelpling, not man nor beast! My father should have killed ye when he had thee between his paws!"

Now, Mowgli's own scalp lifted with a prickling cold fear, and he glanced back at Bagheera, whose eyes were green and hard as jade.

In the startled silence, the tiger shouted out of the blackness, "*Now,* ye know whose vengeance ye face! It is I, Shere Safed [White Tiger], son of Shere Khan, whose skin ye stole, come to seek my father's killer! It has been many seasons, but not so many that *I* have forgotten, whelpling!"

Mowgli started at a touch on his shoulder. He turned to face Hathi behind him. "Now, it is clear," the elephant said. "He has taken our calves only to lure thee hither. We shall leave this place and go to another, and thou wilt go back to thine own trails, Little Brother. Leave this Ghost Tiger to his madness, for ye cannot fight him alone. He is riddled with sorrow and rage, and the stuff of life is out of him. This is why he is white, I am thinking."

The boy shook his head. "He is white because he is white, and for no other reason than that which makes one *Bandar*'s tail longer than another's. It is all one. But because he kills for vengeance and not for food, he will not let this lie. He means a killing, whether here or in another place. He has brought me hither, for he feels safe on his own grounds, against the whiteness of the rocks and the caves. But I am not alone." He turned to Bagheera, who padded silently to his side.

"Canst thou hold him here?" Mowgli asked his brethren, one hand on the panther's hide, another wrapped round Hathi's trunk. "If thou canst hold him, I shall kill him when I return."

"Ahhiii!" screamed the tiger from the caves. "Bring him forward, thou stupid cattle, or I shall take another of thy piglets every night I am kept waiting!"

"Whither do ye run?" Bagheera asked as Mowgli whirled back across the river.

"To the Man-village!" Mowgli called back over his shoulder. "Hold him, my brothers!"

Mowgli ran hot-foot to the nearest village and crept among the sleeping huts until he found one which held what he sought. A soft gleam came from the thatched window, as he knelt and peered inside. Over in the corner, a fire-pot cradled hot coals. Two huddled bundles, a man and a woman, slept on the string hammocks against the walls.

If you have read the other Mowgli stories, you will remember that the boy had used the Red Flower, what the Jungle People called fire, on the night he was driven from the Seeonee Pack. Shere Khan had led a rebellion among the younger wolves, demanding that Mowgli be given to him. Mowgli left then, to hunt alone, but not before he had beaten the great tiger over the head with a flaming branch, leaving him burnt and whimpering. The boy had learned the power of fire and the fear all jungle folk had for the flames, and he had not forgotten that lesson.

Now, he slid over the edge of the window as silently as night fog, eased the fire-pot off its hook on the wall, and carried it outside the hut. The man and woman had not stirred. He hurried into the brush and opened the lid of the glowing pot. Inside, the hot embers smoked and winked. He dropped some dried grass inside, murmuring, "Feed, then, O Fire, until I need thee. For thou must be strong enough to singe another *billi* for me."

By the time Mowgli reached the White Caves again, it was nearly dawn. The herd was still gathered before the caverns, and from within, the tiger howled and snarled and called out his madness, so that even the morning peacocks had been frightened into silence. A pack of jackals had gathered nearby, for they scented coming death like sharks. They fawned at the elephants' feet, grinning and wagging their tails. Bagheera bounded to meet Mowgli, sniffing warily at the hot pot in his hands.

"I thought as much," the panther said quietly. "But how will the Red Flower drive forth the Ghost Tiger? Ye will have to get behind him to force him out into the light."

"I do not mean to force him out into the light," Mowgli said. "I mean to take the light to him. Wilt thou come?"

Bagheera stiffened, his ears flat to his head. "Ye mean to kill him *inside?* In the belly of the earth?"

For the first time in many seasons, Mowgli saw the flashing glimmer of fear in the big cat's eyes: they widened, yellow-green and pale, with small black pupils of doubt. He put the fire-pot down and took Bagheera's head in both his hands, pulling his nose close and murmuring gently, "Not in the belly, my brother, only a little way down its throat, eh? But never mind. Thou canst guard the outside, lest he slip by me in the dark. There is likely not room for both of us down there, anyway."

But Bagheera saw that Mowgli was trying to spare him, and he turned away in shame. "Forgive, Little Brother," he whispered, "for Baloo was right. I brought thee here, to kill for others. And for myself as well."

Mowgli shook his head. "I know this. It is all one."

"Nay, it is not," Bagheera murmured quietly. "I am made foolish and timid before thy courage. Thou art of the jungle and *not* of the jungle, and I have not thy heart. Yet, I love thee and will follow thee, ay, even unto death."

Mowgli's eyes watered and his throat ached to see the panther's shame, and he stroked the black head softly, murmuring, "It is nothing, it is nothing. We shall speak no more of it again."

Together, the boy and the panther shouldered their way through the crowd of elephants until they stood before the White Caves. Mowgli bent and cut a stout branch, thrusting it deep into the fire-pot. When it had begun to flame, he held it over his head, peering inside the caverns.

From within, the roars of the tiger grew more angry, for he sensed that Mowgli was near. "Once a night, I shall take a piglet! Until there are no more at all! Then, I shall harry the fat sows until their dugs shrivel and die within them. If ye move, I shall follow! Ahaiee! Ye cannot hide! Ye cannot escape—until I kill the man, ye shall know no peace!"

Hathi called to Mowgli quietly, "He speaks for thine ears only,

Brother. We can go to another place and guard our own. Ye need not go to him for our sake."

"I go for my own," Mowgli said, remembering the warning words of Baloo, and he turned and walked inside the caves.

The white basalt spires had begun to catch the first rays of the sun, and they gleamed and flashed as Mowgli walked around them. Inside, the shadows were deep and cool. The tiger's chuckling echoed around his head, bouncing up and across the broad ceiling of the cavern, a ceiling jagged with white-columned stalactites. Water dripped slowly at Mowgli's feet, and he heard Bagheera sneeze behind him.

"These are the earth's very jaws," Bagheera muttered, half to himself, half to Mowgli, "for look! There are teeth above us."

They walked deeper into the caves, and Mowgli held the flaming torch above them both, led forward by the snarls and whines of Shere Safed. "Ah, they come, they come!" he called mockingly. "The beggar's brat and his old wheezing shadow, come to pull the whiskers of death, itself."

The shadows were blacker and larger now, away from the sunlight, dancing ahead of the flickering torch like a thousand night demons on the white walls about them. They stepped cautiously over the still body of an elephant calf, scarcely marked. Further on, they found another, only lightly torn.

"This *billi* is wiser than his father," Mowgli whispered to Bagheera, "for he does not feed before his battles. A long moon we would have waited for him out on the sands."

Suddenly, the caverns were silent. After the constant crooning and roaring of the tiger which drew them forward, the quiet was almost suffocating. Mowgli tensed, his hand on his knife; behind him, Bagheera hissed and flattened to the ground.

Now, the tiger spoke, and his snarl seemed to come from a point right at Mowgli's back. "Turn, ye brown grubling. Turn and face my vengeance!"

Mowgli whirled and saw Shere Safed perched on a near mound of boulders. So white was he that he seemed at first another cave formation. His blue eyes shone like two stars in the gleam of the torch.

"Come, then," Mowgli said quietly. He stuck the torch between two rocks so its light filled the cavern and held his knife aloft. "Come down and meet thy father's fate."

The tiger leaped to another boulder, nearer now, a white wraith, his eyes on Mowgli's weapon. Again, he chuckled evilly. "A mighty tooth, bratling. Almost as big as these—!" and he opened his jaws and roared, his fangs flashing menacingly.

Mowgli whispered to Bagheera, "Jump up, Brother, onto a boulder, lest he fall on us both from on high!" Bagheera whirled like smoke and leaped atop a high formation, his ears flattened to his head.

"Stay where thou art!" the tiger snarled at the panther. "This is not thy battle! When I kill the man, thou mayest go back to thine own place, and I shall leave thee master. But if ye intrude, I shall rip thy throat from end to end!"

Bagheera's claws slipped on the wet stone, and he spat in anger. "His war is mine, O ye white whining cur, mine to me! Fall on him, and I fall on *thee!*"

The tiger roared in anger, and his eyes went to small slits as he watched first the boy, then the panther. "Ye speak of wars! Ye do not know the meaning of the word. Mine has stretched my whole life long, and will till ye are dead, brat!"

Mowgli sensed that he must keep the tiger talking. "Thy father began this war, Shere Safed. Have ye never heard the tale?"

"I heard the tale well enough!" the tiger spat. "My mother went to search for him and found his skin pegged to the ground! To the ground, manling, and ringed by wolf-dung! She came back alone to bear a suckling cub in sorrow, a cub born white as death, in memory of his father's shame. And with his mother's milk, he heard the tale of his father's killer and vowed vengeance!"

"Thy father was a tyrant!" Mowgli shouted over the tiger's snarl. "'Twas only justice!"

"Justice! Justice in the jungle brought by Man! Is it justice when Man turns a thundering herd on a trapped tiger? Justice to leave his skin to bleach in the sun like a DOG's? *I* give ye justice, Man!"

With a savage roar, the tiger suddenly leaped at Mowgli's head, knocking him to the ground. The boy writhed free and slashed desperately at the snarling beast, but the tiger caught him with one huge paw, slicing him along the back of the legs. Mowgli screamed and knocked him in the jaw, slashing with his knife-hand along the animal's shoulder. Bagheera roared and leaped on the tiger's flanks, biting him deeply at the neck and then rolling away before he could be struck by the deadly fangs.

Now, Shere Safed turned on Bagheera, his eyes gleaming with hate. "Indeed, ye have picked thine allies badly!" he snarled, and slashed viciously at the panther, who backed away, his ears flat to his head.

Bagheera was trapped between two basalt spires, and he turned to leap up high to escape the tiger's onrushing jaws. Shere Safed caught him round the belly with both huge paws and held him fast, reaching for his throat with bared fangs. The tiger's claws raked his ribs, and Bagheera screamed in pain and fear, clawing frantically at his enemy's chest. Mowgli saw blood streak oily and dark down the panther's side. He reached desperately for the flaming torch and thrust it in the tiger's face, ramming the fire nearly down his yawning gullet.

Shere Safed yowled and pulled away, blinking stupidly, his whiskers smoking. He snarled in pain and confusion and swiped at the boy's hand, trying to knock the fire away, but Mowgli beat him on the head with the flaming torch and Bagheera, seeing an opening, reached up and clamped his bloody jaws on the tiger's muzzle. Shere Safed screamed in anguish, shook his head violently, leaped to his feet, and bounded away towards the daylight.

"We must stop him!" Mowgli panted, reaching for his knife, which had been knocked aside. Bagheera raced after the tiger, black blood already clotting on his chest. Mowgli limped after as fast as he could. They could hear the tiger's snarls and screams outside the cave, and when they burst out into the morning, they saw that they were too late.

An elephant sentry had met the tiger as he ran from the cave and gored him with a tusk. Wounded, the tiger tried to flee, but the aunties and mothers quickly surrounded him. One grabbed a leg, another a forepaw, a third tugged at his tail, and now, they worried his stretched body in the dust, stamping and trumpeting in fury, while the jackals whimpered and barked. When the elephant cows finally drifted away, snorting and trembling with what they had done, the white tiger lay limp and lifeless as a mangled bedsheet, and even his blood had been trampled into the sand.

Mowgli squatted before the tiger's body and watched the kites wheel down to investigate the death. Bagheera knelt beside him, his ribs heaving in and out.

"Art thou cut deep?" Mowgli asked, peering carefully at Bagheera's matted fur.

"Such a large death is worth a scratch or two," the panther said, and he carefully licked the boy's wounded leg. "This needs washing, Little Brother, and Baloo's healing herbs."

Mowgli stood wearily, shaking his head. "This needs understanding, as well," he said. "Baloo was right about many things, Bagheera."

"Ye did not kill the tiger," the panther said quietly. "The Elephant-Folk killed him, and for their own reasons. Ye kept Baloo's favour."

"Not in my heart," Mowgli said softly. "In my heart, I wanted justice. A man's justice. And more . . . I wanted to be master."

"Who did not?" Bagheera said, turning his head away. "The Law says two tigers may not share the same hill. Nor may two masters, eh? Let us go away from this place of death and dust, for the sun is high. A full gorge and a deep sleep will bring what understanding ye need."

Mowgli smiled gently. "Perhaps," he said. He patted the panther's head, and together, the two friends walked back into the jungle, singing the victory song so that all might know that the Ghost Tiger was no more.

This is the song which Mowgli and Bagheera sang as they strode back to familiar trails. Bagheera invented the second verse altogether, urging Mowgli to join him. As they walked, the peacocks took up the chorus, and soon, all the jungle knew of the Good Hunting.

There was one who killed, now he kills no more,
For he speaks to the kites by the river's shore,
He had vowed revenge, with a killing lust,
But now his words, like his life, are dust!
Sing out loud so the word is spread,
Shere Khan's son is dead, is dead!

To the mouth of the earth, we chased him down,
And he leaped in the dark from a cavern mound,
But we slashed and singed till he ran to the light,
Where the Elephant-Folk put an end to the fight!
Call it well to all ahead,
The white rogue is dead, is dead!

A tusk he took, then he tried retreat,
But the females were waiting with savage feet,
Remember this, when war ye would wage,
Ye will not escape a mother's rage!
O his hide is torn and their heels are red,
For the Ghost Tiger is dead, is dead!

MASTER OF
THE JUNGLE

There is no voice so loud, no tooth so strong,
As the jungle, the sun, and the Law.
With the Word in thy head, thy heart, and thy mouth,
Thou art safe from each claw, hoof, and jaw.
Sleep thee well, Little Cub, sleep thee sound,
For the hunt has been good, and thy father's lair-bound.

Soon thy legs will grow long, thy eyes more keen,
Thou wilt run in the night with the best.
But till then, thou wilt listen and learn at
My side, so lie still, be silent, and rest.
Sleep thee sound, Little Cub, sleep thee well,
There are lessons to learn, and more tales to tell.

Baloo's lullaby

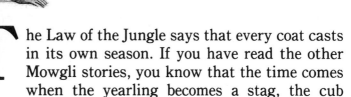

The Law of the Jungle says that every coat casts in its own season. If you have read the other Mowgli stories, you know that the time comes when the yearling becomes a stag, the cub hunts for his own, and the boy becomes a man. So it is that Mowgli came to leave the jungle one spring, in the Time of New Talk. Raksha, his wolf-mother, had said it. Baloo and Kaa had told the same: that Man will go to Man at last. And so, though the jungle had not cast him out, Mowgli found himself standing before the Council Rock as he had many times, driven there by his own heart. But now, he came to say farewell.

He found only his four Gray Brothers, Baloo, and Kaa coiled round Akela's empty seat. Bagheera came at last, his paw dripping from a fresh kill, and he said, "The Bull that frees thee lies dead in yonder brush, Little Brother. All debts are paid. Remember, Bagheera loved thee!" Then he bounded away.

And so Mowgli, now Master of the Jungle, changed his trails. For a season or two, he laired among Man, working in the villages as a cow-herder, a hunter, or a tracker of game. But the walls of the mud huts made him feel smothered at night, and the jungle called to him aloud with each passing breeze. Finally, he met a man called Gisborne, a White-Face who was an officer of the Department of Woods and Forests for the government. For all his high-sounding titles, he was simply a man who had found his favourite place in life—the jungle—and had also found a way to be paid for living there.

When Gisborne offered Mowgli the position of Warden of the Rukh, a tract of forest and heavy timber to the east of the Waingunga, he at first was wary, for Mowgli remembered the powerful aggression he had seen the White-Faces display in the hunt. But as he came to know this Gisborne, he saw that he loved the jungle and its people, and so Mowgli found in Gisborne a brother and a new life. He took himself a wife, Shanta, a slender brown village maiden. In two seasons, she carried a son at her breast, for a forest wooing goes quickly.

Each month, the Government paid Mowgli a sum of silver to oversee his piece of the jungle. He watched for fires, kept the village goats from eating the young saplings, noted the movements of the game, and kept down the boar and the nilghai when they became too many for the good of the growing bamboo. It pleased him to know where each one of his jungle brothers drank at moonrise, fed before dawn, and would lie up in the day's heat. He and his wife lived in a small hut close to the river, and all the jungle passed by his door from one season to another.

Gisborne came and visited from time to time, and he was always startled to find Shanta ringed by four huge gray wolves, who capered about her and watched from the brush, growling if he came too close to either Mowgli's wife or his young son. She would call them out, crying, "Come, ye of little manners. Come and make service to thy master's brother." The wolves fawned around him then, while the mother stood nursing her child and spurning them aside as they brushed against her bare feet.

From time to time also, Bagheera made the long trek to see his little brother, grown to be a man. He would track Mowgli down by the river where he stood fishing, or he would snuff him out as he widened a belt fire-line, coming up on him quietly as smoke with a deep rumble of delight, to share the news of the season. Kaa came too, each year when the Rains were through, but he would not go near the little hut by the river. Mowgli's "small frogling" made his belly nervous, he said. Nonetheless, he came, for friendships in the forest, unlike those of Man, are never let to wither and die away for lack of care.

Old Baloo was the only brother who had not come to sniff out Mowgli's trail. Bagheera said, "He is blind altogether, Little Brother, and the way is long, eh? Soon, he takes a trail we shall *all* follow—" and here he groaned and scratched at his gray muzzle. "Some few of us are overdue. By the Broken Lock that freed me, these bones grow more stiff with each Rain."

But one dawn as Mowgli returned from the hunt, he found the ancient Bear sitting a ways from the door of the little hut, crooning a small song to himself as though two seasons had passed instead of ten.

Mowgli dropped a brace of rabbits at the door and went to his

old friend, wrapping his arms about the shaggy shoulders, now silvered with age. "As is cold water in the hottest month, so is the sight of a friend in a far place!" he said, gazing into the Bear's eyes. And then he drew back. "Thou hast tracked me all this far way, by thy nose alone?" He smiled sadly, for Baloo's eyes were whitened with the cast of blindness, and he gazed up over Mowgli's head.

"Ahrruuh!" the Bear snuffed, grinning widely. "I do not need eyes to find thee, Little Dreamer. Pheuw! The smell of Man is rank about thee!"

"It comes from sleeping within mud walls," Mowgli laughed.

"And sleeping with a mate," the Bear said dryly. "I am not so old that I cannot remember. But come. Come and tell me all thou hast seen in these seasons, for thine eyes must now stand near tall as my own."

So Mowgli sat within the Bear's encircling arms and told him all he had seen in the rukh, all the game he had herded, the saplings he had planted, told him of the battling bucks in the nearby plains and the ill-tempered boar who must be driven from the bamboo, and a hundred other comings and goings of the Jungle Folk about him.

And then Shanta came from the hut, her face twisted with worry. She would not come to Mowgli and Baloo, but only stood far off, staring at the huge bear.

"My husband," she called finally, her voice fretful, "wilt thou not come and help me clean these rabbits?"

Mowgli blinked in confusion. Never before had Shanta been unable to prepare whatever game he brought to the little hut. But he shrugged and went from Baloo to her side.

"Is this another brother?" she whispered when she had him alone. "This great hairy beast with the huge jaws?"

Mowgli chuckled. "This is the best of them all, heart of my heart, for he has taught me the Law. He is blind, but he has found me, nonetheless."

"Well, and he has neglected to teach thee some small part of wisdom, my husband," she said in a small furious whisper, "if thou thinkest I shall let him stay. The Four Gray Brothers are enough beasts for one family, I think, and for one small son as well. He will lumber blindly and crush our Thambi with one paw, or knock him into the river, or perhaps sit on his sleeping basket—! Nay." She shook her lovely head firmly. "Ye must ask him to take himself away, my husband, or I and thy son shall go to another place until he is gone."

Mowgli scowled and scratched his chin, for he had lived long enough with a woman to know the set of that jaw. "Enough, little one. He has come, and he shall stay. Keep my son within the walls when he is about, if thou art fearful. For myself, I fear nothing save thy tongue. If thou wouldst keep my love, remember the love I bear for Baloo as well, and do not speak against him. Nay, not in *my* hearing."

She turned and fled back inside the hut, and the sudden silence in the clearing seemed almost a reproach. Mowgli went back to the old Bear and sat once more at his side.

"What is in thy stomach?" Baloo asked gently. "For thou hast sat down heavily like an ox with a burden."

Mowgli sighed. "It is nothing, my brother. Only a small fear which has laired in the woman's heart. Hast thou never lived among the females for a time? They are winsome and warm, well enough, and many good things come of them. But they are mad and many times mad, mostly when it comes to their babes."

The old Bear chuckled, shaking his head. "Ay, I remember. And a fine babe he must be. To think that I, Teacher of the Law, would live these hundred seasons to trail thy own frogling, Little Brother—" his voice thickened with emotion. "Well, and it is very good, indeed."

"Stay with us, then," Mowgli said. "Thou wilt have all the ripe berries and river trout thy fat belly can hold, if my arm has any strength at all. And the woman will come to know thee as friend."

Baloo reached out and cuffed Mowgli's shoulder playfully. "Thou art still a Little Dreamer of Dreams, I see. But I will stay for a time."

And so, the old Bear made the rukh his own, browsing at Mowgli's side as he fished and hunted and traipsed the woods. They often talked over old times and shared old tales, and if you could have stood quietly in the bamboo and listened, you would have heard Baloo chuckling with pleasure at how his man-cub had grown.

But one heart took no pleasure from the Bear's presence in the little clearing by the mud hut. Shanta still grew cold with fear—and something else which she could not name—when she saw the huge beast and her husband saunter off together for another day in the forest. She kept little Thambi far apart, looking cautiously all round the clearing before she would let him toddle forth into the light. When Baloo lay sprawled by the river, the boy was kept fast inside. And because he was his father's son, he soon grew restless and discontent with the confinement, squawling in fury each time his mother bound him in his basket.

One day, Mowgli and Baloo followed the river to a deep pool which held a school of large and stubborn trout. The old Bear lay in the shade mumbling over some clover, while Mowgli angled a worm under a rock to tempt forth the fish.

The drifting scents on the breeze had put the Bear in a thoughtful mood, and he was humming softly to himself as he plucked first one, then another ripe paw-paw.

"How is it that this Warden Man can give the woods to thee?" he asked Mowgli. "It does not belong to him, eh? And yet he puts thee here and says, 'Yea, over all this art thou master.'" The Bear rumbled as a thought struck him. "In thine own hills, where thy mother gave thee suck, there are those who might dispute such a charge. Are there no Hathis here, no Kaas, and no tigers to say nay to thee as master?"

"There are all these things," Mowgli said, his eyes intent on the silvery shadows of trout. "But what have they to do with me? I count the herds as they move, Kaa's brothers never cross my trail, and as for tigers, I hate all tigers—and if one kills within my rukh, I shall drive him forth."

"And for this, they give thee the gift of silver?"

"Ay," Mowgli said patiently, "but I would not hurt the jungle for any gift, old friend. It is my home."

Baloo scratched his head solemnly. "Bagheera was right. Thou art of the jungle and yet not of the jungle, still. Ye left to lair with Man, ye said, yet ye stand with one foot on each side of the river."

Mowgli sat down and sighed. "It is not an easy thing, Baloo.

When I was of the jungle, all things were clear to me, and each thing was only itself. Joy was joy, fear was fear, and hunger was in my belly alone, not in my heart. These things had not yet trespassed, one onto the other. Now, I am a man, and life is older. There is no joy without the knowledge of pain. Likewise, there is no sorrow without the comfort of hope. But it was simpler then."

"Considering this," Baloo answered slowly, "thou art following the proper trail, I think. Perhaps the only trail for thee. But what of thy young frogling? Will he have no Teacher of the Law to guide his steps?"

Mowgli chuckled. "Wouldst thou take on another cub, old friend? Ye said ye had enough of tossing blossoms to ungrateful whelps."

Baloo grinned. "It is true talk. I said as much."

"I had no father and no mother, save thee, my brothers, and the jungle."

"Enough for any cub," the Bear said softly.

"The jungle alone knows. But my son has both father and mother and the jungle besides."

"And the Law?" Baloo absently batted at a low-thrumming hummingbird, as though to belie his concern.

"He will learn Man's Law, and what he needs of the jungle's, I shall teach him, as is seemly."

Now, it was the old Bear's turn to sigh hugely and roll over, facing Mowgli. "As ye wouldst have it, O Warden of the Woods. But am I not to teach thy frogling even the smallest piece of—?"

"He does not even speak his mother's name yet, old friend. Let it come in its own time."

The bear thought that once Thambi began to speak in Man's tongue, the jungle's would come hard to him, but he decided to say no more about it.

Another day, Mowgli had traipsed far up into the hills, and Baloo was dozing in the shade near the mud hut. Shanta had come out of the hut, peered at the old Bear suspiciously, and when she saw that he slept, she took her water jug onto her head to go to the river.

"Stay within," she whispered to her little son, "and I shall be back before the shadows grow longer."

But Thambi could no longer abide the blankness of the hut floor, and so he stood up on his fat little legs and pushed with all his strength on the rush door of the hut. To his great surprise, it opened enough that he could slip out into the clearing.

He stood for an instant, swaying on his unsteady legs, looking this way and that for his mother. Then, he spied old Baloo under the neem trees. Without a moment's hesitation, he toddled over to the old Bear and slapped him on the haunch, clucking to himself.

Baloo woke with a start, felt about to see what had fallen on him from the branches, and smelled little Thambi. The child was brown as a nut, with tousled black hair and beady black eyes. He sat on the ground and stared up at the bear, not the least afraid.

"Huhnhn," Baloo crooned softly, nuzzling the boy. "Thou art mightily like another frogling I recall, Little Man."

The child giggled and pushed Baloo's wet nose away, tugging at his fur all the while. Baloo gathered him carefully closer and raised his shaggy nose. He sensed that Shanta was nowhere about.

"Hast thy father told thee of the time he sat just so and learned the Master Words? No? Well, and ye shall hear it now, Little Brother," Baloo began. Of course, Thambi could not speak Man's talk as yet, but because he was still a cub, he found Baloo's talk easy to understand, as his father had before him. He chortled and nestled closer to the big bear.

"Long ago and far away, where the Waingunga flows—" Baloo continued, his muzzle close to Thambi's ear.

Suddenly, Shanta came up the riverbank and saw her little son within the Bear's grasp, his head almost within his jaws. She shrieked and ran towards Baloo, forgetting her natural terror of the great beast. Baloo snorted and pulled away, but not in time. Before he could avoid her, Shanta yanked the water jug off her head and threw it full in the Bear's face.

The jug caught Baloo on his tender muzzle, smashing into bits and drenching both him and the boy with cold river water. Thambi wailed indignantly; Baloo coughed and gagged with shock, and Shanta grappled for the child in his paws, screaming, "Get back to thy lair, ye forest devil! Keep off my son!"

Baloo did not understand her words, but there was no mistaking her tone. He laid down the squalling boy at her feet and quickly shambled away.

That night when Mowgli returned and heard the tale, he searched the river high and low for the Bear, calling his name repeatedly in the darkness. "Baloo, Baloo, *ohe,* my brother!" he cried, but only the mocking howls of the monkeys answered him.

He returned to the little hut saddened and silent. He took Thambi on his knee and absently dandled a piece of chapatti for his grasping fingers. The boy chuckled and snatched the bread away greedily.

Shanta watched her husband closely from under lowered eyes. Finally, she could endure the silence no longer, and she repeated softly, "He had him in his great arms, my husband. I could do naught else."

"Thou could have believed me when I told thee that my brother would never hurt the little one," Mowgli said heavily.

"Perhaps not of a purpose!" she replied angrily. "But even without trying, such claws can kill, can crush!"

Mowgli shook his head, unable to say more. He could have told her, he knew, of the countless times those same paws had held him gently, led him surely through the jungle without mishap. But he knew also that her mother's heart would not hear him. And truly, how could he find fault in her for this? He could drive her before him and beat her in anger. He could shout, "Thou art an evil woman, and this matter shall be an open sore between us!" But to what use? He sighed and resolved to say no more for the sake of peace in the little hut. The old Bear was gone, and no word of Mowgli's would bring him back, as in the old days. Two other hearts sat before him now, awaiting that same word, two who looked to him as he had once looked to Baloo.

He ruffled his son's hair gently. "So, little one, thou hast had a great adventure, eh?" He patted his wife's hand absently and saw that her eyes welled up with quick relief. "Ye should call thy mother *nawal* [mongoose] hereafter, for she would surely fight Death himself for thee."

The next morning, Mowgli took himself into the jungle to drive away some wild boars who were tusking among the young bamboo, and he tried to put from his mind thoughts of his absent friend. But Baloo was not so very absent after all. He had listened from the thicket as Shanta scooped up her son and took him back into the hut, fussing and weeping over him with fright. He had waited there in the shadows as Mowgli returned, and heard him call again and again—but he remained silent. He knew that his presence would drive a wedge between Mowgli and his mate, perhaps even cause her to take his son away forever. And so, the bear remained hidden—yet he could not leave, for now that he had held Thambi and smelled the sourness of his ruffled black cub-hair, felt the warmth of his fat fingers, there was no place else in the jungle where Baloo wanted to be.

The season of ripe berries came to the rukh, and Shanta tied Thambi carefully at her hip to traipse the thickets, searching for the best, most ripe patches.

"Thou must call out when ye see them, Little Man of My Heart," she crooned as she wrapped him in gay cloth. But Thambi only chortled and beat on his fat legs, for he had not yet learned to mimic her sounds.

Shanta left the mud hut and followed the trails up the hillocks to where the berries and the lantana grew thick and purple. She untied the boy from her hip and set him down in a clearing where she could watch him, dropping some sticks of bamboo at his feet.

"Play me some music, Thambi," she called as she bent to the lower branches, "whilst I gather these which thy father loves best." The boy picked up the bamboo sticks and began to drum on the earth, crowing and thumping loudly.

Baloo had silently followed the two up the hill, staying hidden in the thick lantana. Though he was blind, he needed no eyes to tell him where Thambi and Shanta had stopped. He settled quietly in the brush, smiling to himself as he listened to Shanta's endearments and the boy's answering prattle.

The sun was warm and the time so pleasant that the old Bear nearly dozed in the berry thicket, his huge head on his paws and his memories far away. His mind's eye followed a river of shadows back to a time when he had watched another man-cub play in another forest clearing, when he had felt the whole jungle was still before him to be explored, before the seasons lay so heavily

211

on his shoulders. He sighed with pleasure and chuckled to himself, lifting his muzzle out of the damp brush. Then suddenly, a new scent brushed his nose, and he jerked up to alertness. Complete quiet had settled on the berry bushes: Shanta had ceased her croonings; Thambi no longer beat his bamboo sticks.

And then Baloo heard a new voice rasp through the silence, and the hairs bristled up the back of his shoulders. If he could have gazed upon the little clearing, this is what the Bear would have seen.

Shanta was frozen, white and still, half-in, half-out of the berry bushes, her hands in mid-air as though to beseech. Thambi had dropped his sticks in wonder, and he too sat still as stone. His wide eyes were fastened on what lay coiled and swaying on the ground between himself and his mother: a huge King Cobra.

"Do not move, do not stir, my heart! O be still, my life!" Shanta whispered in a shrill whistle of fear and horror.

But the snake barely glanced in her direction. He towered over Thambi's head, his hood spread wide as a water lily, within easy striking distance of the boy's brown legs, and he crooned an evil song.

"O ay, be still, little frogling, until I say thee to ssstir," the snake hissed. "Thou art egg of the Master of the Rukh, are ye not?"

Thambi's eyes followed the snake's every sway, fascinated and frozen as a young sparrow. Some instinct bade him be silent, the same instinct which makes a dappled fawn drop to cover when a hunter passes near.

"Ay, thou art of his blood, that I can see," the snake continued, his slithering tongue testing the air above Thambi's head. "Once, long ago, I met thy sire in another place. I would have struck him down, for my people wanted his death. But his tongue charmed me, even as my tongue charms thee now, eh?" The cobra lowered his head slightly so that his eyes were gazing directly into Thambi's, and his tongue wickered in and out hypnotically. The boy swayed slightly forward, his eyes drooping under the snake's stare.

Shanta screamed and stepped forward, but the cobra whirled in a blink, hissing and spitting in anger. "Stay ye ssso!" he commanded, his eyes glittering. "*I* shall say when thou canst stir!" Shanta froze once more. A low keening whimper came from her throat, like that of a snared rabbit.

The snake turned back to the boy, revolving almost leisurely on his black coils. Baloo moved slightly closer in the brush, his back haunches trembling. "O ay, thy father and I have crossed trails," the cobra continued, "and some there were who said that where one man walked, others would soon follow. But I did not listen. Not sssoon enough, fat little frogling. And now, thou hast come. And behind thee shall come others." The snake jerked his chin at the woman behind him. "Ah-sh-sh, from just such as she, thy dam. But if thou dies? Then she shall go elsewhere, taking her nest with her. No more mud huts on the river; no more beating of the bushes in berry time." The snake moved slightly closer, and his voice dropped to a wheedling tone. "Most assuredly, little frog, I bear thee no ill will. And had thou not crossed my path, as impudently as thy father did once, I would have let thee live, no doubt. For surely, thou art comely as thy father before thee. But thou art *Man*."

Suddenly, Baloo raised up on his haunches, his great head and shoulders looming up out of the brush. "We be of one blood, ye and I, O Hama," he called to the cobra in the snake's tongue. "Leave the man-cub alive!"

The snake looked up, mildly surprised. "Art thou here as well, Teacher of the Law? Indeed and truly, this frogling is well-comraded at such a tender age. But ye need not plead his life. Call for his sire, Baloo. I shall have one or the other of them, for the death of either shall rid the rukh of Man. But I shall let *him* choose. For the sake of old memories and an old story-song, eh?" The snake's eyes turned angry. "Call him, Baloo! I await his pleasssure!"

Baloo turned to Thambi, and his voice dropped low and gentle, luring the boy's eyes away from the swaying snake. "Say this, man-cub, say after me: 'We be of one blood, ye and I.' Quickly, manling, speak the Master Word!"

Thambi seemed to comprehend that something was wanted from him. He screwed his mouth up with concentration, trying to mimic the sounds the bear made. Hama hissed with rage as the boy's eyes darted away to the bear, and in that instant, Baloo crashed out of the brush and upon the snake. His terrible great paws swept down on the spitting cobra, who ducked and weaved, trying to strike at the boy. A mighty claw slashed, Shanta screamed in horror, and Hama lay writhing in agony on the ground, his back broken—but not before he had sunk both fangs deeply in Baloo's shoulder.

Shanta scooped up her son and retreated into the brush, frantically checking him for bites. The cobra convulsed and twisted once, twice, his body jutting at odd angles in the dust, until finally he lay still. Baloo sprawled beside him, panting heavily. Shanta put back her head and screamed as loud as a dozen peacocks, calling for Mowgli again and again, her lament wailing through the forest.

Mowgli heard his woman's call from way across the river, where he hunted for nilghai tracks. He knew instantly that such a howl of fear and grief meant death—someone's—and he raced in the direction of her wail with his heart pounding in his throat. He burst into the berry clearing to find Shanta on the ground with Baloo's head in her lap. She wept over the bear quietly while Thambi watched solemnly at her side. One glance to the broken cobra and the bear's swollen, darkening jowls told him the tale.

"My brother!" Mowgli cried, and dropped to his knees next to the shaggy head.

Baloo opened his eyes and looked directly at Mowgli, though he could not see a thing. " 'Twas Hama," the bear said weakly, "come to eat yet another frogling. His . . . his bite went in like a needle, but it goes out like a plough."

"He saved us both," Shanta sobbed. "The great *naja* would have slain our Thambi, save for his swift claws."

Mowgli scarcely heard her. He gathered the bear's head onto his own lap and sat rocking gently, crooning a private song into Baloo's ears. "Dost thou remember, old Bear, how I swam beside thee, so many seasons past, and told thee the Master Words at thy bidding? Bagheera scared Patwari out of his pinfeathers that day, with a yawn bigger than Hathi's."

Baloo chuckled painfully. "Thee called me 'fat old Bear,' even then, I think." He struggled to sit up as a thought took him. "Thou

214

must teach thy frogling the Master Words, Little Brother. Almost did he say them to Hama! I must teach him—"

"H'sh, my brother," Mowgli soothed him. "Lie still and remember. Remember when ye took me to see Hathi and ducked me in the river, filling my ears with water and my head with more advice? Remember when ye and Bagheera pulled me from Hama's black pit? Remember when . . . when . . . " and then Mowgli stopped, for a terrible stillness had come over the bear, and his body fell slack in his arms. Baloo was dead.

Mowgli lay the bear gently down and stood, his arms to the sky. He put back his head and howled into the jungle silence, howled as only a grieving wolf can howl, pealing his sorrow and his loneliness loud and long until the trees rang with it, and every creature for miles around knew that the Teacher of the Law was no more.

That night, as the moon rose over the rukh, a small band of brothers met by the river. Mowgli stood on a rock over Baloo's body and called to the night sky. At his feet in a ring sat his four gray wolves, who lifted their muzzles in unison with his cry. Bagheera slid into the circle, an inky black shadow, silent and solemn. Together, they sang the forest song of the dead, and when they finished and the wolves had turned away, Mowgli and the panther kept watch over Baloo, as jungle custom decreed.

In the silence, Mowgli turned to Bagheera and he said, half-aloud, half to himself, "There was a thing Hathi said once. A true talk, I think."

"Hathi said many things of wisdom," Bagheera replied softly.

"But this thing was of Baloo," Mowgli said, and his voice thickened with pain. "He said that hearts are like horses. They come and go against the bit and spur. I did not know what he meant then. The way love binds. I do now."

"And how does this touch our brother?"

Mowgli turned away, his eyes downcast. "Hathi said that Baloo did not know this wisdom. That only the old heads learn it." His throat tightened with a dry sob. "I wish that he had realised the peril of the love he bore me!"

Bagheera dropped his grizzled chin on Mowgli's bare knee and said gently, "He knew, Little Brother. He knew well enough. And he would have followed no other trail." He thought for a moment in silence. "He was not, after all, blind in his *heart*."

Finally, slowly, Mowgli was able to smile as he sifted through his memories.

They sat in the moonlight until the jackals had ceased howling. As the dawn began to send creeping fingers between the trees, Mowgli and the Black Panther still sat, side by side, and if you could have listened, you would have heard first the boy, then the great cat, chuckle softly as they traded memories of seasons gone by.

This is the forest death song which Mowgli, Bagheera, and the wolves sang over Baloo. It is sung over any great dying in the jungle, and is the first thing which every hunting creature learns, after the Master Words.

Death Song of the Hunters

A cub opens night-eyes,
A nest stirs, a whelp cries,
A calf stands to teat-size,
And in them, the jungle lives on.

The kite cracks the gaur's head,
The jackal is full-fed,
The dawn finds the new dead,
And from them, the jungle lives on.

The sun sears the mango,
The Rains lay the grass low,
The earth turns, the winds blow,
And always, the jungle lives on.

Afterword

Pamela Jekel is a writer and research scholar with a doctorate in English and a specialty in Victorian literature. Her special challenge was to create this continuation of the *Jungle Book* stories in the same way Kipling might have, echoing his style, his themes, even his punctuation . . . less in a spirit of imitation than homage.

She hopes and believes that wherever he is, whatever jungle path he walks now, he would approve.

for Zack, child of my heart,
who's had love enough
for each of us,
right from the start. . .